the soldier's home

the soldier's home

GEORGE COSTIGAN

Urbane
PUBLICATIONS

urbanepublications.com

First published in Great Britain in 2018
by Urbane Publications Ltd
Suite 3, Brown Europe House, 33/34 Gleaming Wood Drive,
Chatham, Kent ME5 8RZ
Copyright © George Costigan, 2018

A CIP catalogue record for this book is available
from the British Library.

ISBN 978-1-911331-05-6
MOBI 978-1-911331-08-7

Design and Typeset by Michelle Morgan

Cover by Author Michelle Morgan

Printed and bound by 4edge UK

URBANE
urbanepublications.com

The Single Soldier and *The Soldier's Home*, took close enough to twenty years to write. It wasn't a chore, I wasn't affected by deadlines or any imperative other than the desire to finish it. So I never thought about the length of time. I think my wife did.

To her, for patience and love above and beyond, this book is dedicated.

THE SOLDIER'S HOME

foreword

The Soldier's Home is the sequel to *The Single Soldier*, and is a continuation of that story, but can also be enjoyed as a stand-alone book. Or two stories, as it is split into two parts; **Simone** and **Enid**.

The Soldier's Home finds the work Jacques was engaged in during The Single Soldier - re-building his house - finished.

The house used to stand seven kilometres away, at Puech. The other side of the village of St. Cirgues.

It has taken Jacques the eight years since 1944 to dismantle the house, move it and re-build it.

He began when Simone left France with their infant son, via the refugee escape route over the Pyrenees, and eventually to the USA.

THE SOLDIER'S HOME

Simone

THE SOLDIER'S HOME

1952

One volet hung loose.
He'd lost one of its metal pins. It would bang in a wind.
But his son's chimney was in place.
I'll read and sleep and I'll go to Maurs.
He settled his back into the wall.

THE SOLDIER'S HOME

I

DEAR JACQUES,

It's over, then.

I've seen pictures of the bombs. So many died and we three have lived.

Everyone here is very proud. Of the bombs.

I have six students - they come here or I go to their houses. Well, their rooms in a house. Apartments, they're called. Only the rich, like you, own an actual house. I pay a baby-sitter to sit here with your son. She's nice. 'Neat', they say here. Susie. Jacques likes her. I have three French students, and, of course, I'm learning English. And so will he. But we talk French and he'll talk with you one day. I tell him about you and where he comes from and who he comes from and the house and you haven't told me anything.

Tell me about Arbel. And Jerome. Did they live? Are they home? Sara? Zoe? Tell me about the life I left. But most of all, you.

I make just enough money. The rent isn't much and trolleys are cheap. Jacques, you've never seen a trolley! I'll send you a picture. If I told you about all the shops - you would not believe it were possible. Some days I still don't.

People tell me the winters are cold and we'll need heating. You've got all that beech, so you'll be good.

I am so grateful every day for our lives here and for our life together. We're a million miles apart and when I look at him you are here with me.

What are you 'taking down?'

You owe me two letters.

We send our love,

Your family.

THE SOLDIER'S HOME

2

DEAR JACQUES,

You are the worst letter writer in the world.

What do you mean 'Arbel came.'? You make it sound like a trek! And then you don't tell me even what sex their baby is! I want to know.

But Arbel came home! I thought so often of Ardelle and her misery and what a relief for them and what a present life has rewarded them with. I've written to them.

Did Jerome live? And how's Sara? And him over the lane – misery - what was his name?

Tell me everything! You write in riddles, my man.

Love from The New World.

They call France and Europe The Old World.

I think it's all one world. They don't.

Simone.

3

DEAR MR. MYSTERIOUS,

Jacques - get a piece of paper - now! - and write 'Dear Simone – Ardelle's baby is called _ _ _ _.' Do it! Have you? You haven't, I can tell. I know you. Have you now? Shall I not write again till I get your reply?

Why are your letters post-marked Maurs? I wrote to La Poste and that angry postman (can't remember his name either) asking for an address for Sara - since I don't get information from you. No letter from Ardelle but she'll be too busy - I know!

I think teething is a flaw in nature's plan. I can't understand why our child should be in quite so much pain.

A tear fell and his hand moved it away and smudged her ink. He panicked. Held the paper over the fire till it dried. He knew the letter by heart, but still...

But all pain passes, doesn't it?

He moved the paper sharply to miss the next tear.

Write!
With love, all of it.
Simone.

4

DEAR JACQUES,
  Janatou?
  What are you doing?
  What have you done?
  I got a printed card from La Poste with this address.
  There's nothing there.
  Tell me, immediately - everything.
  Oh my God - it's winter.
  Jacques - you'll freeze. Where are you?
  What did you take down?
  Live, my Jacques. I can't write through worried tears.
  Simone.

  P.S. I can't believe I'm adding this - but it's nearly December now - and with the time the post takes...
  Jacques.
  Happy Christmas.

THE SOLDIER'S HOME

5

DEAR JACQUES,
  Why?

  Simone.

6

A favourite.

JACQUES, I believe in Hope, too. And now I believe in Promises. I never made any because I couldn't. I make this one. We will see our house, in your paradise. Build it, brother-man - build it. I want to see it. Seeing is believing.

Simone.

7

A postcard. Never forget what a postcard can bring...

I'LL WAIT. Keep safe. I'm on a subway. Going to work. I'll wait. He'll wait. Keep warm! Letter tonight. Happy New Year! A fortnight late - and February, probably when you get this! Our Time is crazy.
   S.

8

JACQUES - *you loved me much too much, you know that now, don't you?*

No-one could love you too much, but you thought I was an angel - dropped into your life.

Did you go mad, dear man?

Is the work healing you?

If it is - we'll see it - somehow.

If it isn't - then sell, beg, steal - borrow (from Jerome's Mother!?) - but come here and let me heal you.

I'm the wound - I'll be the nurse.

Jacques. A boat - you could work your passage.If I can get here you can. Come here. You never made me cry - come here and dry these tears. It's only money - sell Janatou!

Think what's best - just this once - for you, Jacques Vermande.

I care with all my being for yours. And I promise I always will.

Your son has a cold.

THE SOLDIER'S HOME

Have you a roof?
Talk to me gentle, please.
We love you
Simone

9

I'M WRITING to The Mairie now - I'm afraid of your silences.
I freeze over.

IO

DEAR JACQUES,

The Mayor wrote here to say you're 'Very much alive but silent.'
I'm glad you're alive. I knew you were silent.

If anyone has the right to know the things inside your silence it should be me, no?

And you have the right not to tell me. But that's not you. Not you and me. Is it?

Have you sat down to read this? Surrounded by stone and snow and shivering? Suffering?

Consider this - you are my man, so long as you live.

But write. Only connect.

Simone.

II

DEAR JACQUES,
What do I tell your son?
You could write him again. At least. He loved that letter.
I read it to him till I wore it out - and we both knew it by heart.

The days are bright here - but I live cloudy not knowing...
Move your hand and write to me.
Your friend and much much more
Simone.

12

DEAR JACQUES,

On a subway cross-town today I forgot about you. For an hour. I was reading a magazine article about something stupid - oh! - doesn't matter what - and I forgot you.

I was ashamed.

And now I'm angry.

In the end you needn't write to me.

If you're black as hell that I left you - took him.

If that's it or a part of it, fine.

But, as I sit here, writing, you are A Bad Father.

He needs. He asks and I lie. You said once your mother never taught you to lie. Tell him some truth and don't teach me to lie.

Simone.

He rolled a cigarette. Lit it. Laid another piece of pine across the glowing ashes.

Smoked his way back to Galtier's replacement delivering that letter.

A warm day. Spring. Only the foundations and one wall of the caves done. The dog still there. And his reply.

'Simone,
You didn't leave. I sent you. I'm re-building myself. Too. It takes time. Writing takes Time I can't seem to want to spare, even though there's no end to it. But there must be. Some way. Also writing hurts. But I will.
Jacques.'

THE SOLDIER'S HOME

13

FORGIVE US,
  Simone.

  P.S. You remember it's his birthday very soon?

14

DEAR JACQUES,

When my parents were killed, I died.

You brought me back to Life.

I never did come to Janatou, did I? I will.

Jacques - we're both in shock and I wonder if we're not both in guilt.

I bought a new coat today - when I think of you and look at it, it's repellent.

I've no idea what I'm reaching to say so I'll just keep scribbling and maybe it'll come. I always had that space with you.

I think of us - and I know I've escaped. Not from you - but to this bustle. I said once none of us know the future – that the present was madness enough. Well, in my present I'm not suffering. I'm enjoying the struggle.

He'll be in nursery (what we call Maternelle) by the next letter.

No-one ever says he looks like you (he does) because no-one knows you - and I've no photos. There's an album in my mind, but...

When I say 'no-one' - that's a bit grand. The four who've asked.

THE SOLDIER'S HOME

*All women. All different nationalities. All in this building. They've formed something they call The United Nations and I feel like it's this house. America **is** The United Nations! I'm learning Spanish on my doorstep!*

He has a good soul.
And he's serious so his smile is sunlight.
He loves me as much as you do and I feel guilty because I'm so lucky.
Are we Casualties of war? We mustn't be. Don't be.
Build.
Tired. More tomorrow.
Simone.

O.K. Morning headache hangover honesty before he wakes. I feel most guilty because I can feel a future here. And I feel bad for thinking that and not sharing it with you and I feel worse now for saying it but I never had secrets from you and I'm lost for my response and in my responsibility. Responsibilities. They circle round my head and this solitary drinking doesn't still it. I'm a little confused as to what solitary drinking does do. You don't know, do you?

15

DEAR JACQUES,

I talked to a priest. He sent me to a doctor and he gave me pills that meant I couldn't do a damned thing but sit. I threw them away and went back and he sent me to a psycho-something and he listened – much better than the Priest or the doctor - but he cost me money! To tell him I'm sad! So, I'm talking to you. Who always listened.

And I'm crying. Again.

We're helpless here - your family - and more stone for you to carry, Sisyphus - we need you to make an hour a week for us. Can you hear a church bell? Every Sunday morning, yes? We need you to take an hour from work - and write. Anything. For us.

'I'm alive.'

'I'm still alive.'

And sign it.

I feel callous imagining my imaginings are anything like your reality.

Every night when I tuck him up, every night when I pull the blankets over me - I feel guilt for being warm.

THE SOLDIER'S HOME

Once a week.

Simone.

16

DEAR MAN,

Here is a painting he did. Well, it's crayons. They're made of coloured wax, like candles. So - you can cry over this - I did - and it won't run. When I asked him who the blob-man was, he said, 'Pappa.' Are we growing an artist? What do you think, Pappa? I think it's the most fantastic painting in The Whole History Of The World. Guard it, Pappa - it'll be worth a fortune one day.

If you hear your name on the wind - it's the teacher calling the register at your son's nursery.

That's a fib - they don't. But I like the idea - and they will one day.

Your present for him came. I shan't change it for dollars - he wouldn't let me anyway - it's under his pillow.

Of course he walks! He ran the other morning, tripped on a flag-stone, fell on his nose and has learned caution. Which he'll forget.

His hair is losing your curls and, poor him, straightening like mine. He eats like you, concentrated. Food is Serious Business.

He hates baths.

He hates stairs. Carrying him and the groceries up four flights

THE SOLDIER'S HOME

is no fun. And I daren't leave it and take him and come back for it - because you don't ever leave anything lying about in New York.

He loves Susie, his baby-sitter, but he howls every time he sees her because it means I'm leaving. That lasts about a minute. She's sweet - but she is American.

What I mean is - she bought him a toy gun to play with. He loves it. The trigger goes Clack! (it's made from plastic) and Susie rolls over dead and he's thrilled to his socks. I plan for it to become very lost. She also brings him pink gum - which he also loves. It's disgusting. Candy, she calls it.

I've found a new nursery - nearer - that will take him in September. ('Fall' they call autumn, here - I like that)

Take him for the whole day.

I can work more - and I'll earn more – and he has to grow - but I can't bear the idea of not seeing him.

That is Cruel. As thoughtless is.

Writing to you about my not wanting to miss him!

I was always selfish Jacques; did you ever notice? I want all of him all of the time; and only some of that is because I know he doesn't have you.

Do you talk out loud? Do you talk to the dog? Do you even hear your own voice?

I see the same stars as you, only six hours later.

Sometimes the world seems so huge.
The ocean that separates us is. Your work.

I'm glad Sara comes to see you - she always was the best of your friends - but Jerome? Is he dead? I don't like to ask her.

Simone.

THE SOLDIER'S HOME

17

DEAR YOU,

You don't hear cuckoos in New York. Buses, trams, the subways, cars, police whistles, dogs, people shouting across the tenements at night, radios playing music, radios talking different languages - all the time - I've not heard silence since Puech. You see Nature - I see Human Nature - stone and steel and glass towers. If I heard birds they'd be coughing.

We're going up the biggest building in the world tomorrow. We'll see you from there - wave.

One of my French students - yes, I teach everything now! - a German chemist called Erich, asked me to the cinema with him. Marlene Dietrich, whom he adores, and I wanted to ask your permission (and I do) but there wasn't time and I went. The film was in German, the cinema was full of Germans – and it was too much, too difficult and I said I was going to the head (the toilet) and went home. I apologized next lesson. When he asked me why I told him. He said the shame of being German would haunt his life and he loved Marlene because she 'didn't give a stuff' and her pride freed him for an evening.

So, we talk - about the war. He pays me for the privilege of sharing you with him.

I worried about your maybe feeling betrayed and I even wondered should I tell you? The idea of deceit didn't last long.

I bought Jacques a cheap box of wooden and plastic bricks. So, he and I make houses. Like you. He loves the chimney - putting the chimney on - because then it means you can light a fire. Jacques - write and describe him a real chimney, please.

I had the strangest feeling yesterday. I didn't feel French. I was hanging on a strap on the subway - Jacques - these are trains that go under the city! I'll send you a photo. I use it Tuesdays to teach German to the son of a Jewish woman who fled here in '37. He's 8 and I'm to teach him how to talk with her. 'Why? It's dopey...' he keeps saying to me in English. He chews this eternal gum and drinks fizzy drinks and he's too fat. Anyway. I was on the subway train and I didn't feel French - for one whole second. I felt like a grain of sand in this American desert. And remember M.Feyt saying we shouldn't be German or French or Jewish? That's what it was - I didn't feel I was any nationality and no-one else should either.

We can't change what we are - but I did want to tell someone and you're my friend.

Simone.

THE SOLDIER'S HOME

18

DEAREST JACQUES,
  Won't you keep in touch?

19

DEAR JACQUES,

It's a month since I wrote and three since you did. This is all we have.

I get fatalistic. I don't know you're alive.

It's so slender this thread - when you don't write he and I are adrift.

You made me feel once there was somewhere I'd never be forgotten - not for a day.

I can't think what to say. Write. Silence is not golden - it's rust and decay.

It's too lonely to write tonight. Being lonely in a city might be worse than your loneliness.

I have no friends - no-one comes for a chat or a drink or a meal.

I have him and my work and you have no-one and your work so I shouldn't complain and I'm not I'm just talking into the night with a

THE SOLDIER'S HOME

pen. Outside it's dark and noisy. Inside it's hot and quiet. I'm saving for a radio. I wish I were rich.

I have no idea when your birthday is. Write and tell us - we can bake you a cake.

I'd love a drink but the price of wine here! Men drink whisky or beer and the women something called Martinis. Can't describe it - haven't tried one. Don't like beer. Fizzy drinks are what everyone has. They're fine if you don't like your teeth. I dread him going to 'proper' school.

This isn't a letter - I'm talking to myself.
Talk to yourself on paper and send it to us.
Jacques and Simone Vermande.

He read her signature again.
As he had.
Again and again.

20

DEAR JACQUES,

I've had a letter from Sara. I wonder if I don't know more than you do - because she's not sure how much you hear or retain of what she tells you.

She says you're strong and I needn't worry on that account. That's a blessing. It felt like the only one.

No wonder Ardelle didn't write. How vicious Life is.

And Jerome lives - if that can be called living.

But, best of all, Zoe. Sara says she's learning English at school and is real good at it.

Vermande – I'm writing to you about your life! Don't you think that's mad?

Three months, Vermande.

Sometimes it feels like I'm asking, demanding, all the time.

Yeah - as they say here. I am.

Simone.

2I

OH, JACQUES,
  He was a top dog, as they say here. Get another.

  *I'm zizzed. (I will stop saying 'as they say here!') I've been for
a drink. The Italian woman invited me to an Italian café for the
evening. Being Italian they expect the children to come. So we went.
Chianti - it's a fruity red wine - and now we're back and he's gone bo-
bo's and you wrote saying the dog was dead and I'm writing to say
I knew it must have been something bad. And it was. Get another.
Man should have a dog. In the country. They're banned in some
buildings here. Brownstones, like ours.*

  You need a companion.

  *I'm not writing anymore - I'm putting this in an envelope and
posting it before I write anything else as crass as that.*

  *I'm sick of apologizing, too. It's not your fault and I wish I didn't
think it was mine and I wish there wasn't fault - it stops us all being
together even apart. I can't read this writing anymore I hope you can.*

  Simone.

22

DEAR JACQUES,

I'm not working. No-one is.

There's been forty centimetres of snow in the past week. So the city is finally quiet, because this is too deep even for the snow-shifter wagons.

He begged to go out and it was higher than him! We waded to the park and people had sculpted snow-men everywhere. My favourite was two men sitting on a bench talking! And there was a snowman sitting on the swings! A silent art-gallery. We made a house. Our house. His face when I lifted him to put the chimney pot on...

This is his connection with you, Poppa - chimneys. A passion – his first obsession.

See, most buildings here have flat roofs, so one of his big treats is to go up on the roof, because it has 24 chimneys. One for each apartment. He can count that far in two languages now. And there's a Puerto Rican boy up there who has a pigeon-cage. He loves that, too. My Spanish isn't up to much of a conversation - but it will be. And so will his.

It'll be Christmas soon. What do you think we should give him?

I wondered about his own chimney-pot - plant something when Spring comes.I wish I could send you a puppy. But I know what you'd like best.

Simone.

23

DEAR JACQUES,

Isn't he beautiful? Are we not the cleverest parents ever? When I put that picture in the envelope I thought of the loving, the sex that made him. It was one afternoon. Did you know? We were in the garden! Yes - That one!! God, I miss you bad some days.

The snow is still here but has been cleared so the city can move and work again. It's cold. I dress him to go to bed! Coats on the beds because I daren't leave the heater on - it costs. And I don't trust it.

My students were sweet to me; cards in three languages. And presents, too. The German man, Erich, gave me perfume, which isn't very nice (at all) so I only wear it when I go see him - but the tubby German boy - remember? - he gave me a five-cent bag of salted peanuts and I don't know why but I was so touched. Mad, huh? His mother made soup and the lesson was the three of us eating. She wanted to pay me but - you can't when people have been generous with what little they've got, can you? I couldn't. You wouldn't. You always gave.

THE SOLDIER'S HOME

One of my French students – David, a man who publishes chemistry text books and calls himself a 'Francophile' - he has a Television.

This is A Very Big Thing Indeed here. It's the size of a large box, it has two dials on the front (like Feyt's radio) and an aerial – which I can't understand how it works - and it's electric and it's a house-sized cinema! He turned it on, it hummed a bit and it showed something called The Gillette Cavalcade of Sports! David turned to a different 'Network' (there are thirteen) and we watched a newsreel - from all around the world! When Jacques sees it, he'll want one.

David talks about the economy here - which makes it tricky to correct his French because I don't know what he's talking about. He says industry is at a standstill. Because of the strikes. The last time I talked economics was in Lyon and it felt like another life. Another me.

Happy New Year. I pray the thaw comes soon and you write to us. He needs you. I heard someone call someone a bastard the other day and I dread that happening to him. He needs a picture of his father - not a photo - but a feeling in his heart that's real.

Another year. Can you see Time? Did you know it was New Year? Did Sara come?

Too cold to be coherent.

Simone.

24

TELL US ABOUT THE HOUSE. Have you the foundations done? Starting walls? If I send you some crayons you could draw him a picture - he'd love that.

   I'm searching for what will encourage you to write. Regularly.

   I feel I'm writing into a white void.

   I bought a radio. It's fantastic, Jacques. There must be a thousand different stations in a hundred different languages. His favourite is Sports commentaries in Hispanic. The game is baseball. 'Our' team, The New York Yankees (I don't know why they're 'our' team - there's two other teams in New York) are ready for A World Series. I don't know! It means nothing to me! I'm telling you so you can see your two-and-a-half-year-old son, sitting (looking!) at the radio while a man in another language gabbles a hundred and nineteen to the dozen and he, Jacques, squeals with laughter. It's called Enchantment, I think. Jacques has no idea (I don't think!) what's going on – but he literally fell off his chair laughing the other day. I like that station too, cos when he's gone to bed they play Spanish music.

   Oh, I've decided I am French.

THE SOLDIER'S HOME

*I buy a French newspaper once a week. You can buy **everything** in this city.*

I didn't buy him the chimney pot - I found a big box of paints, four different sizes of brushes, some old jam-jars for mixing and a roll of white wall-paper. So, there'll be pictures for you.

David, the man with the television, suggests I apply to become a teacher. It would be regular work and pay.

It's 1947 outside the door and I wonder if you know. Or care.

Jacques, please to tell us where the house is up to. He asks.
And his biggest question, 'When will it be ready?'
This letter's back where it started.
I'm putting all our cents (like centimes) in a big saving bottle.
Saving for one day...

S.

25

DEAR JACQUES,

Americans eat 714 million gallons of ice-cream every year.

There are strikes all the time now. The government has taken over running the railways. I bought Le Monde and de Gaulle has resigned. I'd ask you why but you don't give a fig, do you?

Your son is bi-lingual. When I met his new nursery teacher she'd no idea he was French (she thinks he's called Jack).

Sara sent me a sweet card explaining no-one could get to Janatou - or from it.

I can't think of anything else. Cold makes you tired but you know that better than I do. How many more winters?

A man whistled at me today. I blushed. Why? Because I remembered I was attractive. And then I thought – attractive as what? And he whistled again and I looked back and he was whistling at another woman. I didn't like it and I did like it. Now he's asleep I've come back to that thought and I think of us - paired - like an *octopus - eight limbs and one heart - and I missed you and I miss you and I feel alone again, very, and you are alone and I wonder why and I don't have any answers to any of the questions and I wish I wasn't thinking because I had you – you - Vermande - inside me and my bed. Now.*

'Iffing'. Isn't that what your mother called it?

Simone.

He was always hard after he read that letter.

26

DEAR JACQUES,

Your son is at a stage I can only call 'The Why's'.

Last night. 'You can't listen to any more radio.' 'Why?' 'It's past your bed-time.' 'Why?' 'Because your body needs to sleep.' 'Why?' 'It's tired.' 'It's not.' 'It is - your mind isn't.' 'Why?' 'Because your mind is wide awake with 'why?' 'Why?' 'Because you're learning and its fun!' 'Why?' 'O. Because I Say SO!'

Then his bottom lip comes out and his eyes go darker and I can hear him thinking real bad thoughts. So I said, 'I know - you hate me - tough - go to bed.' This morning he was still black eyed and I said, 'I know. You don't like I can see what's inside your head.' That was a mistake. I need to think.

The cent bottle's half-full. How's the walls?

Simone.

27
A card with a picture of a little steam boat.

IT __MUST__ HAVE THAWED. Write. I don't like to ask Sara to do your duty for you - it's mean. We're going to look at Staten Island. Beachland Amusements.

28

A card with a picture of a long metal bridge over a river.

THANK YOU. Letter tonite.
  S

29
The worst.

DEAR YOU,

*In the end, some nights, **some** nights, what you are doing is too much for me.*

People say, 'Where's his father?' and I don't say, 'Oh, re-building our house by hand.' Because I don't want to see them thinking what I think. That it's mad, Jacques.

Some letters - this one, finally - I want to tell you that it must be over.

*Do you **really** think that I'll leave here to come back and live in a field?*

And I know you do. You must. You think it's the price you pay for sending us away to live.

You can't dream we'll come back (when? – in ten years?) and just pick up where we left off. That's crazy-time, Jacques.

Don't you ever think that what I'm living is not my life Without You - it's My Life.

*Yes, with **your** son - but what will he be when you're done? An American teenager. I promised you we'll come and I won't break that promise but you must understand – must know - that your paradise - me, you and him - is a dream.*

I can't live with you believing that it must happen.
And I can't believe you live without the conviction that it will.

Maybe I'm wrong.
Maybe in 5 years time he and I will hate America and long for France and home and you. I can't say. Like before – I can't promise.
But I fear your dreams.
And worse - I fear wounding them.
I'm afraid of killing you.
I'm afraid these words could kill you.
But I have to write them.
Honestly I do.

It's me. Here. Tonight in two rooms in a tenement block in America.

Don't hope it's not true. It is. Tonight.

I always knew one day I'd really hurt you and this must be it.
I feel cruel.
I don't know why I'm writing pain - I'm only sure I must.
Will I post it? Yes. No. Yes.

I beg you to release me from your dream.
So we may come when we can – but not because we have to.
That would be wrong. For all three of us.

I don't know the future.
I'm not sure about the present.
I do know the past - and - it's gone.
I have to grow him to Love and Respect you and I can't when I feel like this.

THE SOLDIER'S HOME

There - finally you have my fears.

I feel like a prisoner of your hopes. Tell me how to help you honestly, because Jacques, I haven't been honest for a year and more. I've held you up because I dreaded putting you down. That's insulting you. It's false, Jacques. This is true.
Simone.

It's morning and I haven't slept and I have to get him up and out to nursery and me to work and to post this if I dare. Rain. I owe you this life and some days I feel so good and so grateful I could maim myself for the hurt you've been in. That can't be right. I can't grow if I'm shackled to that guilt. And I can't remove it. He's waking. I must go - get on with his life, this life.

I remember.
I remember the grasping at 'I won't break that promise.'
I remember that day, every stone, every slap of mud cement.
One hand asking, 'For what?'
The other grasping, 'I won't break that promise.'
And it rained here. Her rain came in the envelope.
I remember I wrote.

'You should only try suicide once. I won't again.
I'm building a home.
When it's done I may have forgotten.
Some days I work so I will forget.
Some days I work because I have to provide for you both. If you won't need it - then that'll be another Life.
I have money.

The world turns once a day. It seems quick compared to my world.

There is no 'when'. There is only 'if'.

I'm building 'iffing'.

So yes, I'm mad.'

30

DEAR JACQUES,
 Spring is good and here. He'll be three soon. Three years.

 I read your letter many times and you're right. We live with the 'if's'. What else can we do? I hope your money is in a bank, Jacques.

 I will take David's advice and apply to the school system here.

 I feel happier for what I said and for what you said. Yes, there are days when I forget and days when nothing and no-one else is in my mind.

 Simone.

31

DEAR JACQUES,

Did you know about Lafayette and his help during the American Revolution? No - me neither! But when I made a first tentative enquiry to see if I even **could** teach - they greet me with open arms - because I'm French. Did you know the French gave America The Statue of Liberty? So, when they discovered I speak and teach German they fell over themselves. I was given a list of fifteen (!) schools, for **me** to choose from. I've chosen the one nearest here - Hester Street Junior and Senior High and they've promised to take Jack when he's 5.

I worried about my legal status but no-one else did - they're short of teachers - and there's The Displaced Persons Act for those who fled either the Nazis or The Russians. Americans seem paranoid about Russia, which is bizarre - they just defeated a common enemy and when we got here I saw posters of Russian soldiers and - in big letters - This Is A Friend. Not any more... It feels, and I could have this wrong, that if the working-people (paysans to me and you) ask for higher wages they're branded Communists - and that seems to be the new dirtiest word in the American language.

THE SOLDIER'S HOME

This city! You can go shopping at midnight!

I have days when I'm glad he's growing here because if you can survive this you can survive anything.

His birthday? He needs shoes. His feet are like courgettes - never stop growing. He needs trousers. He does not need guns. I 'lost' the one Susie gave him and he made three new ones out of breakfast cereal packets. I think the teacher at nursery showed them how. You read the papers and there are gun murder stories every day. Their films are guns. Their History is guns. Guns are glamorous. And I think of the soldiers who came to Puech - and the guns that killed my mother and father. They're destruction.

Not here. I don't understand and I don't want to.

His present, father? A letter - he'd love that more than anything money could buy.

I've just read this through and it's all of a ramble - like New York. And - I forgot! - I start teaching in September!

You said I'd be a teacher! You promised.

What else can you see? Can you see this smile? Hey!! Come with me now - come on, come Jacques - I want to show you something. Round this partition, move that red curtain aside - gently - shh, there! There's the last of your curls. Doesn't he smell warm, eh? One kiss and no more or you'll wake him and he hates that!

Sleep now, us parents.

Simone.

32

WHEN I WALKED to Souceyrac to see the Curé for the first time, you went to Janatou - and we sat at evening and I SO wanted you to ask me something and you didn't. And that was you.

When I told you about the children and the barn - and you said 'yes' - I think I began to love you a little then.

If it's not exactly true there's a truth in it. Because you gave me what I wanted..!

Sometimes it's not the smartest thing to examine our reasons for doing things, is it? I bet you think that, don't you, you single soldier?

There's a habit here to examine thought that I'm not sure is so damned smart either.

Last night something happened outside the house I want to tell you about and I realised I've never described where we are - and I thought, 'Does he want to know?' and then I remembered you wouldn't ask...

So. Here it is!

The house has six floors, four apartments on each floor, so twenty-three post boxes. Twenty-three because the janitor has a ground-floor room and he sorts the mail. He's supposed to sweep the stairs.

THE SOLDIER'S HOME

He never does. There's always a dead cigarette in the corner of his mouth and he's real old.

We live on the fourth floor with the Italian woman, Teresa, opposite; the Spanish woman, Maria, at the end of our landing and a real American family, The Potters, in the other flat. There's no such thing as 'real' Americans - everyone is an immigrant. (Yes, his name is not Jack, but that's what everyone calls him here. I won't again, I understand) I suppose the area is poor. Yeah.

My school is two blocks away, south. His nursery is one more block away. A block is a street. New York is made of straight lines!

Anyway - last night, through the open window, outside the house, about seven o'clock, we heard singing. We went to see. Jacques, there were five boys - the oldest maybe fifteen - on the steps, singing! People came down to listen and clap and it's called Doo-Wop! You can't listen without a smile. There's part of New York called Harlem and this music comes from there. We're going up Harlem at the weekend! There's so many parts of New York we haven't been to - do they all have their own music, we wonder?

The boys just sang - no instruments. 'Zip-a-Dee-Doo-Dah' was the best. After a half-hour they'd sang all they knew and we clapped and they bowed and Jacques loved it. This city can feel like the centre of the world - every colour, every race, every religion, every language.

Our first jar is filling. We'll count it only when it is full. It's very real in his mind and I'm determined it shall stay so.

Your son demands to know where you're up to with the building. I bought him an alphabet chart for his bedroom wall and some first reading books. Teresa made him an Italian birthday cake. It was sweeeet.

Simone.

33

JACQUES,

Saturday came and on Friday David was very circumspect about our going to Harlem. He wanted me not to - but you can't break a promise, can you? He flat said it was dangerous. I said I had Jacques to protect me and he didn't think that was funny - and in the end he practically begged me not to go - and when I said it was not his affair he made me promise not to go in the evening.

So, we caught the morning subway, all the way him expecting we'd step out into singing.

I said the area where we live is poor. What does the word mean? You and I were 'poor', weren't we? Jacques - Harlem! The rooming houses are **teeming** with people - people sleep in the streets, in alleyways, all the shops have iron bars over their windows, and at ten o'clock on a Saturday morning there was no chance of anyone singing.

People, men, were drunk and all of them, the people, are Negroes. Africans. You've never seen a black person, have you? There's so many here I never thought to mention it. The boys who sang were negroes.

He wanted a drink so we walked up 135th street a block, looking for a café or anything open, frankly. Everywhere everyone staring. A

THE SOLDIER'S HOME

sign said 'Breakfasts' and we went in. It was too dark, Jacques. Down a long corridor and a corner and a big dark, windowless room with a bar and men, drinking, and very suddenly not only was I the only woman but we were the only white people. I can't describe the feeling. Jacques, bless him, walked straight up to the counter and asked for a Coke! (It's the fizzy drink.) The man laughed, went to the ice-box (it keeps things cold) and gave him one, then asked what I wanted. I said a coffee and everyone laughed. A man who'd been playing cards said, 'Give me girlie a rum.' I couldn't refuse because the man put money down to pay. I thanked him and looked for a table. Only boxes. Rum starts off tasting sweet and then sets fire to your chest. I coughed and everyone - and there must have been twenty or thirty men in there – at that time of the morning! - laughed as I spluttered.

So, there we were, Jacques, in this cavern. New York and everything safe - our rooms, you and France never seemed so far away. If I hadn't had him with me I could have been very afraid. A man brought two boxes from a corner and we sat. Breakfasts? We were in a drinking den.

*The man who'd bought the drinks sat with us. Why were we here? Jacques said we'd come to hear the singing. Sad laughter. Not till real late evening the man said. Off went your son. 'Why?' 'Do you sing in the morning?' the man asked Jacques. 'No,' he said. 'Well, neither do I,' said the man. 'Why?' Laughter. 'Why don't **you** sing?' the man asked. 'I don't know,' Jacques said. Then the man said, 'Men don't sing. Boys sing.' 'Why?' 'Cos men is sad and they boys ain't learned sad yet. You ain't sad, are you?' 'No.' 'There you are.'*

Then the man asked, 'Where you from?' and Jacques said, 'France.' I was so proud of him. Now everyone in the bar looks blank. 'Is that far uptown?' someone asked. I said, 'It's Europe.' Everyone still looked blank; so I said 'Where the war was.' A man said, 'Japan? France is one of them damn itty-bitty islands?' Now they were all talking and a new man came out of the dark and said, 'I was out East - ain't no France there.' I said, 'No, not that far East - Europe.' 'What - Eng-a-land?' the first man asked and I said, 'Near there, yes,' and now everyone understood. 'Oh! Eng-a-land. Churchill?' I said, yes. It seemed easier than mentioning De Gaulle and now toasts were made and more drinks poured and the man offered me another and I said I'd rather have a coke and he asked for a rum-and-coke. The man who'd come from the corner toasted the war. I asked him why. And, Jacques, he said 'In the war, in the army, I was an equal; I was a brother in arms to me white sergeant and the boys in me regiment. Now we got peace and I'm a dirty nigger again...'

Everyone agreed and the mood in the bar changed and I had no idea to what or why. And I felt guilty. And I had no idea why.

Jacques asked could we go and we came home.

I've asked a lot of questions since and heard a lot of different answers. Black people are inferior, is the most common. They (Negroes) have separate schools, separate buses, separate churches and Harlem is like a separate place where they live. I thought again of M. Feyt. This is the same as being a Jew, in Germany - and France. But in a country with so many different kinds of people..? I heard tell of a priest who preaches the black man has to suffer because God made him ignorant.

There are times when I need to talk to you - like when I came back from Souceyrac - and this is one.

And the reason I went to Souceyrac and didn't come to Janatou was because I'd decided I had to **do** something. I feel that same feeling. I didn't know what then - and I don't now.

Simone.

34

DEAR JACQUES,

David took me to Manhattan. Jacques, you can take a subway ride from Manhattan to Harlem and go from inconceivably rich and white to dirt poor and black. And, in the middle, the Europeans.

David talked about a law called Harty-Taft which will restrict working people from demanding their right to bargain for better wages, or from forming unions - and they have to swear not to be communists. This communist thing is more serious here than I'd imagined. When I start teaching - in two weeks - I may have to sign something similar. My father was a communist - I'll be betraying him.

Something in me is getting angry - good! People here, even David, are wary of talking about the communists and what they want. Well, the Communists won't be, will they? I'm going to find a meeting...

I'll write again soon, but suddenly, what with planning lessons and him and all these new things - well - you know how hard it is to find time to write! I'm sorry, that sounds mean - it's not meant to be.

Busy me, busy you.

Simone.

35

A post-card with a different bridge on it. Brooklyn Bridge.

JACQUES,

When you have good reason to be jealous I will let you know. David is twenty-nine years older than me. Get on with your work!

THE SOLDIER'S HOME

36

I'VE STARTED TEACHING, but I'll write about that next time.

We can't thank you enough for the letter. We got out our crayons and spent all evening drawing. I've drawn a picture of how I remember the house and we've put the one we did from your letter next to it. And next week we count the pot! But he can picture it. All the cave walls finished - how did you get those beams up? Did Arbel come? We haven't drawn the bache because then he couldn't see the house.

Are you proud? No. Not you.

When he'd gone to bed I sat and read your letter again and there you were, sitting in the autumn sun bending, writing, thinking, working. And Jacques, I dared imagine you aren't lonely. It's more I hope you aren't. Don't be afraid to tell me. I hope there's nothing you can't tell me. And there must never be anything you can't tell him.

Your family.

37

DEAR JACQUES,

I've done two weeks and the Headmaster seems pleased.

I have a room, 'The Language Lab' and when the bell rings - I jumped out of my skin at the end of my first lesson and all the children laughed, so that was good - the children leave my class and another forty come in. There are desks, which are screwed into the floor. I've no idea why but I'm taking my time asking...

I'm teaching French, no German (!), some Spanish (I've asked may I bring Maria into the school) and English – because there are children here who speak no English. On my first morning I got my 'curriculum' (that's Latin - a dead Italian language!) and the Headmaster gave me the registers and a leather strap. 'To beat the children with.' I put it in a drawer and I've sworn never to use it. I'm pretty unusual let me tell you. I've no idea what I'll do if Jacques ever comes home and says he's been strapped.

School, first lesson, starts at nine - we have an hour for lunch at twelve and then from one till three - when the darned bell rings for the last time and I can get Jacques from nursery.

The important thing is Jacques is happy. We walk to our schools

THE SOLDIER'S HOME

each morning and he only has to wait ten minutes for me to pick him up every evening and he's adjusted to this new routine. He's like you - adaptable. And the second important thing is - I can do this. I was nervous but the children seem to enjoy me. One of the older boys got real cheeky - sassy - he asked about my husband. I asked about his wife and everyone laughed.

The strangest thing is I've begun to think in English. A couple of nights ago I dreamt in English. That was weird. 'Weird' is American for strange.

We've started the second jar! We have nearly thirty dollars! I have no idea what two tickets across an ocean and back will cost and for the moment I don't want to find out because I'm afraid they'll be so expensive it'll seem like we'll never get there and I don't want to depress him - but I wonder if maybe our jars and our house will be full and finished at the same time... What do you think?

They say it's going to be another bad winter. What will you do for heat when winter comes, Jacques? I'd like to know - it would make me feel warmer.

I'm going to my first communist meeting next week. David said don't tell anyone. I'm telling you. You won't tell, will you?

*God! What **is** this? Politically immature nonsense.*

Simone.

'And back.'
How many times he'd read that.
'Across an ocean and back.'
Like a black mantra.

38

A post-card with a picture of buildings at night
glowing with electric lights.

DEAR JACQUES,

    *This is Times Square. An aeroplane broke the sound-barrier. I
told Jacques. 'Who's going to mend it?' he said. I don't even know
what it is. Was. It's broken now. In a rush. S.*

39

DEAR JACQUES,

I went to the communist party meeting. It was dull and exciting. A man called Jerry spoke first about The International Conspiracy of Capital (don't ask - I don't know - yet) and how The American Government were passing laws to suppress the spirit of the working-man (he didn't once mention women) and how we all had to fight it because an injury to one is an injury to all. He talked about the economic imprisonment of the ghettos and The Marshall Plan. (All the papers and all the teachers at school are very proud of this. It's a package of inconceivable amounts of money to help 're-build Europe' - it seemed rather marvellous to me, too) Jerry said the real aim of the plan was to isolate Russia from the rest of Europe - because, of course, of the fear of Communism. He talked of a man called Henry Ford, a car designer, who's just died and left 600 million dollars in his will! He said most Americans consider this admirable, enviable; but we had to remind ourselves daily it was an obscenity. He talked about the 'evil' of something he called Consumerism and how it could consume the spirit of brotherhood in The American People. And he finished by saying that spirit was truly alive only in us.

By the time he finished I was of a mind to believe him. I felt my father would have. And I thought of Jerome, too. Other men spoke and whilst I believed what they were saying I wasn't moved by any of them. And that made me think. Hitler was an orator, wasn't he? De Gaulle certainly was - I've never forgotten that night at M. Feyt's. There was a lot of talk about 'an iron curtain' between the West and Russia.

And in the end I got bored. It would be wrong to deny it. There was a collection and I wasn't sure I wanted to give money – but I did - a little - and as the meeting finished I asked a man why there were no black people there and he said, 'Cos niggers understand nothing but cotton and dancing.' Another man said, 'Because there ain't no civil rights for Nigrahs.' Then he took me aside and said of the other man, 'He believes in a Brotherhood of white men.'

Then, as we were about to leave, the chairman reminded us to be cautious about Government spies… The meeting was three subway stops from home and though four or five men got on my train, none of them sat together. And they call this The Land Of The Free!

I know all this will mean, perhaps, less than nothing to you, and if you ask me not to discuss it with you - but to only write about your son and his life, I will understand. But you always listened.

I'm confused and ignorant. Is that the same thing? I don't know if I'll go again.

When I got home he'd missed me and if the important thing is to stand for something then I stand for him. And how do I stand for you beyond putting my cents in our jar and not the hands of The Communist Party?

It'll be Christmas in two months and the shops are ready to sell us everything. Jacques wants a cowboy outfit. More guns. And a television. Susie is getting married in two weeks and we've been invited to the wedding. Jacques said, 'What's 'getting married?'" and I told him, and he said, 'Like you and Poppa?' and I said we hadn't had time to get married. I couldn't tell him the truth. For once he didn't say, 'Why?' I worry if somehow he knew I wasn't telling him the whole truth. I don't know.

I'm lonely.

Simone.

40
More horrors.

DEAR JACQUES,
  Isn't this great? It's called a typewriter
- I'm in Mrs. Hughe's office - it's lunch-
hur and sjhe leant it to me. It's a machine
to write letters with and it's Electirc! It
makes a clack-clack noise every tuime I kit
(hit5) one of the keys but it's fun, don't
you think? Oh, yes, the HeadMaster agreed to
let me brinf Maria into one of the classes,
so, that's good.
  Your leter - sorry - letter - was just what
we needed - like always - this is weird§ (ops
- oops, I ment to put a !) but writing on
this I can't think what I want to say - just
so concerned with not makig mistakes like
that one; she had - she HAS a bottle of some
white ink she left me to go ver any msitakes
I might make but I can tell already that this
whole page will would be full of more ink
than words.

```
I think I'm going to stop this and write
you a letter at home and then come in here
and type it - that would be bettter wouldn't
it? We're fine - both of us - God! I just
looked at the clock - it's time to go back to
work - I thought this was sup^posed to make
writing quicker!

Proper letter later.
```

Simone.

I hated that letter more than any other.
I must have - because -

41

DEAR JACQUES,

You write back real quick when you get mad! Maybe I should annoy you more.

Your presents came for us - and I asked him what he'd like to buy with it. He put the money in what he calls Dad's jar. So I did too.

I hope you don't mind being called 'Dad' now and not Pappa - it's the word he chooses and I don't like to correct him. I explained that you didn't like it when I said the boys and teachers call him Jack and not Jacques and he said it was 'cool' to have a special name with just his Dad.

By the time you read this it will be 1948.

David has invited us to his house for Christmas dinner. If we had Time I would ask you - but our Time - yours and mine - doesn't work like that. And by the time you read this we will have eaten it and I'm going to invite him to come to us for New Year's dinner and I haven't time to ask your permission (not 'permission' - but you know) about that, either. And anyway, why should I? You wouldn't want me not to have friends, would you?

Oh yeah! Susie's wedding. I was talking with Teresa and mentioned the wedding and next evening she came with a machine that sews -

THE SOLDIER'S HOME

they have machines for everything here - (when they invent a machine that teaches I'll be useless) - and some smart blue cloth and she made him a little jacket, with three golden buttons and matching trousers. Someone at the wedding, I can't remember who, took a photo of him - 'For my Dad,' he said and Susie says she'll bring it. The wedding was in a Ukranian Church. I had no idea Susie was Russian - or rather, Ukranian (she'd be offended to be called Russian! I don't know why – sometimes there's too much to learn in this world don't you think?) but she is - or maybe her husband is - I never asked - and I couldn't understand a word of it but the singing was beautiful and we went to a hall and everyone (except Jacques and the other kids) got very drunk and there was a lot of music and dancing. It was joyous. Just as it should be. That night I wished you and I had had a day like it. But it wouldn't have happened like that in St.Cirgues. - or anywhere in France, honestly. It was Russian. Ukranian! In America!

Remember I wrote I'd forgotten you for an hour? That happens more. I wish it didn't, but it does. When you come back to me it's all in a rush and I love that. But it's a strange living we don't do. And a great living we did. He's here, I'm here, keep warm, keep building - we keep saving.

Will you see Arbel? I thought long and hard about writing him and Ardelle a letter - but I looked at Jacques and couldn't write, feeling so bad and so grateful in the same moment.

The world's a whirl. Sometimes I envy you the solitude and the purpose you must have.

I wish you the Happiest Christmas and I feel a fool writing such a sentiment.

Simone.

42

DEAR JACQUES,

Here's the photo. Is he handsome or are we biased? And me dancing with a Ukrainian. This, if certain people here had their way, would have me thrown out of my job. There is a government committee, called Un-American activities, intent on rooting out communists they say are in the government. They're attacking a man called Alder Hiss and the papers seem hopeful he'll be put in jail. He's accused of 'Being a communist twenty years ago.' Aren't people allowed to change their minds ever? Not here, not now. One of the teachers, Mr. Hutchinson - he teaches science and I'm glad he doesn't teach me – said, 'Once a Red, always a Red,' and everyone agreed with him. This passes for political debate at lunch-hour. I was going to say that I'd distributed communist literature during the war - but you do not say or do such things.

School is good, there's even talk of unscrewing the desks from the floor - some Government initiative about Education being 'more fun'.

Jacques is good - we read night-time stories together now.

You owe me (and him) two letters.

And I hope that makes you angry.

THE SOLDIER'S HOME

David came for New Year and offered to buy us a television set. Luckily Jacques had gone to bed so he didn't hear me say no thanks. David did say he'd take Jacques to see the Yankees play baseball and I couldn't refuse – he, Jacques, would never have spoken to me again.

I need to register to vote in the election.

I've no idea who I'll vote for.

But I intend to go to some meetings and hear the arguments.

Has it thawed? Please to tell us where you're building now. It's good for him to think about you each day and though you're always in our prayers I wonder some days if that's the only time and I don't want it to be like that.

Help us to stay this bizarre family.

I'm tired, Jacques and I still have to prepare tomorrow's lessons.

The second jar got emptied a little for Christmas presents.

Simone.

43

A post-card of a black man wearing boxing gloves.
A Joe Louis.

NO, I KNOW, but we want to save. It's an active way of keeping you in our lives. You do your bit and we'll do ours. O.K.? Us. This man was a champion. Like you.

44

DEAR JACQUES,

I was going to start by apologizing for not writing, but why should I? You don't. I wondered if I didn't write again - would you? And I didn't know the answer. Jacques' birthday is coming up and I thought will he know if I don't tell him? I know you have the weather and the sun and seasons - but no idea what the date is. And I have no idea what you have around you or within you. I guess sometimes, and then Jacques Vermande, I get mad enough not to guess because guess is what I **have** to do. And then I get guilty. And that makes me mad and I'm into a spiral.

I'm working with the communists. The opposition party - The Democrats - have split and we're supporting the left-wing candidate - Henry Wallace. Jerry said he's as much use as a blind dog but the best of a bad bunch. It's all to do with Berlin and the Russian blockade and Truman tightening his Anti-Soviet position and you're not interested I can tell so I'll stop.

School is still good, though more tiring, because of the political meetings etc; and harder because I have to keep my lip buttoned *as the rest of the staff seem to be all for Dewey. He's the right-wing candidate.*

Have you got your money in the bank? Because the Franc has been de-valued. Did you know that? Why am I asking you? Sorry, it's that real world again, and it's crazier than you, who doesn't write to me. You, who let me worry. You, building a house by your stubborn self.

Jacques' class at Nursery did an Easter concert. I ran there at lunch-hour and saw him singing. You'd have burst with Pride. I did. His teacher took his hand at one point and I saw, realised, he has a friendship with her that I'm no part of. And, that if I were to die tomorrow, he would survive. I felt empty and scared, relieved, proud and worthless, all in one second. And I never wished more in that moment that you'd been there. We'd been together.

Me.
Where are you?

THE SOLDIER'S HOME

45

DEAR JACQUES,

I went to see Wallace speak. He wasn't as good as Jerry, who was there. He remembered me from the first meeting. I don't know why - he never spoke to me.

*The President is now talking about Civil Rights - for the Negroes - which I think is the most important issue. Jerry says it's a vote-catching exercise and he won't **do** anything - that it's smart, but cynical. Jerry has a conviction I find hard to doubt. He expects The Republican, Dewey, to win. Everyone does. Dewey's talking about repealing the Low-Rent laws - which could be A Big Problem for me and Jacques.*

Wallace can't win - so people say, 'so what's the point of voting for him?' Jerry says, 'All you can ever do is send the message.'

So I do, in haste;

S.

46
Another awful one.

*NO, I am not neglecting **your** son and you've got a hell of a nerve even thinking such a thing. Glass houses and stones, Jacques Vermande. How **many** times have I begged you to write to him and how many letters has he had? You're in no position to criticise me. If I write about what I'm doing and not about him it reflects not the constant in my life but the new. If you're suggesting I should be home seven nights a week - that is not the relationship I have with my son. I explain to him, always, where I'm going and why; and I believe he understands his mother is not with him because she has something she wants, needs and feels passionate about doing. That's A Good Thing to teach him, I believe. If I were out dancing - hedonistically enjoying myself - that would be different. I'm not and he knows that. He's not yet four.*

He heaved a sigh. Lit another cigarette.

47

DEAR JACQUES,
I'm writing - he's dictating.

Dear Dad,
I went to see The Yankees. It was a night game. There was an organ playing and we had Popcorn and sausages. David said we won. It was exciting. School is keen. My teacher is Miss Rivanski. We have two jars now and Mom says when we fill maybe another we can come see you. I like it when you write about the house.
I love you,
Jacques. Like you.

P.S. Mom says anything else? No.

Mom says - don't neglect him. Me, I guess. Mom says neglect means forget. Kind of.

48

Horror. Still.

DEAR JACQUES,

He's poorly. There was a bug at school and he's got it. Bad. The doctor's been the last three days and if he's no better tomorrow he'll go to the hospital. It's a viral infection on his lungs. I'm so frightened. This letter will take days. I'm praying. Join me.

Simone.

THE SOLDIER'S HOME

49
A plain post-card.

I'M WITH HIM at the hospital. Its congestion of his lung. My hand is shaking. Pray, Jacques, pray. He's very weak.

50

It had come the following day. Another plain post-card.

HE'S IN what they call intensive care. The doctor said, 'It's up to him, now' and somehow that's hopeful. Something has to be. We have to be.

He remembered the seven or eight days between that post-card and the next letter. How he'd done nothing. But pray to every star, every tree, every bird, and every stone that waited for him.

THE SOLDIER'S HOME

51

JACQUES,

He's home. His chest is weak - one lung is bad and will probably always be so - but the other is enough for him to live a normal life the doctors said. I have to believe them.

He was bad, Jacques. They let me stay four days and nights and he was bad. But he came through. He's going to be fine. He's watching television. David bought it. He's watching a ball game right now. He's here.

Jacques, I was so scared - so helpless and so scared.

And you must have been.

I had awful thoughts. And you must have had.

But he's here and they promised me he's safe.

There might be a problem at my school but I don't care.

It was horrible. And it's over. I'll write tomorrow.

Simone.

52

DEAR JACQUES,

   He's sitting up in bed watching a man called Buster Keaton. I can hear him laughing. **Some**times he coughs but not so much now. Soups and solids. In the end, with the cost of the hospital and the doctors and the worry about work - there was only one question - is he going to Live? He is. But the mending is slow. **You** know that. Write him - he'd love that.

   S.

53

DEAR JACQUES,

Next week he can go back to Nursery for one morning. So I can work. I have to - I had a letter saying they can't hold the post open indefinitely blah-blah. Like I'd had a choice! The rent's paid and I have a little if Times get tough. Only Mrs Hughes has been to see us - from the school. David comes and Teresa and Maria. Jerry called in, too, which was sweet of him and I appreciated it. Not much to show for three years is it? Two neighbours, one secretary, one student/ friend, one communist...!

I'm exhausted. Forgive me.

Simone.

54

I'M TO BE REPLACED. I kind of understood the Headmaster's point of view. What can he do? He's got the Education Board on his back - they don't give indefinite leave. He has to accept the replacement they've suggested. He promised he'd recommend me 'highly'.

Jacques goes to nursery three mornings a week and next week he'll try four - but he gets tired and needs rest. I do three students on those mornings and although President Truman did win there is still the threat of a rent-rise and I daren't think about that and it's hard not to. When he's back full-time I can look for another job - that shouldn't be a problem - but I can't and won't till he's 100%.

Suddenly it's nearly Christmas again and we shall have to empty both jars.

Write - it cheers him so. More than anything I do! You're special in his heart.

And mine.

Simone.

His cigarette had gone out.

55

DEAR JACQUES,

I asked you to put that money in a bank.

I told you to.

You're what they call here a blame fool, Vermande. They've changed the currency - its worthless paper.

I told you The Germans weren't coming back and they didn't, did they?

Why don't you listen to me?

You said once I knew more than you - and in some ways I do. When will you learn?

Jacques' gone to watch football with David. It's his Christmas Treat. Mine was wrapping him up to go, feeling certain he could cope. That was a Christmas present.

Did Sara come?

1949 when you read this. I went to a Library and looked at a book about house construction. My God!

I can't write - my head is full of fear and thankfulness.

With Love and my Hopes for you, always.

Simone.

'Fear'. Her head was full of fear? He'd read that word over so many times. Fear of what? Who? Fear of telling me something bad?

56

SALUT FROM SPRING IN NEW YORK,

I have a new job - donc, the immediate financial crisis is past. I'm working in the office of the factory where Jerry works. He told me about the vacancy, I did an interview, must have done good - I start on Monday. They make industrial components - something called ball-bearings, and I'll be in charge of dealing with any customers who use German, French, Spanish or even Italian. And the coffee-machine.

It means we have to move - nearer to the factory. I can't get him to Nursery and me to work. It means finding new schools too. It means looking nearer Harlem and I'm kind of excited by that. The President is to stop segregation in the Armed Forces and even I can see the thin edge of a wedge. Civil Rights is Time versus Prejudice - and I'm in for some of that struggle.

We're going up-town apartment hunting now. Post this from there.

Us.

57

A post-card of a group of black men,
singing, on a street corner.

HERE WE ARE! Apartment 5,
    1127, West 113th Street,
    New York City.

Love, Les Vermandes.

58

JACQUES your letter was beautiful. The stars - I could touch them with you as you walked. Beautiful. More please. My heart is so warm with you tonight. Four years. I'd forgotten just how much I was waiting for that letter. Jacques and I painted the ceiling of his room dark blue and we're cutting stars from tin-foil to put up.

Your family.

He'd done so much the day that letter came.

59

DEAR JACQUES!

I bought some paint called luminous. We painted your stars with it and then lay on his bed, pulled the blinds, turned the lights off and Jacques – they glowed! He made me 'really honestly' promise the sky in France had so many stars. Because, with all the electric lights even on the roof of a house you'd be lucky to see a dozen on a good clear night. I promised him this was what his father sees every cloudless night.

It's going to be O.K. this place. It's what they call a rooming house - but its first floor (hooray!) with its own (filthy) bathroom. Like everywhere there's shops and stalls on the corners and Saturday is market-day and 'the mommas come with cake'. These are the negresses with their home-cooking. I bought some ginger cake-bread - buttered it and it was delicious. His new school is poorer than Hester Street - the whole area is - but what can I do? I owe money I borrowed to pay rent when he was ill but this all should fit together. Owing money is horrible. Everyone does it - Jerry says the country is building itself on credit - but I hate it.

There's a coloured family on the ground floor with a boy of Jacques' age and I aim to make friends with them. I'm a bit obsessed

THE SOLDIER'S HOME

with the separate laws these people live under. It's a waste of people. I daren't say in front of Jerry but I like the President. I wouldn't want the job, that's for sure. The idea that one man can be considered in any way responsible for this whole country is certifiable. To me it proves America's need to dream.

I'm engaged with this place, Jacques - it's vibrant. I mean the whole country, not just this new part of this city. It's unfair and greedy and gaudy and full of hope and possibility. It's cruel and violent. Everyone is here - all nations - and the blacks, like the Jews in Germany - are definitely the bottom of the pile. There's fear of unions and communists - so it's like Vichy in that way. Except you wonder who's collaborating with who. And what for. And, you have to keep telling yourself - this is peacetime..!

You don't care, do you? - but if you were on Arbel's bench and had a cigarette and a fire you'd let me talk and you'd listen - so - this is what I am at the moment. Engaged in the energy and contradictions of this place. And he, our son, just accepts it of course. And, so far, it's been good to him. And he's a lovely fellar, your boy. You'll be proud of him. You are - I can feel it across the fireplace.

Money's tight.

My job is boring - but the men on the factory-floor... Jacques!

Imagine ploughing one furrow. Now go back and do it again. The same one. Why? Don't ask. Just do it. Do it all day. And all day tomorrow. For five and a half days a week, every week. For a year and then the next. Because you've got mouths to feed. And now imagine endless clanging machinery. Add in oil fumes from the machine and the broken heating. Oh, and it is way too loud to hear anyone speak.

The women in the office are dull. They travel in, with their sandwiches in plastic boxes called Tupperware. They have parties where they sell this stuff to each other! And they talk about clothes and kitchens and occasionally children but more passionately new furniture and they seem content, damn them.

The manager/owner is more interesting. Engaged, pressed, needs help, constantly worried.

The whole place is ugly.

Jerry talks about better working conditions but without all the workers being in a union – (illegal now) he has no chance because 'Unionist' means 'Communist' and Communism is worse than being black. Although there's this one singer, Paul Robeson, and he's a negro **and** a communist - and **everyone** thinks he's great! It's like - they'll allow one.

Jerome would love it here! Where is he? Do you know?

It's late now - but our stars will shine. I love that it sends him to sleep with you in his head. Should I do my ceiling? Sure! We're a family - let's sleep under the same stars.

Simone.

60

A picture postcard of Harlem. Huge buildings.
Crowded together. No cars.

YOU'VE NEARLY DONE THE BIG ROOM? Here am I worrying about your son coping with change and I think of his father - focused, forthright, determined, dogged - what's to fear? If he's your flesh and blood he'll survive anything, right? One proud Mom.

61

DEAR YOU,

It's started. Half a million steel workers stopped work in protest about wage-controls and working conditions and across the country other workers joined in sympathy. Including Jerry and most of the men on our shop-floor. All the Unionists. The manager sacked them all. Twenty-four of them. No wages - just sacked. For 'breaking their contract to work.' That's the law. Twenty new men started last week. To do the work of twenty-four? Oh, yeah. The business lost orders, couldn't accept new orders, lost payment when goods were late; and so, the very worst crime of all – they lost Money. Lost much more money than if they'd let the work-force support the steel men for an hour. Where's the sense? The sense is that the boss has got rid of his communists and put the fear in anyone ever to even think of such an action again.

Because Jerry helped me get my job and lost his I felt bad. And that I ought to resign. In protest. Or sympathy. And I was scared. Money. The rent. Living. I couldn't.

I could - but as Jacques' parent I couldn't.

Jerry came one night, said he didn't blame me – fact is he seemed

THE SOLDIER'S HOME

thrilled I'd even considered it. He's looking for work. It'll be hard. America is harsh and getting harsher. And I don't (dare) say at work I agree with Jerry. What's that? Betrayal by omission. It rots at my soul, Jacques.

I borrowed the book on house-building from the Library so you can tell us what you're doing - and we can draw it and write you about it. Share it.

Another day another dollar tomorrow.

There are ball-bearings in everything. God, they're dull. So, I'm at a grindstone, too.

Night night.

Me.

Oh! We met the coloured family - the little boy is called Dwayne - he's coming for tea next week. Jacques can't wait to show him the stars. His mother, Clara, is warm as fresh brioche and the father isn't there. I didn't ask where he was. You don't.

62

PROBLEM. Jacques' school. We have a choice between two. The better one is Catholic. The other one is bigger, poorer and non-denominational. Hurry and give me your wisdom. I have to register him soon.

Me.

THE SOLDIER'S HOME

63
A plain post-card.

GOOD FOR YOU! That's what I thought and in the end, had to do.
Like we've said - he'll survive. Two months since I seemed to have
space to write. Tonight, I promise. S.

64

THAT PROMISE WENT WITH THE WIND, didn't it? I apologise. Our lives could not be more different - I'm in a whirl and you're alone. Where do I start?

Jacques is in his 'big' school - he insisted on wearing his suit the first day and he must have got ribbed because he sure hasn't suggested it again. His teacher is a Polish Jewish lady, which (snob and fellow-immigrant that I am) I'm thrilled about and Jacques likes her but I wouldn't want her job - there are more than forty children in her class...

Me? The manager asked for suggestions for how the business could be improved. I sat down (with Jerry, I admit) and wrote five pages - from painting the place, to longer lunch-hours, better and therefore longer holidays, a health-care insurance scheme for the workmen particularly, everything I've ever thought of to humanise the place. He called me in next morning - made me his 'staff liaison-officer', gave me a budget of money to spend and doubled my wages.

Clara said, 'Oh, God Bless America!' A country that keeps her close to the gutter because of the colour of her skin...

Jerry laughed and said it only mattered how I used the job and the money. David's reaction was that I should move back down-

THE SOLDIER'S HOME

town (to a 'nicer' area) and buy a car! We're staying here. Jacques and Dwayne are inseparable, (except at school-time!) and I owe the manager re-payment of his trust.

So, I've hired painters, streamlined (what an American word!) the filing system, have health-care insurance people coming to talk and I organised a company night-out - all 35 of us went up-town to see a musical show called 'South Pacific.' It was brash and noisy and romantic and we all had a good night, which was the point. And, I'm learning to drive - because he wants me to meet customers. 'A pretty French girl can't do no harm at all...'

His name, I never told you, is Les - short for Leslie.

And I'm caught between feeling compromised by his money and my responsibilities to Jacques. And the jars. Which are re-filling.

I dared suggest to Les re-introducing a union and got a cold glimpse of the differences between us. I was ashamed of how quickly I said, 'Oh, just a crazy French idea.'

The Russians have exploded their atomic bomb.

I envy you (some days) your life without Politics.

Another Christmas looms.

Clara, who has next to no money, is prepared to borrow so Dwayne gets what she calls 'enough'. What you and I would call more than excess. But I have to consider Jacques' feelings when he compares his presents...

They're selling Envy and Pride. And it's probably plastic.

And you? I expect these great silences. And, I've joined in, haven't I?

Pas bon, but we're both to blame and both been busy. Tell us, then, please.

*Jacques. Because I'm to meet customers I had to buy new clothes - and they had to be smart. And they are. And because the materials are plain nicer, I **feel** better. It's roused a vanity in me that I don't care for. But I look better, I attract the 'right' response from customers, etc. It feels like a honey-trap. Jerry laughed and said, 'You're a civilian now.'*

We send you our love and best for winter. We need to know where you sleep now.

News, please. My best to Sara.

Simone.

THE SOLDIER'S HOME

65

The greatest.
A post-card of a tramp called Charles Chaplin.

*When I'm rich and famous I'm coming to see you - Daddio.
Jacques Vermande - like you. Us two.*

66

DEAR JACQUES,

Happy New Year.

Cars frozen on street-corners. Jacques and I walked to his school and stopped just to watch the traffic-lights changing, reflecting all wide on the snow, it was pretty. And in a city - you need pretty.

Jacques started second-term today, his teacher says he's 'no problem' - it's one of a hundred catch-all phrases that keep Americans full of the illusion that Life is Peachy-Keen. See what I mean?

Jerry finally got a job. He saw an ad for a grave-digger on the door of a church. He told the church-board he was a communist, and that he thought Christ was, too - and he believed Christians the only people with the moral courage to offer him work. He got it. I reminded him Marx said, 'Religion was the opium of the masses' and he said he was burying 'em, not raisin' 'em. His sister, Belle, comes to sit with Jacques when I have to be late or go out. She's sweet, shy and seventeen.

The house sounds two-thirds done. Do you have days when you give yourself a pat on the back, Vermande? Pride's a sin, but it's nice, sometimes.

Christmas Day we invited David, Jerry, Belle, Clara and Dwayne

THE SOLDIER'S HOME

to eat with us. David surprised me. I didn't tell him about Clara and Dwayne but to say 'he took it in his stride' would insult him. He was, as we Americans say, 'cool.' We all ate too much and watched TV. And David invited us all to his apartment down-town for New Years.

Boy, that was different.

David's place is super smart and all of us felt a little out of place, especially Clara. Your son, once he'd realised what toasting was - toasted you. We all did. And I talked more about you than I ever have. And it felt great. 'To The House That Jack Built' Jerry offered. We toasted your house. Our house.

Then back to Les Grossman and his ball-bearings. Les is lonely and I fear he's attracted to me and that's what all this promotion and clothes and money is about - not his interest in running a healthier factory. I told him about my Jacques' - both of you - and he hasn't sacked me, so maybe I'm better at smiling at customers and talking quantification than I think I am. 'Lay on the Frenchee,' Les says as we go into each meeting. It works. The women in the office hate me and that makes me laugh. It's a form of no-contact whoring to be blunt, and I do it, our jars fill, we've paid our debts and we can help other people. What's wrong with that? I ask myself that a lot and I wonder why. Clara **always** says, 'Honey, take the damned money! Better you than the Revenue.'

I took Jacques to the big ball game. Apparently, we won and we're World Champions. Someone throws a ball at a batter, he misses - and that's about it. Then, as you're looking around at sixty-thousand people buying still more pretzels and popcorn, one of the darn batters does hit it and you missed it. Jacques adores it. He has a score-card and he scribbles everything down and is disgusted by my ignorance - and he has a point – because he's told me I don't know how many *times the names of the players; but they all wear caps and I can't tell one from the other. They all chew and endlessly spit and I don't care to learn their names. I've warned Jacques about spitting. I can't stop him chewing.*

I have to go sleep, Jacques, we're up early every day but Sunday.

Why did she forget to sign it? Only when it wasn't there did he notice, even today, how different the letter felt without her name.

THE SOLDIER'S HOME

67

JACQUES!

I've just got a letter from Sara. Jerome has gone to fight in some place I'd never heard of. Vietnam? I had to look it up in an atlas. Jacques - he's gone to the other side of the world. Sara said Communists have attacked French territory and there was a call - and he went. To fight communists? Jerome? I couldn't believe my ears. I still can't. The only thing I could think was he's going there to defect to the communists. That I could believe. Sara says Zoe is good. And six!

Writing about you she said, 'He'll finish it.' I could feel her surprise and I heard my own too; because, my dear solitary Jacques, in the years we've been here and our letters and thoughts and cares and worries, the drawing with your son, the library books on building - I never imagined that you'd finish it. Not that you wouldn't – but not that you would either.

Two years? If you don't maim yourself - but you won't now. You know that stone. You've lived with that wood. And somehow, we will come. We have to.

And. In your achievement, I'm afraid.

Because? You expect us to come 'home'.

I can't say that we will.

I can't honestly say that I want to.

And I'm not even sure we should.

*I've never **really** thought about this end of it as seriously as I do now.*

I do know, at this moment, Our Life is Here.

I used the word 'engaged' didn't I? I did. And I am.

And his whole life (you know what I mean) has been here.

And none of us know how he might re-act. Me, you, him - none of us.

Or how you and I will be. Could be. Might be.

So much has happened to you, too.

Jacques - help me, please.

I owe you him. And a part of me - of who I was.

What's best For Him is what's important.More than for either of us.

We can't live side by side with an unhappy child. That's not just.

*And, Jacques, I **am** selfish - there are things here I don't want to give up.*

I'm ahead of myself - I don't know a darned thing - I'm just worrying about hurting you.

I share my shameful fears. And worry that I shouldn't share them.

Talk, you.

Simone.

I remember the letter back took a week to think and a day and a half to write. And a week before I found an envelope. And another week before I went to Maurs to post.

THE SOLDIER'S HOME

Simone,

I remember, but don't want to, why I started this. So you can come. Still, I always told myself you had to want to. Not because of pity.

It's Paradise - why would you leave? Because you sinned and God threw you out? That won't happen. It's a story. And it's been told.

I'm building so you can come home. That's the only thing I know. And that you've said you'll come.

I can't release you from worry about hurting me. You'll kill me one day. Of course.

I do know there's no such thing as the future.

Jacques.

And I posted it before this came.

68

Hell on three pieces of paper.

DEAR JACQUES,

I've never thought so hard before writing to you. Here it is.

I need to introduce Jerry to you, properly.
I care for him.
I am perhaps a little 'in love' with him. Infatuated. I don't love him - but I like him.
And you would.
You did when he was Jerome. But he's more rooted than Jerome ever was.

Jerry asked to address one of the Church's after-service meetings. These are his notes.

Americans have always tried to accumulate goods and goodness.
That's our charm and our paradox.
Believing we can make Heaven here on earth.

I am a communist.
I believe the instinct to help the less fortunate, what we call

'humanity', to be the meaning of 'communism'. To expand the community of humanity to include all. And isn't that the aim of Christianity?

I do not take Soviet Russia to be a marker for a Fair Society.

And no-one should ever seriously claim America is. Both strive, both fail. We strive and constantly fail to reach an ideal. Yours is Christ - mine is Marx. But that striving and failing and striving again is our Humanity. When we choose to place the boundaries of prejudice in front of that instinct, we lose pace with the March of Possibility.

The triumph of our way of life - our system of capital - has been to convince us of the material truth of Possession.

Christ knew a good deal better than that, Christians.

What do I ask? To join for one hour, next Sunday, after church, at 2.00, in a demonstration for Civil Rights - in Central Park. Christ and Marx will both be there – alongside Negroes, communists, crashing bores, and the passion-filled - sometimes one and the same thing! – but a Truly Broad Church - daring to walk, as Senator Humphrey said, 'Forthrightly into the bright sunlight of Human Rights.'

And there will be State and Police Photographers too, guaranteed - and a photo can 'prove' you spoke with A Red.

We are a society at war with its convictions. Please join us.

He, like you, is a part of my life and, as I've told him about you - I want you to know about him.

This must hurt you, but if you wrote about you and Sara, I'd want to know. And there's some serious self-serving bullshit for you.

We shared precious feelings, and I pay you the respect of telling you I sense those feelings rising in me now for someone else. I don't know where they'll lead, or if they'll lead - or anything - I'm only sure I have to tell you, pain and all.

Jacques likes Jerry - though not as much as David, who takes him to sports. I've never told you - though you guessed - he too is attracted to me - but it won't develop and he is a good enough man for me never to have felt I was using him. Even when he lent us money. For one day each week he can be with some sort of family - and the rest of his life is his work and his down-town apartment or the wife he simply will not discuss.

Jacques and Dwayne are making a real friendship. Still no sign of Clara's man - I suspect he's in one of those drinking dens on 135th Street - but she's courageous and laughs and cooks for America and when Dwayne was bad she hugged and slapped him au meme fois! Jerry and Monsieur Feyt are right - Humanity is colour-blind. By definition.

I won't write anymore now - I must wait to hear from you.

Simone.

69

JACQUES,

Your letter came. You're right - there is no such thing as a future and I must stop burdening you with cock-a-mamie plans that are years away.

The only way I could truly re-pay the life you've given both of us is to return it to you. We will come and we will all do our best with snatched time and all three of us will see what we shall see. Until then, we'll fill jars, you'll build walls, and we'll send each other ourselves in envelopes.

I'm driving! I have to take a test to prove I'm not going to kill anyone.

S.

P.S. The priest is under serious Christian pressure to sack his grave-digging communist.

Jerry told the priest to sack him - but, no.

'A Good Man is Hard to Find' a song says here. I feel I've known more than my share in my tiny life.

70

JACQUES - I'm not coming back. He's a war-baby.

I'd like to not have to cast my heart backwards. It no longer wants to. I feel the connection between us stretching; as he grows.

There's no way to resolve this at a distance. Two jars are full (74 dollars) a third is underway and I put my bonuses in there, too.

Out the window I can see storm clouds.
Korea. China.
You live in the reality of a false silence, Vermande.
Sky's started weeping.
I'm a fool, surviving.
Simone.

No wonder Religion is seized like a comfort blanket. Trust God - he'll sort things.

THE SOLDIER'S HOME

71

DEAR JACQUES,

No, I haven't. Yes, I would like to. Yes, he would like to. We haven't, probably, because of Jacques. We will, we hope. I have no notion of being faithful to you, Jacques. Sacred with our memories, yes - but constrained by some Loyalty - no. No more than you are, should be or may not have been. How would I know?

The television is on the moment he comes in. We are separated by it.

I despise my job, and my persona at work.

I go to meetings and listen to talk and do nothing.

I dare not join The Communist Party - so I betray my father, by protecting my son.

I haven't been back to Harlem - I just **think** about it and use Clara and Dwayne to massage my coward conscience.

I should set up at least a union of Office Workers - but I won't. Too judgemental of the other women (I'm a snob too) and too damn scared for my job. I just take the money. I'm an American.

And I can't do right for doing wrong with you.

And as you get towards the roof I get heavier.
Tonight I'm weak as this pissy wine, Jacques.
Release me from my promise - we live here.

Simone.

I replied. 'You sound frightened. And you're right. I was with Ardelle. Once.'

THE SOLDIER'S HOME

72
A plain postcard, it arrived before he'd posted his reply.

A PROMISE IS. I ask your pardon - I was down on myself and took it out on you.

I went with Jerry. It was good to feel as a woman and not as a mother for one night. But seeing you again, in some crazy way - will happen. I haven't **known** *that before this moment. And I look forward to seeing you. Simone.*

73

DEAR JACQUES,

Jar three half full.

Our son's eating habits.

He loves burgers and 'dogs' with ketchup. They're sausages - but not Toulousian - these are red rubber. We're French! We eat food! There have been rows and bad words. He got mad. 'Dwayne eats burgers.' 'David buys me hot-dogs.' I'm asking him (David) to stop. Sweets, candy, ice-creams. Television. Crisps! He wants crisps. If he had his way all I'd see of him would be the back of his head watching T.V. and eating chips. He 'hates' the radio. Says it's 'dumb'. Doesn't want to see the chimneys. Doesn't want to hear the Harlem boys sing - 'I'll miss 'I Love Lucy''

It's the first time I've disliked him. People come round and boy! does he sulk when I turn the T.V. off. He's addicted to it and it tells him to eat chips and ice-cream so he believes it and he **wants** it. Clara gives Dwayne money every day to buy Candy. Advice, fellow-parent, please. People call the T.V. 'the electronic baby-sitter' and I know when I go out he and Belle just sit there, I know it.

I talked to Les's secretary. She 'swore by it' - gives her 'some time of her own' while the kids sit there, glued. There is no time of your own in two rooms with the T.V. on. And Clara **loves** to come up and watch it - most nights there's her and Dwayne and Jacques. She brings packets of cheese biscuits - so he thinks she's great. I'm the dragon who turns it off and makes him go to bed. I think it's the first time he hasn't liked me, too.

Les has put me on a bonus system. 15% of first or new orders, 10% of renewals. Last week I made an extra 47 dollars! I can't accept that. I'm going to insist he spreads the bonus - however thin it is - round all the staff.

My eyes are tired.

I have to be up soon, it's late.

Sleep well.

Me.

74

DEAR JACQUES,

Your letter telling your son to listen to his mom - because she's doing her level best - hasn't come yet. Or the one telling us how the house is. Or news of Sara, Arbel etc - anyone. I'm putting this down until it comes. No. I won't post this until it comes. But we were always good at quiet, too, weren't we? Too damn good.

Thursday 17th
Oct 1950

Maybe you're having too much fun? I wish I believed 'no news is good news'.
20th Oct

I need to write to tell you it is Christmas soon. What difference would it make? How many Christmas days have passed you by? We're worlds apart.
1st November 1950

THE SOLDIER'S HOME

I really resent this un-needed worrying. 'I'm fine' would be accepted. I'm angry. Pissed, we call it.
4th Nov

Shall I tell you I slept with Jerry again? Would that make you angry enough to write? Or type about your kid Jack?
11th Nov
He hasn't asked about you in a long time. He is definitely your son! And that's no joke.
20th Nov

I'll be grateful, resentful, glad and guilty when your letter ever comes. Work is shit.

I'm posting this. It haunts me and it's for you - even though you've forgotten us. Will you feel bad when you get this? Do I hope you will? Will you reply?

If you are suffering Jacques - then you are a selfish fool and I have no memory of your being either of those things - so, I assume you're not suffering.

Get your head up - Look West.

It's where the post comes from.

S.

75

*I'M A LITTLE DRUNK and he's in my bed - third night in a row.
A bad dream, he wakes up, comes to sleep with me. Bullying? No
father? French? He's unsettled. I'll talk to his teacher.*

*He's big! In the bed. And warm. And suddenly needy. And so-o
good to hug.*

*I feel frightened for the first time in five years. Of my future. It
could be Comfortable.*

*I see you in pouring rain - and I have an umbrella.
I see you in sleet and I have snow boots.*

*And him here, breathing - almost snoring - I didn't know children
could snore - but he's troubled and so am I. Wind of change blowing.*

*I've been worlds apart from you. Tonight I miss you and remember
you snored. Did I?*

I feel five years younger and ten years older.

THE SOLDIER'S HOME

Have you started the roof?

Two days later.

I went to check the price of sailing tickets. Take your time roofing, mister. It's expensive.
Jacques – do you still have the money Duthileul gave you?
It's not in a bank, like I told you, is it?
That paper is worthless. It's antique.
We *have to save for this.*
We will save - and this will happen.
I believe it now I know. It will, believe me, take Time.
So, I can't quit the damned job.

Drinking is contradictory. Promises one thing - gives it - then gives something else you didn't want. It's two-faced.
Tired now.
Lights out.
Clara's husband's in jail. For rape. I hope he stays there.
Simone.

76
Plain post-card.

I WRITE long letters. I want long letters.

77
Plain post-card.

Korea; Oh no.

78

DEAR JACQUES.

Changes.

*Last year The Russians exploded their own bomb like the ones in Japan. And people here are afraid Russia will attack. It's insane. How **could** Russia attack? No-one can **attack** America, surely? I know The Japanese did but after what happened to them no-one could ever consider it again, surely? But it doesn't matter what's true or plausible - what's important is what people (are encouraged to) believe. The economic necessity of the Threat of War. And now The Russians have invaded South Korea.*

I know this is all words to you - but even though it's a million miles away - it affects us.

Because. Jerry was called up to join the reserve army and he refused, so he's in jail waiting trial and Les heard, and asked did I support Jerry and I said yes and he sacked me.

So, I have no job. I'm looking - and running out of savings fast (yes, your jars) - I told you it affected us - and I will find a job. I have to - for him - but it means I can't see how and certainly not when, we'll come. All I see is ads in the papers. Oh, and I saw a poster -

THE SOLDIER'S HOME

'Better Dead than Red.'

All of a sudden I hate America. I haven't seen David and I dread asking him for money - but I may have to.

And Jacques' has bad dreams.

I went to school and asked had he been strapped. He had. I told the Headmaster I would take him from the school if he was hit again and he snorted and said, 'Yeah? And send him where?' I found his teacher and asked him why, and he said Jacques had been 'naughty'. I asked how and he 'Couldn't remember, why? What's the big deal?' I wanted to say the big deal is if it happens again I'll chop your head off. I talked and talked with Jacques - but he's like you - he buried the memory deep. And it is his. Maybe I have no right to it. I don't know - I've never been this parent before. Clara said, 'Darlin', sometimes they need a good whoopin'...'

I'll write when I've good news - this is enough bad;
Me.

David did a marvellous thing. He took Jack and Dwayne to a game. He had to pay a lot of money but they all three sat together.

79

DEAR JACQUES,

You're a roofer! It sounds fantastic. That's the second really happy letter. They're the best.

Life here isn't. I'm working - with Clara - cleaning office buildings. We go in at night and work till 6.00. Means I take him to school and fall asleep, set the alarm, get him, feed him, Belle comes - Clara and I go. There's no racial separation of labour at the shit end of the stick. The pay is obscene. We're struggling. Belle stays every night. Jacques trusts her and so do I but I'm looking everywhere. My old Headmaster has nothing but 'will ask around.' That means he'll find out I was sacked for being a Pinko. The education board, falling over themselves three years ago, has zilch. I'll do anything - this is stop-gap - it has to be - it's one rung up from slavery. Organise a union? We'd be thrown on welfare.

David has been kind - but I hate it.

Jerry's 'hearing' has been delayed - twice. He wrote he expects it to be delayed indefinitely - I can't get to see him - I can't get to see anyone or anything. I'm a creature of the night. We're not eating well. No treats.

I sold the television. Jacques didn't speak to me for five days. I slapped him. No better than a thug with a strap. He hasn't forgiven me and neither have I.

And you're on top of the job. Good for you - I'm proud to know you. Steady now - but you are - and you're an inspiration - or you should be. I'm very low, Jacques.

Good news round the corner?

Simone.

One of the cleaners suggested I go whoring. 'Good money - you being a Frenchy...'

I don't think I've considered it, but you never know what your brain hides, do you?

80
The Last.

DEAR JACQUES,

Don't ask - I'll tell you when.

I'm coming. Today is March 10th. The letter takes two weeks. Two weeks after that - April 5th – I fly to Paris. I land very late on the 6th. There is a train on the 7th with connections that get me to Maurs at 6.04 in the evening. The 7th April. You'll be there. Are there taxi's? Anyone with a car? Jerome's mother?

I'm coming alone.

I'll tell you why then.

We have six days before I have to go back. I'd love to see Sara and Zoe.

And we'll talk.

April 7th. 6.04. Maurs Station.

Simone.

He looked up. He didn't remember when he'd lit the candle. But the window was black with the night sky.

Tomorrow was almost here.

🐑

He was at the station by four. At six minutes to six Lavergne drove up, parked his taxi and nodded at the bearded tramp. Who'd paid him 4,000 old francs.

Ten minutes.

She would go back.

This was the six days she would take to say goodbye.

'Iffing?' No.

How can I be so hot with such cold thoughts?

Why am I shaking?

That **is** iffing.

He swayed.

Between the two platforms was a small fountain playing in the middle of a threadbare goldfish pond. He sat on the cold stone rim, reached across and ran the water through his hair and beard, ran it till the cold penetrated. He stood and shook his head hard, splashed cold water round his eyes, the back of his neck, his chest. Breathed hard. Straightened. Looked at the people staring. Sat. Should have brought my blinkers.

Nine minutes.

He found his tobacco. Rolled a cigarette. Lit it. Hauled the smoke down, chased it with another.

There were ten people on the platform, sitting, standing, smoking some of them, waiting like him.

What have I done?

Should she not be coming?

Should I have released her?

Have I forced this?

Have I earnt it?

Yes.

Whatever it is. I've kept my word. I've provided. I've made a home in paradise.

That she doesn't want.

Iffing.

That she won't stay in.

She can't leave him.

I won't fight or argue.

I'll just hope. For something. Salvation?

I never used that word before. Said it in church - but catechism means you don't think - you repeat.

Eight minutes.

The cigarette burnt his fingers. His hair dripped and his jacket had grown grey blobs where the water had mixed with deep-rooted dust. One lapel, such as it was, was mottled with a kind of mud.

His boots were open at the right toe.

His trousers were threadbare at the knee and round the patches he'd fashioned - and across the arse the cold stone reminded him. They'd served him well. The belt was good as ever. He'd washed his socks and vest and shirt - the shirt so very gently and even so another rip - and he hadn't shaved.

So, this is definitely me, he thought.

Seven minutes.

There was a public lavatory behind him but he knew that was a waste of time now. He was empty - waiting to be filled. There was a sandwich and two tomatoes in his pocket for her. And soup at home.

At home.

Home.

Going Home. For six days.

Only one bed. Sleep upstairs if...

Home.

And then she'll go.

Then will it still be a Home?

I don't know - I don't know. I can't know.

I will know.

It won't be.

It wasn't when she left the first time - she took the Home and left me the House.

I've built the house to be a home and she's here to christen it into a Home. And when she goes?

Well, I'm not moving it again!

People turned to stare. What had the clochard found funny?

Was he drunk? A madman? Laughing out loud. What? What at?

Six minutes.

She said what I hoped for was mad.

I must be certifiable then because I have so wished for this moment.

Will there be any joy in these six days?

Do I deserve some?

Some.

We'll see...

He stood.

Walked round the fountain, looked at the clock - five and a half minutes.

He watched the koi carp. Began to count them. Again.

Five minutes and she'll be here.

Will she hug me? Will I dare hug her? Take your coat off, fool - she'll hug mud.

He laid the poor wretched thing on the pond edge.

Will we kiss?

He ran his hand over his mouth, folding the huge moustaches aside, pulling down at the beard, clearing a path for their lips, should they...

Will I recognise her? Yes!

Will she recognise me? No - and yes, of course.

Will she be ashamed?

Not her. She's my friend. Whatever - she is my friend.

Four.

We won't kiss. We'll meet exactly like before - I'll take her bag and lead her into a brown house that will become ours. For six days. I'll feed her and she'll be tired and I won't be and that'll be one night. I'll make breakfast and take it to her and she won't say what she said years ago - she'll be different - we'll be different - it'll be hard.

I want to run...

I won't leave this spot till a train gives her to me if I have to stand here forever. She's mine. I've earned her.

I've done what I've done - for her.

That is true. It is. It is.

It isn't.

It must be. It is.

I - I was right.

Don't say now it wasn't; don't say that now! It was. 'Right Right Right.'

He heard his own voice.

Saw the gawping people.

He sat down hard and heard the squash as the tomatoes flattened.

THE SOLDIER'S HOME

Lavergne watched his customer stand, scrape his jacket-pocket inside out, wash it in the fish-pond and wipe it on his trousers to dry.

The sandwich was safe.

Another cigarette.

He rolled it, lit it, hauled hard on it and the clock said one minute past six.

She'll never kiss you - not with a mouth that'll smell like an ashtray.

He stood, stamped on the cigarette.

He strained to listen. A car.

One of those tractor things. No train. He put the jacket back down. He walked to the platform edge - peered up the oh so straight line - saw a moving column of smoke and heard noise coming. Coming. Like a season, like a year or a birthday or Christmas she was coming. Like night and day. Six of each.

He stepped back, as the other passengers moved forward, avoiding him.

He was not one of them.

He stepped back to his jacket by the pond, planted his feet, crossed his arms and stood solid as his corner-posts to wait.

🐑

Simone had politely fended off the young man travelling back to Toulouse to study.

She needed the room for her own thoughts.

When the guard called, 'Next stop Maurs,' the fierce instant quickening of her heart-beat told her which thoughts she'd avoided. All of them.

Her heart clanged with the engine's bell.

Her mouth eased open for more oxygen.

No harm can come to me - this is Jacques I'm going to.

No harm.

Her pulse slowed.

She noticed the apple blossom.

This tiny part of the country was not familiar to her but the tone and the trees and the roofs and the agriculture were.

But, it doesn't feel like Coming Home. And I had feared that it would.

No. He, little Jacques, is Home.

The train lost momentum.

Jacques Vermande. You've called me back.

The brakes were applied.

Who willed this?

Whose will. Ours?

The first clusters of houses. Brakes scraping now. The young man stood and took her case down.

'Thank you.'

'It's nothing.'

If I was meeting one of Les' clients, she suddenly thought, I'd be rouging my cheeks and dabbing lipstick.

Simone gathered her handbag and shoulder-bag and watched the platform arrive.

The brakes moaned. Gripped hard and the whole thing shook itself finally motionless. The young man opened the door and put her suitcase on the platform.

'Thank you.'

'My pleasure.' He got back in and shut the door.

A station scene.

People saying hello, people saying goodbye. Along the platform no-one she knew. Either way. Both ways. The station-master checked the last door closed - the platform had one solitary waver-off left, the green flag signalled steam and pistons and smoke and noise and her eyes moved to the station building, across a thin garden and there was Jacques.

The train moved behind her.

Simone, motionless, with a suitcase.

A brown coat, a mustard-coloured suit - no hat, less hair, more flesh - the train ripped across behind her and gone and she stood against the background of France again.

He looked smaller. His beard was wild, his hair too yet she could feel o familiar heat in his eyes and from his heart. Or was it her own?

'Can I help you, Mademoiselle?' The Station Master.

'No, thank you. I have help.'

He looked round, saw the tramp, looked back at her un-French elegance, saw the 'Yes, him,' in her eyes and touching his cap he shrugged and moved away.

Time stood. Still.

🐑

'Just here.'

Lavergne hauled on the hand-brake. Jacques was out and round and had her case and helped her out.

'Thanks.'

Lavergne drove away.

They both stood waiting for the racket to die away. Waiting for their silence.

'Where is my post-box?'

'I don't have one. He brings it.'

Jacques waited for the silence to heal the belch of Lavergne's back-firing vehicle. He picked up her case.

'This way.'

He led her down the path.

She stopped, just as he had at thirteen, by the hollowed out ancient oak-tree.

He stopped.

'It's quiet,' she said. 'It's really quiet.'

He nodded and waited till she wanted to walk on.

Down to that last branch. The curtain that was always leafy in September was now, bless it, in blossom.

The sunset had gathered to display Janatou as if at Jacques Vermande's command - a low fast-falling fast-reddening sun lit the valleys in retreating depths of pastel blues all the way to the snowy Cantal, bathed his field and the house in ochre perfection - and as he heard her gasp so every moment of their life together rushed through him threatening to fix his mouth in one insane grin and tears to flood away his sight.

Simone stood one arm's length, one pace, in front of him.

'My God, Vermande.'

He had never had a desire beyond hearing her say that.

Then he thought of their son.

'I can't speak,' he thought he said.

To her left the house waited. Behind her he waited. Ahead Nature's effortless majesty lingered.

They moved.

THE SOLDIER'S HOME

He led her to the house.

Again.

She stood at the bottom step of this space-ship moved in Time to meet her.

It was the same. He'd done it.

'My God, Jacques.'

He jiggled at the door - opened it. No dog - that was a difference.

She followed him inside. Again.

The room looked different - no plaster on the walls. Bare stone. They walked back into their history.

A low fire, soup, a chair. No Mother. Same smell. Peace-time.

He stood by the fire, as he had eight years before.

'Shall I sit down?'

'It's your home.'

Simone slipped off her coat and turned to a hook in her memory and there it was behind the front door. She sat. No cat. Images charged at her, bombarding her with Love and Rape, babe and man, man and woman, even her own mother's eyes. She shook to a gooseflesh, instant iced erotica.

'Come to the fire.'

He sat on Arbel's bench - she on the chair.

She'd left here their child's lifetime ago.

They both stared into the ashes rather than at each other. Both breathing slower yet, tasting their past, daring to believe this present.

'Food?'

'In a little.'

He nodded, sat back and reached for tobacco. He had none. None in the niche and none in the jacket because his jacket wasn't there. He'd forgotten it, left it at Maurs. It'll be there in a week, unless they burn it. And her sandwich.

His eye caught her ankle. The brown brogue shoes. Polished. The nyloned legs. Nylon knees, hands on her knees, her arms on her thighs, leaning forward, pretty soft beige blouse, hiding her breasts, her neck with a chain - who gave it to her? - her mouth I kissed that nose I kissed her eyes her eyes her eyes are here.

'You're staring.'

'Are you surprised?'

She couldn't see his mouth move within all that fur but the smile was in his eyes and she returned it with all of her Love and Fear and Admiration for him - the brother-man.

No need for words tonight. Just be here in the crazy reality of someone else's dream. This is his - I never dreamt this, for sure. Not ever. I'm humbled to be in your capacity to dream. You move houses and you move me. Across oceans. Her head shook.

'What?'

'You.'

Jacques' mind slipped back to War. Different clothes, different details - but she was here, again. Speaking. Being here. With me.

For six days.

A new reality blinked him back to whatever this year called itself.

Different clothes, same woman.

Same story.

Same end, she'll leave, same scary love.

Same pounding time. Don't waste a second of it. Don't even sleep.

'I've no tobacco.'

'I brought you some.'

She took a packet of cigarettes from her shoulder bag. He

THE SOLDIER'S HOME

watched, mesmerised, as she took some almost invisible clear paper off it which crisped instantly on the embers; ripped a corner of silver paper away, knocked the packet and two cigarettes, rolled, offered themselves. When she took one and passed it to him their fingers almost touched.

They ate and the sun was gone and the candles danced their shadows about his walls. She washed away the plates and for the first time asked herself about the sleeping. With? Without. What?

Before any stress could rise she reminded herself who she was sharing this fairy dance-macabre with.

'Bed,' he said.

He took the candle and her bags and put them in the room. Her room.

Where everything had happened once. Between them. Somewhere else.

He stood by the door, beckoning her.

'You're exhausted, Simone.'

Her name. Spoken in French. That was **her** name.

'I am, Jacques.'

She walked the floor, stood in front of him and placed her hands on his shoulders, came to her tip-toes to reach into the beard for his mouth and his arms were around her and lifting her and carrying her to his chest where he held her as gentle and deep as the slowest ever ocean swell. Then she was back on her toes with his bushy kiss on her forehead. She looked into his eyes.

'Sweet dreams.'

'Of course.'

She stepped back into her room. The bed, a chair, the dresser. The candle. She turned.

'Too full for words,' he said and she said, 'Yes.'

He walked quickly to the fire so she couldn't close the door in his face. Yet.

She sat on the bed.

He's right - too full. At least lie down, eh? She zipped her skirt down and folded it onto the dresser. Her blouse on the back of the chair, the nylons and belt and her bra went in a drawer and her pyjamas were cotton warm as she slid back into that bed where everything of human wonder had happened to her.

I'll never sleep.

These cigarettes are strange. Leave them and they burn away. A rolled one goes out. He lit another and sat and looked and felt and smelt and breathed in and breathed out.

She's here. They would be married for this week.

🐑

'Where did you sleep?'

'Above you.'

'Not next door?'

'I - chopped that bed up.'

'Firewood?'

'I used it for firewood, yes.'

She nodded, waited. No more.

She sat up in the bed, patted it and he sat.

He said, 'You're here to say goodbye - not write it.'

'Yes.'

They stared at each other.

Slowly their eyes dropped. Precious time passed.

'Your life is there.'

THE SOLDIER'S HOME

'Yes.'

'Why six days?'

'The most I dared leave him. Wanted to leave him,' she added softly.

Silence.

'Sara comes Sundays.'

'Thank you.'

'I didn't tell her you'd be here.'

'Ohh. Why?'

'Don't know...'

He stood and left her. She heard him light a cigarette. He came back with a saucer, sat down and tapped the cigarette on the saucer's edge.

'These taste burnt,' he said.

'They roast the tobacco.'

'Why?'

'Different flavour.'

He nodded. 'It's different.'

He took a deep pull.

'Tell me about David.'

She told him David had asked her to marry him and she had said she couldn't until she'd seen him, Jacques. And, of course, he had paid.

'What about this Jerry?'

'He thinks I should.'

'And - what about you?'

She looked him straight in the eye. 'I think I should.'

'But you came for my permission?'

'Your blessing I hoped.'

He looked at her, stubbed the cigarette dead and put the saucer on the dresser.

'So - what about you?' she said.

'What about me? What do I think?'

She nodded, waited.

'I try never to think.'

'And you fail.'

'Every hour.'

He sat on their bed. Bearded, hairy and heavy.

Silence fell.

Simone and Jacques.

Jacques and Simone.

'I have coffee,' she heard.

'I'd love some,' he heard.

He took a bucket and she listened to him go down the stairs and into the field. There was a well, then. Or a source, a spring.

She thought of dressing and stayed where she was.

She remembered his chest lying on hers and how deeply they had loved.

Would, always. Why not? He was Jacques.

He was Jacques.

I must write to Jack - but I'll be home before it got there.

The cement-work round the window lintels was neat and painstaking. Pains taken. Pain.

Get up - get dressed.

She was still sitting there when he came back in and set the water to boil. She listened to him washing two cups. Grinding beans with a mortar. He stopped. Silence.

'What?' she called.

'I can't remember - do you take sugar?'

'I didn't. One now, please.'

He moved again.

She yawned, then shivered. It was cold. Her feet were cold. It was bright but cold outside.

At home she made instant coffee. Across the ocean it took the time for the electric kettle to boil. What will I be at the end of six days at this pace?

She heard him pouring liquid. He appeared with two cups. He put his on the dresser and when he reached across to put hers on the bed-side chair and say, 'It's hot,' he inhaled the night-smell of her.

She felt him take that breath, that aroma off her flesh. Should she - could she - have withheld it? Would she if she could? Why?

And as he sat he thought - have I the right to that scent, that memory?

She read that thought. Knew the earthquake in him. Recognised it.

Isn't it mine? It was.

I daren't ask him what he's thinking.

He said, 'You'll give me time to think about - what I think. About - David.'

Simone felt the smile rise from her toes to her eyes. 'I would give you the moon on a sixpence.'

'I don't want that.'

'I know. Forgive me my nerves, please.'

She watched him pick up his cup and the cup find a way through the beard and he slurped and the cup went to his knees and his hands wrapped around it. She did the same and was almost scalded.

'What?'

'We take milk in coffee. Us Americans.'

'Do you want some?'

'No. I'm French here.'

He slurped again. She watched him wipe his moustaches and beard and re-wrap his hands round the cup.

She remembered that silence with him was never a problem - but in just six days shouldn't I ration them?

Why? Who are you to judge? Decide?

He felt her toes through the blankets, pushing at his thigh. What?

'Sit on my toes, they're cold.'

He lifted and sat gently. Through the blanket through his threadbare trousers passed the heat of him.

When it was time for the silence to end he said, 'Tell me about our son.'

'I've brought photos.'

'In words?'

The day rose and she talked.

'I brought letters and drawings from him, too.'

'Good. But keep talking. I've missed talk.'

An hour later, dressed, they sat on the doorstep watching the morning stroll by.

'Tell me the top of your thoughts, please, Jacques?'

'That I'll never see him.'

She took his heavy hand to hers. He watched her hand squeezing at his but the nerve-ends didn't yet register.

He cleared his throat.

'Can you love David?'

'He's a good man.'

'You wrote - you said he has a wife...'

'Divorced.'

Silence. A cuckoo far off.

'So he isn't Catholic?'

'No.'

THE SOLDIER'S HOME

'Are you?'

'Not any more. You?'

'I don't go.'

Silence.

'Anywhere,' he added. 'Maurs, to post. Buy tobacco. Things.'

'You've been busy.'

'I won't go anywhere now it's done.'

'Sure?'

'Why would I?'

'Live in - Paradise - without people?'

'It's not for other people.'

His swollen hard heavy hand. Hers. Small and soft. The cuckoo called again.

'Sara?'

He shrugged that thought away.

'You came back all this way to finally leave me?'

'I said - he's a Good Man.'

'He deserves you?'

'Jacques - I think it's the best thing for Jacques.'

Jacques' father nodded.

No sound. Pine trees moving in the thin breeze.

'Are you hungry?' he wondered.

'No. Talk to me.'

'What about?'

'What you feel?'

'Loss.'

'Me too.'

Silence.

After a lot of silence she took his hand to her mouth, brushed it with her lips and returned it to his knee. He stared at it.

'What do we do with five more days?'

'You always asked me questions I didn't know the answer to...'

When he prepared lunch she walked a little, down the slope. This view, she thought, must be awesome night and day. He came to the door, watched her being here at long long last and then she turned. She turned and waved and she smiled. And when she turned away a dam broke in him. Warm, cleansing, bitter, fearful, proud, love-sick, self-pitying, shocked, furious, helpless, thankful tears - the man emptied the surplus out like a great long piss. Tears for my own funeral he thought and turned back to the food.

Simone sat. This earth was his. This view, this sight. These flies and moths, birds and worms and the moles he'd never see were his. They all live in his paradise. And so do you.

Come on - you are the paradise. Be honest, Simone. It's paradise Now.

And when I've gone?

How do - how can I - leave it healing?

Oh God, have I come here, like some nascent sadist, to nail this man into this earth? Surely not.

Don't you know?

No, I don't know a darn thing now I'm here, with him, in this place.

I know -

What?

I know this is another unknown time with this good man.

And? What else?

That I cannot give him what he wants. For more than these six days.

That's pretty arrogant, girl. And pretty shallow, too.

And so what about what I want?

I want to be loved by him again.

And that's plain selfish, mademoiselle.

I want him to accept my version of our future.

And do you think he possibly can?

Who dare say what that man can do? Look around at what he's done.

O.K. But then - is it fair to fuck him?

I won't 'fuck' him!

I have need of him. I love him. He is the father of my child and - he is mine. I've tried so hard to forget that. Deny it. In my American world. But here - it's true. Though this is all I'll ever have of him.

O.K...

So, do I pretend these days won't end? Or - try to make him glad I've gone?

Simone - let the ants in your hair again. Let your sense of responsibility trust you!

He watched her stand, turn, walk towards him.

'You have seven years to tell me about.'

'Simone - I'd rather not talk than talk about the past.'

'Was it bad?'

He smiled, it felt to him, for the first time since her train pulled out of the station.

'Are you going deaf?'

She smiled. 'I hear you,' she said.

'Good.'

They ate. When he looked up again she was still smiling.

'What?'

'When you smile I see your son.'

She thought - it's five years since I had a salad without Thousand Island dressing on it. And Jack never has.

'Have you - did you use a horse?'

'No. Why?'

'Those blinkers,' she gestured at them.

Jacques looked at her, finished his mouthful carefully, and said, 'They're mine.'

Simone blinked.

He put another forkful together, concentrating. When he raised it to his mouth her eyes were waiting for his.

She looked at this, her man, as if for the first time.

'I see.'

'I couldn't with them on.'

'O.K.'

They ate.

As they washed up she said, 'Will we - be together tonight?'

He turned slowly and smiled again. 'Do you think I'll say no?'

'Vermande - I don't know what you'll do.'

'Well, I'll lie with you.'

'Oh, good.'

My. soul. is. in turmoil.

My. soul. is. at peace.

nearly. nearing.

His body. is part. of my. turmoil. and this. coming. peace.

I. wish. this. sex. could. never.

never.

ever.

end -

'Go on go on never never stop...'

'I don't intend to...'

'I have missed every centimetre of you. And the smell of you.'

'That's us. I missed us.'

Another deep bearded kiss. Never stop.

'I said once - ' he gasped a breath and lifted up onto straightened arms to look down at her, ' - words were better than loving.' Her pelvis ground a new angle into his and sensation robbed him of words and she laughed. 'And you were wrong, weren't you?'

'Very, very very very wrong,' each word a new search for a new crevice inside her velvet. A new and an old search. A memory and the making of a new memory.

'What? What was that thought?' Her hands grabbed the beard and shook the head as their flesh re-entwined, slid into a different shape of legs and sweat.

'I was remembering and forgetting.'

'Which was best?'

He kissed her bony shoulder. 'The forgetting.'

Her finger nails scratched slow and deep across his arse and he arched, 'Ohhhhhh.'

'Let's forget everything but this.'

Both hands now traced up his spine, came back down his chest and her mouth took a nipple and bit gently into it and her thrusts became deeper, asking his to join, deeper and longer and more harmony and trust and the talking was done and the turmoil on hold and the sky too as they hunted down each other's orgasm.

'What day is it?'

'Day two,' he said.

She punched his shoulder. 'O.K. - when's Sunday?'

'Day four.'

'Friday, then.'

'If you say so.'

They lay.

'What time? On - Tuesday?'

'The train? Tea-time. Twenty after five.'

That anvil thrown in his pond. Tidal waves of silent bedlam.

They lay. Listening to the other's breathing.

'Your body's changed, my man. All these muscles. Sinews. Like you're a body-builder.'

'A what?'

'A man who builds up his body - his muscles.'

'Why?'

'To show.'

'Show who?'

'Other people, silly.'

'Ohh - women?'

'Well - no, men really, I think.'

'What! Why?'

'I guess to make them envious. To encourage them to look like that.'

'Why?'

'You're like Jack! 'Why?"

A beat of silence.

'Have you seen these people?'

'In magazines - sure.'

'Are they - attractive?'

'No! They look gross.'

'Thanks.'

'You don't. You look like you - tough. They're all oily and disfigured.'

THE SOLDIER'S HOME

He nodded.

'And I've put on weight, haven't I?' She said.

'There's more of you - but that's good. It wouldn't matter to me if you were a mountain.'

She kissed him. He took the flesh magic of her lips and kissed it right back. In the briefest moment he was hard as iron under her fingers and she climbing above him and ecstasy engulfed them again, as natural as the night that must at some point fall around them.

He asked. 'Are you hungry?'

'No! You?'

'Not for cooking.'

'No..?'

'I'd like to eat your feet.'

'Do.'

She sat at one end of the lovely wreckage of the bed, Jacques at the other with her toes in his mouth. Her ankle bones and instep to lick and kiss. The flesh of her calf in his hand, the muscle warm and liquid. He lay that leg on his shoulder, kissing the calf and shin and took her other foot, the underside of it, each toe in turn, oh but there was no particle of her he couldn't love. He placed that leg on his other shoulder, his eyes gorging themselves on her. Her, her self, her body, her wee breasts, the soft darker hair at her armpits, her spread arms, her hair on the pillow, but all her sexuality and sensuality irrelevant to the smile at her mouth and in her eyes - the smile that was his and for him alone.

And for her she watched this incandescent transformed smile between her thighs, saw some of the cares of the years had left him, saw they would return when she left, left him in the void that was inevitable, and she squeezed his face, as much to distract herself as him.

'What?' the face asked.

'Nothing I want to put into words,' she said.

His hands rested on the flat of her stomach, a thumb reaching into the hair around the very her of her and she took one hard hand, pulled him forward so she could kiss into the palm of it and take it to her breast and her legs dripped from his shoulders and it could all continue, this their brilliant oblivion.

'Are we still Day Two?'

'I think it's night two, but yes.'

'Would you like a cigarette?'

'I'll go - what would you like?'

He sat up in the bed to pull the sheet away and she took his flaccid self to her lips, hearing the breath rush out of his mouth and everything was forgotten as she took what she liked, as he crashed back into the pillows, wide and wanting her to never never stop, again. Wanting to not climax, ever, so it would last till her boat had sailed.

The room was black with night but sight was past any relevance now.

'Day Three...'

Silence.

'Sorry,' he said, 'No more numbers.'

'And no more 'sorry'. Yeah?'

'Yes.'

'I feel sore.'

'I am sore.'

THE SOLDIER'S HOME

'Can we have a bath?'

'A swim?'

'No, a warm bath.'

'No.'

He looked out at the morning sky, clear as if there were only blue in Nature's palette.

'Well...'

Jacques had lit a fire and filled his biggest pot, his smaller one and the bucket with source water by the time she rose, only a little dressed, and he grinning like a naked loon.

'What?'

'I can wash you.'

'Ohh, I'll settle for that. Where's the soap?'

A silence.

She laughed. 'I should have guessed! What do you use?'

Silence. She laughed again.

'You mean we can wet each other?'

He grinned.

'When is market day in Maurs?'

'Don't know.'

'But the shops are open today, yes?'

'You can't leave me.'

'I'm not. We're going.'

'What for?'

'Jacques - I'm an American - we go shopping!'

'There's nothing I want.' His face clouded. 'And - I don't want other people... taking a second of my time...'

'They won't - you'll get to watch me talking to them. You'll get to see me from a little distance. And me you. It'll be good practice for us. And when I've done one whole hour of that we can come back here and we can lather one another. Get it?'

'I'm not sure I want to share you with even one soap-seller.'

'Share me? Vermande, there's a 'me' and a 'you' no-one will ever know and never share - not till the ending of the world.'

He stood there, naked in the fire-place.

'Grin you oaf - I'm right!'

He tried not to grin and it burst past him.

'Get dressed - yeah?'

'We'll have to walk...'

'Don't you believe it, man.'

She was right. The first car stopped right by her thumb and in she bounced and in he followed and she was right again because he sat enchanted in the back watching her charm the driver.

She took his hand as they strolled down past the school to meet the circle of shops that is Maurs La Jolie.

'Made a list?'

'Huh?'

'In your head. Shopping?'

'There's nothing I want.'

'Tobacco?' she prompted.

'Oh, yes,' he almost blushed and she hugged into his shoulder. 'And my jacket.'

'What?'

'I left my jacket at the station. With a sandwich. For you.'

'I don't want it, thanks.'

'No, but the jacket must be there.' He laughed. 'No-one'll have taken it, that's for sure.'

She suddenly turned him and placed his back flat into the wall of a house. She was grinning into his eyes.

THE SOLDIER'S HOME

'Listen to me, Jacques. I have money. O.K.? Let me buy you a jacket. Will you let me shop for some things that will be a tiny touch of me when I've gone.'

She saw terror ransack his mind, watched him tell himself not to feel those things, and she stood on tip-toe to lay her cheek against his to still his whirling thoughts. Only when the warmth in their cheeks was equal did she draw her face back enough to fill his vision.

'It's stuff, Jacques. You and me... If Janatou is my house, my home, I'd like to furnish it and you a little. Please. That's all.'

'And will you be so fine and easy when you have to leave?'

She flushed.

'Of course not.'

She took a whole pace back to look again, at all of him.

'Aren't we equals? Aren't we?'

'No Simone. You have half my life to go back to and I'll be left with much less than half my life.'

'Yes, and I'll lose you. Again. For ever. Do you think I think that's a great idea?'

'It's what is.'

'That's right. For both of us.'

They stood, staring again.

She reached for his hand. It met hers.

'Should we really spend this time discussing the inevitable. Jacques?'

'I can't deny it.'

'Me neither, love. I hate it, do you hear me? You and him are the best of my life. And I hate that it can't be here.'

Their eyes locked.

'What if you become pregnant?'

'What if you sold Janatou?'

'And come to New York?'

'Come to us, yes.'

'I did everything - I built - so you could come to me. Come home.'

'I can't.'

He stepped away from the wall, closer yet to her eyes, his hands gripping into her shoulders.

'Sell everything there - come home! To me. Bring him home to me.'

Tears in his voice - tears in her eyes.

'I have nothing there to sell, Jacques. I have nothing! Nothing but debts. Jacques - I'm poor!'

He looked at her clothes. She didn't know the meaning of the word.

'But you have money to buy me clothes? David's money?'

'No! The remains of our jars and Jack and I agreed I should spend it on you.'

'And the debts - David will pay?'

'I... Yes.'

'So you're selling yourself to him?'

A beat.

'If you want to look at it that way.'

'Tell me another - because I'll have to live with it. While I dust the things you bought me. Teach me how you want me to think of you. Wife.'

'Mother is what I am. I'm no-one's wife. I'm his mother and he deserves better than I can give him. By myself.'

'I should give him the rest.'

'Yes! You should. Only tell me how.'

A boy-man holding hands with a girl-woman. His back against a wall again, their eyes searching for the invisible. People passing slowly, looking.

'Only tell me how I afford to bring him here.'

'I don't know how.'

'Neither do I.'

A long quiet.

'But Simone, I don't want 'things''.

'O.K. I know you don't. But I have a need to leave a thing or two in the home you made for me.'

A quiet.

'O.K.'

Another quiet moment.

'Then can we go shopping?'

'Yes.'

They made to walk.

She said, 'Even if you throw them away when I've gone.'

'I did that already. I won't again.'

'Did you?'

'Oh yes.'

'Did you go mad, my Jacques?'

'I went – very private. After yesterday - that feels mad. But I shall have to deal with it again.'

'And me. And me.'

'Let's not talk in circles. That is mad.'

'It is. Let's distract ourselves. That's what shopping is.'

'I wouldn't know.'

'It only works temporarily - but it is the best thing to do with money. Come on.'

They took one pace before he spoke again.

'And you will be a wife. David's.'

She stopped.

'If you bless us, yes I will. But it cannot be like you and me.'

'No?'

Her smile surprised him because through the grin she said, 'I shall slap you!'

'Why? I shall slap you back.'

She laughed to cover her shock.

'You wouldn't? Jacques Vermande! Would you?'

Jacques considered. 'No. But, why would you?'

'To slap the sense into you that Nothing, no-one and certainly never David could be like us. Could they?'

Her eyes demanded an answer. 'The you and me who want to go looking for soap? Then we can wash to sex. Do you think?'

'I hope not.'

She laughed so loud a couple of shoppers turned to stare. To his horror she now spun on her heel and included them as she spoke. 'Do you think any of these people are like me and you? Yes or no?'

He blushed puce and whispered, 'No.'

'Sure you're not saying that just to shut me up?'

'Yes.'

'We are the only lovers in the world, yes?'

'Yes.'

'We agree?'

'We agree.'

'Let's shop.'

Jacques walked the shops of Maurs and watched his woman buy soap, tobacco, a plain blue denim work-jacket, a pair of cord trousers that would last, two paintings, a razor - despite his mouthing, 'No' - a bunch of flowers, a vase, a pot-plant; she went into a pet-shop but came out empty-handed. 'No parrots,' she tutted and dived into an antiques shop. She came out with a crude

THE SOLDIER'S HOME

painting of a vase of flowers and a couple of old magazines. 'That's it. What about you?'

'I was thinking about chickens...'

'Let me buy you some!'

He held her arm and spun her back to him, 'I need to think about it.'

'No time like the present.'

'Simone. Stop now. I'll think about it.'

'Am I all of a flurry for you?'

'I don't know what that means - but yes.'

'O.K. What about tea tonight?'

'Enough - we're going home now.'

He took her elbow and guided her back towards the road to Janatou.

'Are you mad? Cross, I mean?'

'Not a bit - but I have had time to think about food. In the four weeks since your letter came.'

'Wine?'

'I have some.'

'Shall I shut up?'

'Just put your thumb out and get us home, eh?'

He cooked and she arranged flowers and hung the two miniature paintings. One was a violent oil of a storm wave crashing on a boiling ocean; the other a bearded male nude. He laid the table and she opened up the back of the frame of the painting of the vase of flowers to remove the canvas.

'Do you like this?' she held the painting up to him.

'Er...'

'Nah, it's crap.' And she tossed it on the fire.

He stood amazed.

'What?'

'You paid for that!'

'We don't want it.'

His jaw moved but words didn't appear.

'Still I burned it?'

'Yes.'

They looked at each other.

'You burnt a bed you said.'

A beat.

'I did, yes.' His body was turning back to the cooking.

'So?'

'So - nothing.'

'We don't need it?'

And slowly he smiled and she smiled and she went back to the empty frame and he to the food.

They washed away and he smoked into the evening and watched as she went slowly through the two magazines she'd bought, taking the scissors to cut out a fragment of a page, making a careful pile of her choices by the foot of her chair.

No words.

As the sun dipped he went outside and the sky was that empty-before-stars and very still.

'We can wash tomorrow - it'll be warm out there,' he said when he came back.

She nodded.

They made love once and slept as a secular pieta.

THE SOLDIER'S HOME

'What time will Sara come?'

'I don't know. I don't have that kind of time.'

'Will she bring Zoe?'

'I don't know. She may not come - she doesn't always.'

'After Mass. Does she walk?'

'Yes.'

'So, afternoon?'

'If she comes.'

They lay, her fingers in the hairs of his chest, printing visual and sensory images in her mind.

'Tell me about Sara.'

There was a loaded quiet.

'Don't mention Sara in that way.'

She sat up.

'What way?'

His voice was gentle; his eyes were full and dark.

'It has nothing to do with you - and I hate that you wish something to happen so you would be...'

'No,' she interrupted, 'So you could be...'

'You can't know what I'd be.'

'Neither can anyone till they try.'

'I'm not experimenting with Sara.'

'She loves you.'

He sat up, their bodies no longer touching.

'If you are going to say this when she comes - I shall go elsewhere for the day.'

'But isn't it true?'

'It has nothing to do with you.'

'So, some part of it is true.'

He threw the bed-clothes aside, stepped from their bed and began to dress.

'You're angry?'

'I'm invaded.'

'Good God!'

He buttoned his trousers.

She pulled the sheet up to cover her nakedness.

'A lot of it is true, then.' Simone said, sad.

He opened the door.

'Don't you dare leave!'

He turned, shocked.

'The last thing we have is time for either of us to sulk. Jesus!'

Jacques heard an ancient echo of Arbel, 'Don't take his name.'

She drew her knees up in the bed and said, 'But I will mind my own business.'

He looked at Simone.

'Is David your business alone?'

'What do you mean? I don't understand.'

'He'll be the father of my son. Is he your business alone? He's already more friends with Jacques than I will ever be.'

'What's your point? What do you want to know?'

'I used to think - about me and Sara. When I was thirteen. Because she laughed. And because she had - big tits.' A blush started but he rushed on. 'And Madame Lacaze - the night we took you - to Souceyrac - took both of you - *that* night - she said Sara. And I. Me. Should have. But Sara chose Jerome. Or he her. Doesn't matter a fig. Because - you came. You.' His body faced her squarely now. 'You, Simone with no surname and no birthday. You came. You who are all my Love. All My Loving. My whole Life. Don't you know that?'

She spoke as slow as gathering tears.

'Yes. I do. And you mine. But Jacques, we have these few racing hours and then - new lives. Less life each maybe. Me with my sugar-daddy, as they'll call him. And can't you be with someone who loves you?'

'Don't speak about that. And doesn't this man love you?'

'Yes, I believe he thinks I'm worth loving, yes. But not as Sara could love you. Don't you see?'

'I don't think – I should talk about Sara with you. I feel...' she watched him reach for the words, 'that I'm dishonouring her.'

'O.K. I understand.'

'She is a friend. I can't discuss her like - this. Like she's an idea. Of someone else's. Even yours.'

'I understand.'

'Tell me about sex with Jerry.'

She blinked. Wide-eyed for a second.

'Why? Do you need a picture of me and him?'

'I need to find a place to rest it. Him.'

'Me too.'

'You loved him.'

'I love something in him, yes. I do.'

He stood there. A statue.

She sat, waiting.

Only his mouth moved.

'I don't want to hear these next words. And I'm scared of how much I must have them.' His knees almost folded beneath him. 'Tell me.' He sat on the bed. 'Is this what they call anguish?'

'I don't know man.'

One hand came out of the cocoon of sheets and laid over his.

'Jerry and I wanted too much to be in love. I wanted that he would take your place in my heart, Jacques. I did.' Her hand pressed hard now, her nails sinking into the leathered flesh. 'I did. We found a night and I ached for him to be you and more - in me. Body and soul. And he wasn't and he isn't and he can't be. Nor should he be. I love his head but not him.'

'And him?'

'He made love to a woman. Not me. I didn't blame him. I don't. I understand need. But I don't need 'need' in my life.' She almost laughed. 'I have plenty, thanks.' Her hand dared relax. 'You know?'

'I do. Know that.'

Their fingers entwined. A little. Softness.

'And David?'

'Jacques. I shall have to write and tell you how that develops.'

'Mmm.'

A quiet in their room.

'And you would write me about Sara?

'If - there's ever reason.'

Another quiet.

She stood in the doorway, shielded her eyes from the bright glare of a low April sun to watch him weeding.

'Hey!'

He turned, his hat falling in the soil.

'What?'

'I love you.'

He retrieved the hat and straightened.

'Peasant that I am?'

'Peasant that you are.'

He nodded. Smiled. Turned back to the weeds.

'Hey!'

He held the hat to his head as he turned again.

'What?'

'What about me?'

He straightened.

'You'll have to wait.'

She leaned her weight into one leg.

'Yeah? Why?'

He grinned.

'Because,' the grin widened, 'there's time.'

'Oh yeah?'

'Ah oui.'

'D'accord.'

And she was gone.

Sara made this vegetable patch.

I don't want to consider Sara now.

She'll come soon. Soon enough.

And there will always be time to consider her.

This time is Simone's. Ours. Flying by.

'Hey!' he yelled.

She came to the door.

'Quoi?'

'I love you.'

Again she put her weight onto one leg.

'So soon?'

'Oui.'

'Yankee that I am?'

'Mine that you are.'

She nodded. 'That I am.'

And she was gone again.

Three more days. Two and a morning.

When he looked up again she had the big pot, both his pans and a bucket, all of them full of water, out warming in the sunlight in front of the house.

'Bath time in...' she stuck a finger in the big pot, looked up, 'a couple of hours?'

'What is all that water for?' Zoe held her mother's hand tight.

'Some American custom?' Sara was still gawping at this vision - Simone.

Simone turned to this tiny feminine image of Jerome Lacaze. 'Can you guess, Zoe?'

Zoe looked from her mother's encouraging nod to Simone. 'What does 'American' mean?'

'It's where I live. It's a country. Big.'

Zoe turned to Jacques. He squatted down to her eye-level, took off his hat, and nodded her attention back to the pots and her question. 'What do you think it's for?'

'I don't know.'

'So?' said Sara. 'Ask some questions.'

The adults waited while the child thought.

Sara reached out her free hand and Simone took it and kissed it.

Simone said, 'Didn't someone tell me you spoke English?'

Zoe reddened, looked at Sara.

Sara nudged her, 'Go on - I can't!'

Zoe stared at Simone.

'I speak English. In America.'

'I speak English. In school.'

'O.K. Pretty good! Try a question.'

'Why - why is the water - dehors?'

"Outside. Good." Simone went back to French. 'Why do you think?'

'I wouldn't ask if I knew!'

Simone grinned and she too squatted down. 'It's outside. Right. In the sun? Why?'

'Getting warmer?'

'Yes. And so are you...'

Zoe turned back to her mother. 'Do you know?'

'No, I don't!'

'Ask another question, maybe?'

'Are they for cooking something?'

Jacques said, 'No.'

'Washing something?'

'Yes..!'

Zoe blushed at Simone, nodding her head - urging the child on.

'Him!'

All three women laughed.

'Good idea,' said Zoe and everyone laughed.

'Ardelle's baby?'

'Brain damaged at delivery. Badly.'

'They haven't tried again?'

'They never forgave each other. Or themselves. You wouldn't want to see them, Simone. Arbel drinks and she's gone somewhere burnt inside.'

'Let's go for a walk, Zoe?' Jacques offered his hand.

The child took it. They bathed out into the light and his field.

'It is so - miraculous - to see you. Here.' Sara said.

'I know. It's him.'

'I know.'

'He's - there are no words for him.'

'No.'

Sara moved an empty plate.

'Tell me about Jerome.'

'Invalided home from the Eastern war. Something called beri-beri. A blood disease. He lives - elsewhere.'

'Does he see Zoe?'

'No.'

'Your mother?'

'Good.'

They looked at each other.

'Tell me about little Jacques!'

'I have photos.'

'Show me! What did Jacques say?'

'He hasn't wanted to look at them. Yet.'

Sara shook her head.

'Him! God…'

'Want to walk in the sun or the shade?'

'Sun, silly.'

Holding hands they skirted the pine, walking down the edges of his field.

'Who is she?'

'Simone? She's my - wife.'

The child nodded, as surprised as he was by the use of the word.

'But we never married.'

'Then she's not your wife.'

'No.'

'Why say she is, then?'

'Because it's true.'

'I don't understand.'

'Neither do I, Zoe.'

The ground dipped sharply and their grip tightened a little.

'Why does she live in America?'

Jacques took a moment before replying.

'I - sent her there. During the war. Just after you were born.'

'Why?'

'To be safe.'

'Oh. O.K.'

He lifted her over some new-green stretching blackthorn.

'But it makes you sad?'

'Very.'

'Are you going to cry?'

'No.'

'So. You're not that sad?'

'Why do you ask so many questions?'

'My teacher says we should. Always.'

'Not always.'

Zoe looked at his face. Nodded.

'Is she staying? Your wife?'

'No.'

'Why not?'

'She has to go back to look after our son.'

'To America.'

'Yes.'

'You are crying.'

'Yes.'

'Shall we not wash you?'

'I think I'd rather you didn't.'

'I agree.'

At the bottom of the field they looked back to the house and their two women now in the garden.

'They're still talking.' The child sounded disapproving almost. Petulant. A smile toyed at Jacques' mouth.

'I like this spot,' he told her, 'because - sit down.'

They sat. The view of the mountains disappeared and only hedgerow and sky filled their vision.

Zoe looked puzzled. She looked at him. He nodded her sight up the slope. Zoe looked back.

'You can't see the house.'

'No. We're secret.'

They sat.

Sun and silence. A low buzz of flies.

'But - Jacques - you're always secret here.'

'I'm what?'

'No-one sees you. Do they? You don't have to walk right down here to be secret.'

He looked around him, looked at her.

'No,' he confessed, 'But I do.'

'Why?'

'I don't know. Everyone needs a secret place maybe.'

'Even from themselves?'

'Especially from themselves sometimes.'

The child nodded and he waited for her 'Why?' but it didn't come.

'Can you be secret from yourself?'

Jacques almost laughed. 'What do you think?'

'I've never tried - but I think I will...'

Silence moved around them, sitting there.

The man looked at the child, concentrating. He watched her till he said, 'Let's go back.'

'Why?'

'Because you're right. You can't be secret...'

'But I like being this secret. Mamma doesn't know where I am. I'm invisible.'

'O.K. Let's be properly invisible.'

They lay down on the spring grass.

'Close our eyes?'

THE SOLDIER'S HOME

'Yes...'

A beat.

'What can you see? I can see purple bubbles dancing.'

'Mine are green.'

'Show me!' The child laughed. 'You can't! Jacques! Our pictures are invisible too.'

'What would you like to see?'

'I don't know. Do you?'

'Yes.'

A beat.

'And can you?'

'No.'

'Why?'

'Because I can't see to America from here.'

Zoe thought.

'Oh... Your son?'

'Yes.' Then too quickly, to distract both of them he said, 'Wouldn't you like to see your poppa?'

'Poppa's gone,' she said simply.

'Now what do you see?'

'The bubbles are going yellow. My teacher says when you see white you're looking at God. Do you believe that?'

'Do you?'

'I asked first.'

Jacques thought. 'They say when you die you see God. I might believe that.'

'Ohh.'

'But, I don't want to see God before then.'

'Why?' The child drew the word out, her curiosity elongating with the vowel.

'Because -' Zoe felt the man sit up. She was sure he'd opened his eyes, too. When she opened hers hot light flooded in and she moved into the shade his back offered.

In a moment or two her face re-appeared in the sunlight beside him. 'Why?'

'Because I would spit in his eye.'

Again he waited for a 'why' that didn't come.

He offered her his big hand.

'Up?'

'Yes.'

He stood but she pulled on his hand to sit him down again.

'Can we be secret another time?'

'Any time.'

'O.K.'

They stood.

'They're *still* talking....'

'We're not washing him, Mamman.'

'No?'

'No.'

'Fine. Then we should leave these people in peace.'

Simone said more to Sara with her hug than she could ever have said in words.

She dived into the house, returned and pressed a piece of paper into Zoe's hands.

'My address - will you write to me, in English, please?'

'Yes.'

The adults smiled.

Sara made a step towards Jacques and he, startled, took an involuntary pace back before correcting himself and kissing her three times, then kneeling quickly to Zoe and repeating the gesture.

THE SOLDIER'S HOME

'Thank you for coming.' He stood. 'As always, Sara.'

She looked straight into his eyes and said, 'I am so happy you've been blessed with this, Jacques. You deserved it.' Then, quickly, 'Come on, Mademoiselle.'

He took her hand.

The sun said late afternoon.

Simone dipped a finger in the big pot. Looked up, smirked at him and went inside for the soap.

When she came back he was nearly naked.

'Hey. I wanted to do that.'

As he unbuttoned her dress her hand slid round his underwear and eased it down. The dress fell and he lifted her vest over her head and she stood out from her knickers.

Two naked people. One pot, two pans and a bucket of warm water. One bar of soap. A French April Sunday.

He walked a little of his land with her wrapped around him. Them dripping a little, drying a little, kissing a little, fucking a little. Her ankles joined behind him. Her head on his shoulder.

Standing, naked and finally married in Paradise.

Pouring rain. Here for the day, he could tell by his first breath in, before he heard it on the roof.

Good. Won't have to share her with even the daylight. This last full day.

He tried to quiet his thoughts, lest their vibration wake her. And stir his dread.

He opened his eyes and listened to her breathing. He could feel its heat on the hairs of his left arm so she was lying facing him and if he could but turn on his side he could feast his eyes on her face. All this he considered in the nothing of one more breath. Now he concentrated on quieting that breath for an intimate anxiousness had invaded his soul and his chest was moving with that.

The rain drummed steady and French. The sky would be grey all day. Mountains hidden in the mist - maybe even the whole field. So what? All he wanted to see was a head-turn away.

He pressed his head backwards into the pillow so his hair couldn't rustle, and slow as a sloth turned his neck muscles, his chin a centimetre at a time, his straining eyes now rewarded with the shape of her body under their sheet. He stilled another breath. Moved again and her sleeping face was all he could see.

Don't let this breath out disturb her.

Simone.

A symphony of rain.

Bed-warmth and body-warmth.

Thirty hours.

Simone.

Jacques.

Another whole breath in and out.

My little Jacques.

Only his needs stop me from killing her gently now and keeping her, burying her here.

I can't bear the idea of not being buried with her.

Another breath. In and out.

Selfish melodramatic nonsense.

I can bear anything.

That's my tragedy. That I can...

I've lost her once and survived and I'll lose her again and I'll survive.

It would be warmer to kill us both.

Some minuscule something moved on her face – perhaps it was an eyelash - and he stifled a gasp at the juxtaposition between his thoughts and the magnetism in her skin. How every crevice of her face needed to be kissed. Not kissed, held. Needed to be in contact with his. Blurred forever.

Another breath.

How many more till she leaves?

May she not wake for an hour. May she age here. May I watch.

I'm looking at her like I looked, with her, at our new-born son.

His mouth leapt into a grin and too late he tried to stop the breath charging from it.

'Mmnnhunh?'

He held his breath, muscles, mind – he held everything but her.

Don't let her hear that rain yet.

Let her go back to where there are no questions we cannot answer. Let me look one minute more at her peace.

A fleet of swans, red as begonias, swept over the mountains of a vast school atlas. A great page was turned and hungry peasants rose out of Africa. Now an elephant climbed out of the page and wrapping his huge trunk beneath her lifted her and the book onto his back. 'Where?' it boomed gently.

'Wherever,' she told him and the great grey beast rose into a great grey sky and dissolved into a wounded bomber aeroplane, burning and falling earthwards. The screams of her crew surrounded her, filling her ears and as the tilt of the plane neared the vertical so men fell past her. David, Jerry, Erich, a bar-full of black faces drinking rum and ball-bearings, now Les, all of them dressed as airmen, all of them spitting dollars as they tried to speak, all falling past her help, the whine of the burning craft accelerating, the chaos of a crash inevitable, death certain, still she hauled on the controls, still she wrestled and strained with all her strength, still she believed this was avertible; and now the Curé in Lyon – that sad gentle face - at the window, knocking - showing her his radio. She could tell he was mouthing something. She hauled the window open, roaring wind mixing with choking smoke and flame; 'What?' 'de Gaulle!' he triumphed and flew away from her - inviting her to fly with him, soaring and hanging there in the clouds, calling her to come listen to the news - to fly - to be free - to fly. She looked at her feet - at her American shoes. 'I can't,' she called and closed the window, eyes on the screaming descending altimeter, she hauled at the controls, still the craft burned, still the men screamed, still it fell... A drummer somewhere played, an endless roll of the drums, another roll of the drums, just another roll on your drums and the war has begun, still drumming, steady, no music just that drum raining down...

'What were you thinking Vermande - watching me?'

'I told you, I try never to think.'

'Oh, yes?'

That loveliest of smiles - the first from the border-lands of sleep. That single smile held every promise he'd ever have imagined.

'I thought of killing you.'

The temperature of the space between them changed.

'Both of us.' He attempted a re-assuring smile that rotted in her gaze.

Silence.

Unless her blinking made an actual noise.

'But then I wondered if that's not what we're doing to each other anyway. Without the Death.'

Simone nodded slowly. Very slowly.

'And,' he calmed his fear by talking, 'we both have duties to him.'

Again she nodded.

'So,' he discovered as he said, 'I wasn't serious. Only desperate.'

'I see why you try not to think...'

'I used to think I was older than you,' she said, her fingers combing in the hair on the arm draped around her shoulders.

She laughed suddenly. 'I was going to say - when I first came here! When I first came to this house - I thought I was older than you.'

'You were.'

'Not now.'

'Is that good?'

'Dunno. It is - that's all.'

The rain fell.

Jacques made coffee, brought his cigarettes and they lay quiet

'Tell me how tall our son is - show me.'

'I have photos.'

'I'll look at them and nothing else when you've gone. For now I'd rather look at you. How tall is he?'

'I'd like to see your face as you look at the photos.'

'I'm going to cry plenty, Simone. Please.'

'He's up to my shoulder, nearly.'

Jacques nodded. 'And his lung?'

'It's O.K.'

A silence.

'We have to say everything now,' she said.

'What do you want to say?'

'I don't know. I've never been here before.'

In the quiet he said, 'But that's not true. We've been exactly here before.'

She nodded.

'Can you agree with - no...' She stopped, moved her body position to try again. 'Can you accept - what must happen?'

'What choice do I have?'

He stubbed the cigarette into the ashtray and leaned out of the bed to place it on the floor.

'What choices do either of us have, Jacques?'

'But whatever I say or feel it's a fait accompli, isn't it?'

'We both have to settle for less than - this.'

He was very quiet.

She sat up, looked squarely at him, 'You don't want to come to America.'

'I don't want to be alone. I don't deserve it.'

'I don't want to be an old man's prize. Don't want my child not to know his father. Or to never love you again. Be this easy, this honest. I don't deserve those weights.'

Quiet again.

Rain.

Simone said, 'Do you wish I hadn't come?'

Jacques looked at her, his elfin woman. 'Yes. No.' He shook his head hard. 'Do you wish I hadn't done - this?'

'Yes! No! It doesn't matter, does it?'

'No.'

'What,' she wondered aloud, 'do we do with what does matter?'

'You raise him.'

Simone moved to still the sadness tidal-waving inside her. More tears than raindrops on the roof.

'Have you kissed him? David.'

THE SOLDIER'S HOME

'Ohh, Jacques. I respected what you said about Sara - that has nothing to do with us.'

'You mean - no?'

'I mean it has nothing whatever to do with now.'

'"Now" is dripping away.'

'Yes. Don't let's waste it with sad iffing...'

Dressed and eaten the little either of them needed he sat by the slow fire and watched her at the table with scissors and a pile of paper. The empty picture frame waited.

She looked up. 'Have you any flour?'

'A little...'

He rolled a cigarette while she made a paste of flour and water.

'What are you doing?'

'Making you a present from him.'

A beat.

'I should make him a present.'

'You could.'

'Oh God. I haven't thought. What?'

'You're his father - you decide.'

'I don't know him. And he's already got a chimney.'

He lit the cigarette, hauled on it, blew up.

'Shall we get drunk?' she said.

His eyes widened with surprise.

'If you like, yes. Why?'

'It's you and those damned cigarettes. Makes me wish I did. I won't - but we can drink.'

'Let's drink, then...'

'Here's to our son.'

The parents clinked glasses.

'Jacques,' Simone looked up from pasting paper and photographs and pictures onto board, 'how do we stop us rotting? Away?'

He rested the glass on his knee. 'Our lives are up to ourselves, aren't they?'

'I guess.'

She turned back to the paper.

He looked at her steadily, waiting till her eyes rose to see what he wanted to say.

'Do you wish you could leave now?'

'No. I was wishing I could transport him here. I wish I'd brought him.'

'Why didn't you?'

Simone drained the glass, pushed it forward for a re-fill.

'Because,' she watched him stand and pour, 'it wouldn't have been - fair and honest to David.'

Jacques now filled his own glass, took it to the bench and sat down slowly.

'So. My son is a bounty to make sure you return?'

'No...'

'But yes. He is.'

'Why would a man pay for me and my son to leave him?'

Jacques' back met the wall hard. 'Jesus, Simone - you can ask me that?'

'I didn't mean - you know what I mean.'

'Jacques stayed so that you would come back. Have to go back. Proof.'

Simone put her glass on the table, turned it in her hand, made the eye contact. 'I didn't think of it like that.'

'Did you say – 'I have to go and see him - but he needn't see his flesh and blood? Did you?'

'No.' Simone took a breath. 'I said - 'I'll go and I'll come back

and then we'll live with you."

'So. A Fait accompli.'

'He offered.'

'He offered what?'

'To pay for me to - come and see you.'

'I am to be grateful?'

'No.'

'But it is decided. So - what is this?'

'This is the best we can make of it.'

'This is what he's allowed us.'

'He'll never know you - but he'd respect you.'

Rain.

A fire.

Her looking evenly at him.

He threw the dog-end on the ash.

'I'm thinking of kidnapping you now.'

'You're that bad a parent, huh?'

'A choice between one of you and neither - that's not difficult.'

She looked carefully at him. His eyes were dark and full again.

'Are you frightening me? For the first time?'

Jacques drained his glass.

Re-filled it, and hers.

'You wouldn't be worth kidnapping - you'd kill me as soon as I slept.'

'How do we get to Maurs tomorrow?'

'Walk.'

'O.K.'

The second bottle emptied.

Satisfied with her pasting, Simone threw the cuttings and scraps on the fire, placed the finished work with its face against a wall and came with her glass to sit opposite him, across their fire.

Some Time passed again.

'We're staring.'

'Can we blame us?'

They almost grinned.

The rain was only dripping now.

Jacques looked deep into her and said simply, 'What do I have that you needed to come here for?'

Her eyes widened as she considered her response and he went on, 'Not me, not the physical. And not this emotional ocean - that has to end.' He felt hot. 'What? Simone?'

Simone came to sit next to him, pushing him along the bench to make space. She took his hard hand in both of hers.

Firelight. Dying rain.

'I'm saying goodbye to the woman you made. I will not ever be this woman again. Never this young, this greedy, this selfish, this needy. So, perhaps I came to let us say - goodbye to both of us.'

She felt his face move. Was it a grin? 'What?'

'Is that drink talking?'

'I don't think so, Vermande, no. And I don't think you should think that either.'

They climbed into bed and she lay her head into his shoulder.

'How long will it take to walk?'

'Two hours.'

'O.K.'

'No lifts.'

'No.'

As sleep drifted nearer and the rain almost silent, and when they both knew they wouldn't make love now, she whispered, 'Have you thought of something for him?'

'He gets you.'

'OK.'

♣

Sunlight. Dawn.

The weight in his chest like one of his corner-stones.

He looked at her and knew the idea of one last loving was impossible.

He slipped quietly from the bed, knowing she'd woken and was watching his body, watching his nakedness disappear.

In the big room the fire had died.

He wanted to sit and watch her body but instead he left her in the room to dress and do her awful packing.

He had to go outside to not hear the sounds her cases made.

In a while she appeared behind him. With a camera.

'Come and stand in the door, please.'

He did as she asked.

'Are these my present for him?'

'Yes!'

She took almost all the roll. Pictures of him and him and the house and him and his view of paradise.

'We'll find someone at the station to take a picture of us. Yes?'

'Yes.'

He stepped outside again as she busied herself with her bags.

'Where are you going?' There was the trace of panic in her voice.

'For a piss.'

'Ohh.' Her nerves spilled into a giggle. 'You may, sir.'

'Thank you, madame.'

He strode to the compost and wondered by what process a human being walked and talked and thought and felt and breathed and didn't explode or fly, dissolve or burn or do anything rather than this mundane fatal, goodbye dance.

Whose will was this? Who was pulling these strings?

The only certainty was it could not be anything meriting the name God.

He watched his fingers tying his new trouser fly buttons together.

Everything functions. My hands, my dick, my bladder, my speech, my legs.

Only my heart feels actually alive, and that's because it's dying.

And it's not, it's not, and I know because I have been here before.

A woman stood framed in the door. A smartly dressed woman.

'What time is it?' the scrubbed face asked.

'I don't know - you have a watch.'

'It stopped days ago. I forgot to wind it.'

'We've - some time yet,' he nodded at the sun. 'It's not really afternoon.'

He walked back towards her and they met at the top of the stairs.

'Would you lie?'

'Would you wish I did?'

'Not now.'

'No. Me neither.'

'This is his present.'

She went to turn the picture frame.

'Don't show it to me now, please Simone. I'll see it tonight.'

'Ohh.'

'And please don't be disappointed.'

'No...'

'There's so much we've asked each other to understand. It's only one more.'

She looked around for the next thing to do to use up some more seconds of this gaping space.

Two people in a room in a house. Their history swirling around them and in the spaces in between them. Nothing they could do to stop it or change it.

Helpless in Time's indifferent vice.

'Have you money for food?'
'You asked me. Yes.'

'Have we said everything, then?'
'I don't know,' he said. 'I know I can't think of a thing to say.'
'That's not the same thing.'
'Let's go. I'd rather sit there than here - this is killing me.'
'Yes.'

He closed the door.

She watched him as they had both watched everything the other had done today. Printing the sequence in the mind's eye, in memory. She walked down the steps quickly, to turn and see him, standing there - him and his house and he picked up her case, just as he had walked with a different case of hers into that same house ten years before. He could see her mouth trying to set itself, like his, to find the right shape for these last few hours - till the train would release them from this torture. It will be a kind of relief, for both of us. No-one should live this intensely, surely.

His eyes swept round Janatou with her in it for the last time. She

walked away, leading him up the path to the curtain of blossom and leaves.

He held the branch and she stepped under his arm. No last backward glance. He followed.

A car stopped and offered a lift but they declined.

'What time is it, please?' Simone asked.

'Three. Bonne route.'

O.K.

Spring everywhere.

A photo of us - that's all now.

He hasn't said he blesses me.

But then I never promised him things I couldn't, once.

He can't release me. Only I can. Forgive myself for the joy and the torment in the loving him.

They walked.

'I wanted to shave you. Cut your hair.'

'Why?' His voice was thin and suddenly high, like half his vocal chords didn't care to work.

'To take to Jack.'

He nodded a little.

'I bought that razor - you could do it. Post it.'

They walked.

'But would you? Will you?'

'I don't think so.'

Her smile as thin as his voice.

'No-one walks - like this - in New York.'

'Oh.'

'They couldn't afford the time.'

'What?'

'Time is Money. In America. Walk two hours? Crazy.'

They saw Maurs in the valley beneath.

Finite.

Waiting.

They were very quiet now.

And silent, they walked into the circle of shops.

He switched hands with her suitcase to take hers and she squeezed gratefully but couldn't look to see if he wanted or needed eye-contact now. She would have been reassured to have seen his eyes pinned ahead only. Like he was wearing his blinkers.

The station clock said they had forty minutes to wait.

They sat on the rim of the pond, the fountain playing behind them.

She found the camera and said, 'Wait here.'

He almost smiled.

Where else would he go?

In one whole minute - he watched it all tick by - she returned, explaining something to the station-master. He nodded, looked at Jacques, looked at her and nodded again. Jacques could see him shifting social credibility to one side as he concentrated on the task described.

Simone took Jacques' hand and stood him up next to her.

'Wait monsieur, please' - she held up a hand to him, turned to Jacques and whispered. 'I know this is difficult for you, but put your arm around me as though you love me half as much as I love you...' and then her breath was taken as his arm whipped around her waist, lifting her to his lips et voilà, the photo the station-master took.

'Are you going to ask about your jacket?'

'No.'

Speech, as the clock counted down the last seven minutes, was too difficult.

Looking at her was too difficult.

Holding his hand was the easiest thing.

Placing her cheek against his bearded warmth meant neither could see each other's grief.

Each passing second tolled slower, heavier and still heavier.

A signal clanged down, a hundred yards up the line. Both of them strained not to hear the train enter the tunnel, its whistle announcing its entrance to their stage.

The station-master came forward, red and green flags in his hand, a whistle in his mouth.

Jacques stood first. It would have been too awful for her to have stood first.

He picked up her case and walked towards the platform where the train was squealing to a halt.

Simone followed. Mesmerised one final time by how capably he performed an action that was breaking her and must be breaking him.

The train stopped.

Jacques opened a carriage door, stepped in, placed her case on the rack over the seat and stepped out again.

They looked at each other.

Into their eyes.

THE SOLDIER'S HOME

'Please - messieurs mesdames!'

He bent to kiss her.

They kissed.

Her arms so tight round his neck.

'Madame, s'il vous plait?'

They parted.

She stepped into the train.

Jacques Vermande shut the door.

Simone lowered the window, leaned out and held his face in her hands.

Nothing but her.

A terrible rush of steam and brakes and the station-master and she was moving and he was too and her hand left his face, kissed her mouth and came so briefly back to his mouth before the gathering pace separated them down to hands, finger-tips, a millimetre a centimetre a whole metre of air between them and now only eyes and waving hands and his racing clattering feet and the breath burning in his lungs and her waving waving waving as he slowed to stand and watch her diminish to a moving shape a blur on a carriage of a train that was steam and was gone.

We never asked each other's birthdays.

I don't know her surname.

Yes, I do. Vermande.

David would have her companionship for life.

For money. For loving her.

He'd better.

If she and I have lost everything, he has gained everything.

Is there a kind of man who could simply shrug and let this go?
And do I wish I was that man?
No.

What will I do - with this rest of my life? Move the house back?
People stopped, startled, as a man laughed aloud in the street.

Sara?
Let that be. Reap and sow.

A woman squeezed her child's hand tighter as the bearded
tramp loomed in her face. 'Madame, when is market day?'
'Thursday.'
'Thursday. Thursday. And this is - Tuesday?'
She stepped past him as she said, 'Yes, of course...'

He walked home.

As he moved to lift the branch aside to see empty Janatou he
waited for desolation to engulf him and the tears to wash him.
But grief was arrested by the evening light and the thought of how
many times in his short life he had stepped back into that house
to be alone. Surely it was done now. Surely there would be a rest.

The picture - 'his present to you' leaned against the wall near
the stairs.
I can't look at that tonight. I cannot.
Sleep – please consume me, please.

THE SOLDIER'S HOME

There was a knocking. Someone at his door.

He stumbled from the bed, made himself decent enough with a shirt and opened the door to a man in a brown coat with a box in his hands. A cardboard box, one corner of which was damp.

'Vermande?'

'Yes.'

'You're not easy to find! Here.'

He offered the box. It made a noise and seemed to shift in the man's hands.

'Eh?'

'A young lady came in last Saturday - paid for this to be delivered this morning.'

Jacques opened the lid and the puppy blinked and squealed.

Simone watched The Atlantic roll beneath her.

The picture was a collage. It centred on a photograph of their seven-year-old boy, black hair, small nose, incandescent smile. Spinning out from that centre were a cascade of photos of him at almost every age, so Jacques could trace his face forming and the body developing. Then he began to notice fragments of drawings, a stick man standing by a crudely crayoned house stopped his heart for it said at the bottom, 'Poppa et notre maison.' A woman holding a child's hand was, 'Me and my Mom'. Simone had filled all the spare space with photos cut from the magazines - Statue of Liberty, Empire State Building, Broadway and Times Square - all nothing to the wonder of his son's face. And now, at the top middle of the frame, was a letter. Written, Jacques presumed because he couldn't understand it, in English. The top line of this Simone had pasted above the line of the frame, making it look like a title for the whole picture. It read 'Dear Dad...'

He leaned the picture on the dresser in his room but after one whole sleepless night watching it, he put it over the fire on the mantle-piece.

By market day he had forgotten the idea of buying a beast or chickens. He moved and ate and shat and walked and dug at his vegetables a little, played with the pup, threw the dead flowers away, watered the pot plant - he existed. He seemed to continue.

It took Zoe, walking back home with Sara the first Sunday after Simone had gone, to identify that, 'He's empty inside, mamman.'

My dearest Jacques,

I'm writing on the plane. One hour out of New York. Too many from you. I'm writing full of you - not our son or the life I have promised elsewhere.

Part of me is stupidly proud to find I have nothing to say that we didn't say.

Will we meet again?

When will you and he meet?

What might our futures hold?

Why ask? The world will turn and us with it.

Somewhere inside my baggage, rolled up inside a box, on a piece of material I can't begin to pretend I understand, is a picture of you and I. There is a moving one in my heart - and I believe in yours too.

THE SOLDIER'S HOME

My father's name was Cascals. Our son's name on the school register is his fathers' so I am known as Madame Vermande. Mrs. Vermande.

Forgive me, but I'm writing without thought now.

My mind is blank.

This heart is full.

Simone.

The day her letter arrived he walked to Maurs and bought three hens and a cockerel.

The day his first letter arrived was the same day she and Jack moved into David's apartment.

Sara came without Zoe.

'I seem to have spent years asking you to talk.'

'I was always grateful you were here - when I was silent sometimes.'

'Sometimes! You flatter yourself. More life in the stone.'

He nodded.

'Jerome's in hospital.'

'Where?'

'Perigreux.'

'That's…'

'- too far, I know.'

They sat. Thought.

'This dog got a name yet?'

'No. Any ideas?'

'No.'

The sun was warm. Summer was waiting on tiptoes.

'You are going to harvest this?' She nodded at the field.

'No.'

'That's waste, Jacques.'

The farmer in him stirred.

'Have you got a hungry cow?'

She nodded at the inanity of his question.

'Bring it. Please.'

'O.K.'

Simone sent a package enclosing the framed photograph of them at the station and a letter from Jack to help distract him from their new address. Knowing it would fail and that she felt feeble.

Jacques wrote once a week, telling his son about the chickens, the pup, the silence in the woods. About Sara's beast gorging itself. Telling him to take care of his mother. By the time it had become a routine he believed he had achieved something. Whatever this existence was, he was 'coping'. He daren't judge it by his feelings for he tried so hard to allow himself none. Until her card came to remind him he had forgotten their son's birthday. Remorse overwhelmed him and he realised he needed Sara to come so he could choke it out to her.

He had to wait a fortnight and she came with news of far worse. Jerome had died.

Then

Dear Jacques,

David and I will marry soon now. I beg your understanding, because I want it more than anything - and I need it.

I have an office job - in a printing company - yes, a subsidiary

of the one that publishes David's books. It's hard to write when you
imagine every word of it will bring negatives to someone you love.
I don't know how to betray you kindly. When I don't feel I am.

Simone.

One weekend in late Autumn Sara came alone, saying Zoe was
staying the night with a school-friend. And so, finally, did these
school-friends.

'It's not right,' he said as they lay naked.

'It doesn't have to be anything other than itself.'

He tried to think like that - but he couldn't stop thinking of
need.

His.

Jerry's.

Ardelle's.

Sara's.

David's.

Simone's.

Jacques'.

They performed as best they could and the warmth in the sleep
afterwards was the best of it. Sara walked home and decided she
wouldn't return for a month. She didn't expect him to come to see
her, and he didn't. She waited another month and then she and
Zoe found the house empty, the dog and chickens gone and two
letters cob-webbed on the table. One from America, opened and
the other, with a waiting envelope, written by him, unsealed.

Jacques,
Jerry was jailed for four years.

Your son is well and happy in his new school though he misses Wayne.

I am pregnant.

Please bless us.
Simone.

Dear Simone and David,
I am so happy for you both.

It was unsigned.

'Mamman?'
'Yes?'
'I know where he is.'
'Tell me.'
'It's a secret place.'
Sara took her daughter's hand. 'Show me.'
'I don't want to see.'

Sara followed the pointing hand, walked down the frosting slope and there he lay. Cold. And face down.

The funeral was long gone by the time Simone opened Sara's letter.

Sara burnt the few clothes, boxed the letters, the two paintings, the framed photo of them at Maurs station, the collage and the few plates and, leaving it all upstairs, closed up Janatou and her heart and walked back to her daughter and ageing mother.

THE SOLDIER'S HOME

THE SOLDIER'S HOME

Enid

THE SOLDIER'S HOME

one

1988

EARLY MAY. Friday evening. Just gone four-thirty. Or 'almost five and twenty-to-five,' as both her parents would have said.

At the bus-stop with five teenaged stragglers. Four girls, one shuffling lad.

Enid didn't teach any of them, knew no names.

Netball practice? Dawdlers. Detention?

No. Unlikely any of us teachers would volunteer to monitor that of a Friday evening... Perhaps these were the latch-key kids? Or those with neither desire nor impetus to rush home. One way to find out and Enid was not going to do that.

They ignored her. The ancient teacher, invisible.

She listened not to their conversation but to their language, their use and gleeful abuse of it. Slang. Was that derived from slung, she wondered. Words thrown?

Enid listened for examples of it, but their chatter was coded so as to all but forbid her entrance. Fine. That suited, too.

Their bus appeared in the distance, Worsley to Swinton. Then on, for her, to Pendlebury.

Tickets, passes, coins were found and rubbed. Primed.

Something about a Friday.

Odd but she now recalled some man called Fordyce, or similar, announcing, if she remembered correctly, 'The weekend starts here.' 'Ready Steady Go!' In her very early thirties. When people danced. Shook. For a brief moment there was Dusty Springfield. Making black and white television feel as though it were in colour.

The bus squealed to a stop and the small scrum gathered impatient and spuriously excited, then opened to offer her – the ageing 'Miss' – to get on first, a practised display of 'respect', and when she demurred, it clattered chaotically upstairs. As though it had never ever done such an exciting thing before…

Enid sat downstairs, beside an exhausted woman obliterated by what Enid presumed was weekend food shopping. For a small platoon.

Nine stops – let thought loose. Loosen.

Anniversary of father's death, soon.
Tend their grave. That sweet ritual.

You have, like J.B. Priestley, been here before. Anything make tonight any different? No… Well, I have never shared a bus-seat with someone with quite so much shopping.

Papers to mark, essays to read, lessons to plan. Much Ado About My Life. Church on Sunday. Back Monday, five past nine, urging a comprehension of the difference between metaphor and simile into fourteen-year-olds. One of the young ladies careened down the stairs, called, 'Night, Miss,' and swung off the bus, running and swearing at her friends upstairs.

So many things you never did, Enid.

I hope we reach my stop before this poor woman has to negotiate her way past me and off. I don't want to watch, witness, her struggle; and if I offer to help I'll needs go all the way to her house.

Ye Olde Pendlebury Offie.

A banal contradiction in terms, but what is life without the detail?

O.

'Under New Management'. Well, let us believe they will still sell my Vendredi Vouvray.

She pushed at the door.

'Barp-Klack.'

Enid was shocked, harshly, out of her routine.

No soft tinkle of a bell on a spring.

It had said, and it repeated itself lest she be in doubt, as she let the door close, 'Barp-Klack.'

A hideous noise. An unnecessarily loud, metallic, somehow inhuman, noise.

The lay-out of the shop had been modernised. Making its title yet more idiotic. The wines now separated by country of origin. There were scattered half-barrels containing 'offers'. A sprinkling of sawdust on the floor. Really? Were people likely to spit? Or bring their horses in here, perchance?

She located her ritual tipple, then spotted the same in a new glass-doored fridge. O. Then saw a chilled Chablis.

For once, Enid... And for no good reason. Beyond a warm, thinning, memory.

Pleased, she headed towards the young man, reading at the counter, his hair languishing seemingly off only one side of his head. Indeed, the other side of his head appeared to have been recently shaved. Odd. When he looked up (and almost smiled) he had a ring in his nose. Someone new pushed at the door.

'Barp-Klack.'

'Barp-Klack.'

The young man, whose hair appeared to be partially cobalt, made no reaction to the door, only took her bottle and pointed a hand-held black plastic pistol at it, which glowed red and emitted another atonal noise, making the till spring open with a third variation of what to Enid sounded like frankly, schoolboys trying to fart.

Surprised at herself she blushed at the thought, and at her using the actual word too, and, a nervous reaction, she laughed.

The young man looked up. He took her ten-pound note and the till trumped gratefully when he closed it. He handed the grinning old thing her plonk and her change. He did not wrap it in its usual soft tissue paper but slid it into a thin white plastic bag. A tube with handles.

'Thank you,' she said.

'No worries – enjoy.'

He looked vaguely puzzled by her politesse, but went briskly back to his reading. A comic book. Enid didn't move. And wasn't sure why.

'Ought else, love?'

He could have been a pupil two years ago. She wondered if, in his head, he'd spelled the word, 'Owt.'

'No, nothing, thank you.'

The new customer approached with his purchase.

'Right…' the young man said.

With that bizarre fashionable inflection making it sound like a question was being asked, when it couldn't be.

Enid turned, still puzzled, still wondering if there was more she needed, wanted or ought to say. The door greeted her pulling it.

'Barp-Klack.'

She would like to jam it open so it couldn't ever offer it's unmusical greeting or farewell again.

THE SOLDIER'S HOME

But now came a droning single-note buzz from behind the counter and the young man tutted wearily, 'Make up your mind, love – in or out?'

Enid left.

'Barp-Klack.'

She placed her bags and keys on the piano.

Open this bottle before you do anything else, madam. Mademoiselle, you should say. Being a pedant.

Drink to not being a pedant? Good luck with that…

She poured a first Friday evening glass. The chilled liquid was oddly warming. Again.

Her flat brogues she eased off. These stockings really are too thick, but you can't have teenagers, of either gender, distracted by varicose veins.

Enid unclipped her grandmother's pink cameo brooch from her neck and opened a single top button of her blouse.

Mm, Chablis.

O but it was worth paying the extra for the real thing. Once a Friday came. And what a school-teacher's phrase that is, she thought. Were I to write about this life I lead, have lead, am leading - that would pass muster as a reasonable title. She sank into her father's eternally comfortable armchair. It had fitted him and now her.

One more sip before I draw my bath.

Curious phrase. I wish I knew its provenance…

She put Mendelssohn's, 'Songs Without Words' on the radiogram. I must replace that stylus at some point. Yes, scratchy but fondly perfect, Felix.

Poured some salts beneath the hot tap. The art-work on the box promised a bliss of Scottish purple-heathered relaxation and by the end of a long week Enid was prepared to believe it. Scotland in a box, why not believe it?

The thought passed through her as she was undressing that she had become what someone of her age and background would call a spinster. Possibly elsewhere, some crueller place, an old maid. And, as she hung up her teaching uniform, tweed suit one, in these gay 80's, she had also asked herself again – all these years after Val - whether she was at heart a lesbian. A closet one. That, she believed, was current idiom. In denial? Possibly, but her increasingly infrequent fantasies being in and of a hetero-sexual tone had dissuaded her. To her relief. A little late to start too much new now, she thought.

She ran some cold, stirring up, like a child, bubbles.

Like Chekhov's Sonia she was plain and she knew it. Be-spectacled now - she laid them on the toothbrush shelf - and hair in-a-bun too, Enid. Just run and turn the music up a notch. The curtains are all drawn. 'Large naked female pads about Pendlebury.' Heavens!

For some reason she could never fathom she had placed a large mirror at the tap end of the bath so when, as now, one lowered oneself in, or later hauled oneself out, lobster-red and with what her mother called 'corned-beef legs', it was impossible to ignore the sagging of the spare tyres. It was, she thought, an odd kind of cruelty; relieved again as now she slid below its angle and into the scented heat. O. Oh. Mmm.

Long ago she had accepted solitude as her lot, and a single pat on the back was surely due here, for she had, in the phrase, worn it well. Even used it well. As a defining part of her professional

THE SOLDIER'S HOME

persona. No false modesty naked in a bath, Enid! She knew how good a teacher she was, and how her students did well. She had the results to prove it.

And now – now that 'achievement' was, paradoxically, a reason to stop. Go.

These league tables, these ladders of excellence, and this latest smokescreen christened Parental Choice. It was people playing politics with Education. Despicable. That woman.

Oh, shh Enid, leave her.

Don't spoil a cold Chablis in a hot bath.

'We put our shoulders to the wheel, else we're hopping a free ride.' Her father.

Life wasn't so very bad. A yearn now and again. But, like normal. An ugly phrase, she thought.

O.

O but there is *nothing* like a bath.

A Greek beach? A heated swimming pool?

Yes, pedant, but I have neither the mentality nor, frankly, the body to lie, or lounge, in any public place.

And I don't own a swimming costume.

Mum and dad must have bought me one once. Well, she would have. But I have never paid for one. Yet this immersion, this enfolding touch-all heat, it truly suits me. Especially of a Friday. With a glass. Her gaze lingered on the ceiling. Unchanged. Undecorated since…

Her only home.

Their first home. Council estate in Pendlebury.

Where Mum and Dad met. At a church dance.

'He made a bee-line for me,' said her mother when Enid had asked. When they talked.

As we did. As we had to, us two, the whole war.

'Why is it a bee-line? Shouldn't it be a crow-line; as in, 'As the crow flies?''

'Well, as maybe – but he made a bee-line as in I were like honey.' And Mabel had blushed.

Enid always loved it when her mother blushed. It meant it was true.

'Met at a dance, and we knew. Well, I did. And I could see he did! That whole massive question mark laid aside in an evening. In a dance if I'm being soft. And I wish the same for you, you know I do.' And that would be followed by a squeeze of my hand.

'Other problems, mind. My father. Your Grandpa Cliff; you don't really remember him. He was - prejudiced.'

Her mother always lowered her voice when she said that word. The two of them, in their own house and still she whispered. A memory that tickled still.

'Because Daddy was Irish. When we told them, and us so proud of each other, and we said we wanted to wed he said, 'A Paddy with a pick? A miner? Mabel…' And he left the room. Left my mother crying. Pat, your daddy Pat, he followed Cliff and we all heard him say he couldn't and he wouldn't waste breath trying to stop Cliff thinking as he did - just to inform him the only member of his family invited to their wedding would be Mabel. I was shocked and proud at the same moment. Swinton Town Hall. February 12th,1932. It rained. He came around, eventually, your Grandpa. Mainly because of you, Enid.'

Then there would be a tiny quiet in the story-telling.

'And we got this, our council house, and your Daddy worked Agecroft Colliery and we thought, we hoped, and I certainly prayed that because he was a miner, and they'd said miners were 'vital', that he wouldn't be called.' Then there was always a longer quiet. And that quiet always ended with an action beginning.

THE SOLDIER'S HOME

Baking, ironing, doing the crocks... Distraction. And she would eventually say, 'But he was.'

Enid stirred the bath with one foot. With such large toes, she thought. Again. Closed her eyes to better concentrate on greeting the movement of heat. Feel the tiny waves meet her. Explore her. Move with her stolid flesh. Loosen it. Or feel as though they could.

'But he was. Called. And left me here with you. And you - you always loved books...'

Her mother would say that in a tone of some wonder, as to where, genetically, such an impulse could have sprung from. Virginia Woolf's father, Stephen, once said to her, 'Child, how you gobble...' Meaning books. I was the same. And now, still. Forever, I believe. She, Virginia, was loved but lived mainly loveless. I felt.

And who loves you, Enid?

My parents did. Do, in their peace. Mrs Cowley did.

Mrs Cowley!

Oh, the passion in her classroom! If I were writing that thought, passion would have a capital 'P'. And embossed like the Book of Kells.

I have tried, too hard, to do that. To be that passionate. And, failed, I do believe. My students respect me, and – she took another drink – so they should – but they don't adore me. I adored Emma Cowley. For the radiation of her love of Language. Because 'words make stories and stories transport.' And that - the lifting above and away - to Emma Cowley, that was a Holy act. She moved me. Changed my life. Set it on this course, certainly.

Enid stretched.

Pressed her toes into the metal. This old iron bath. Marvellous. How it holds the heat. That hotel, where was it, Bordeaux, that modern plastic thing – oh no no no.

Mrs Cowley slipping me summer-holidays Jane Austen. At ten. And still meeting me, with new ideas (and fixed ideals) when I went on to Monton, to the posh grammar school. Encouraging me.

That was love. Heck, she even praised my dreadful teenaged poems! And she lived to read my first book, my fictionalised biography of Mum.

O, there was A Moment. We had fulfilled each other. And, and she suggested I might now call her Emma. Sealing an eternal circle of love.

Mum.

My mum. Talking to Eileen, her neighbour, every Thursday.

'She likes to clack,' her mother always said of her. As though she didn't. No. She was 'chatting' - Eileen clacked.

They shared a Victoria sponge, copious cups of tea into which they dunked usually a whole packet of digestives each Thursday morning and I must have been off school poorly, because I remember her saying, like yesterday, 'One man went off to war and a different one came back.'

And Eileen had said, 'My Fred went off whistling hymns and he came back whistling 'em an' all. He learnt to cuss. That were all difference war made to him.'

Mabel said, lowering her voice but not quite enough, 'Our Enid spent the war reading.' Then added, 'Mind you she's spent peace doing it an' all...'

I remember worrying, hearing that, whether it was a strange or a wrong thing to do. Wicked even. She had lowered her voice...

And Mum, who had never worked when Dad was mining, taking a job at the primary school. A part-time dinner lady. She came home tired.

Enid opened the clip holding the too-tight bun of her greying hair and it fell grateful onto the water, spreading weightless.

THE SOLDIER'S HOME

She lay right back, hair drowning and inviting the heat to find her temples and neck and ears.

What a shock I would deliver if I ever went in to school with it down.

She floated her head back to Easter 1946 and the shell of her father finally finally returned to them.

His eyes, the skin and bone of him. Hollowed.

'He's a gourd,' said Mabel and Enid had had to look the word up.

The horrors of war had barely touched Pendlebury. Rationing and worrying. Patrick was an emotional sink-hole. Into which had fallen, most noticeably, a desire to speak.

'We shall have to be very patient,' her mother said.

A lot.

Enid shampooed.

My mother, faced with this silent broken stranger, spoke to the vicar, the doctor, her old teachers, Eileen, other wives of returning heroes and elicited bottomless sympathy and not one thing practical. He wouldn't go with them to church; but when the young vicar, Father Kirkby, came round and suggested the two of them go for a pint father roared, 'No!' and Enid only ever saw the vicar at church after that. Mum, en route for Desperation turned to The Army. A Sergeant behind a desk at Eccles barracks listened and when she mentioned Burma, nodded and her heart rose. For the first time since her husband had returned. There was a society, at the British Legion, of ex-servicemen. 'Take him there.'

'Oh no, he won't go out.'

'Right,' said the man. 'Right. Leave this with me, me ducks.'

A week later a man came to the door. Ted. A slight man with a bad limp. He introduced himself, told them he didn't know Pat, but perhaps he knew part of him.

'Don't you introduce us,' he said, 'I'll just pop through and see if he fancies a chat, should I?'

Behind even the plaster-board walls she and her mother heard hardly a thing. Ted surely did all the talking that first time but he came back once a week and six weeks later, the first week he missed, Pat was distressed. Missed him. How thrilled his women had been at that distress.

Ted got him out.

First to his, Ted's, allotment, and then, with Mabel, to The Legion.

Mabel asked Ted one night what they spoke of so quietly and he patted her arm with his thin claw and said, 'There's things women have no need to learn.' He must have sensed it not being a satisfactory answer, because he added, quieter, 'Men can be cruel shits. All right?'

The Legion led, slowly but marvellously, to a first night out without Ted. At the Miners Club. Enid left at home, reading.

Unable to concentrate I was so thrilled, I remember.

And that, The Miner's Club, became once a week, regular, in his slow healing. In his re-assembly.

Rinse out the shampoo. The real heat, the distracting heat, is out of this bath now. It's always been a grand boiler. Why do I so love this heat? And the record is almost finished. I listen to the staff at work. Hear their talk of juggling money to get new appliances - and now they talk of and expect, 'built-in obsolescence'. And I lounge in my Friday bath and feel childishly grateful. And, how awful - I feel pity. Pompous private Enid.

What was I thinking of?

Dad. Recovering himself.

From turning 14, and the tightening of their belts with his being unfit for work, Enid had taken a Saturday job. To help the finances. A good feeling, she recalled.

THE SOLDIER'S HOME

She squeezed at her hair and readied the shower attachment.

Helping a greengrocer do the markets. And bring the left-overs home. Sunday veg. Sometimes fruit. I liked the market, enjoyed the hard work and the early hours - earlier than teaching even – and I liked that he, Mr. Skipton, said, 'Call me Joe, Enid, it's my name.' I liked that he obviously appreciated the help, and that he liked me. And it was a pleasure to feel useful. The two pounds her parents said she could keep, but she shared it with them.

Once University got mentioned she gave Mabel all of it.

OK.

You are done, miss. Now, nothing compares to a warmed deep towel and a softer bath-robe.

Oh, but that reminds me!

Enid stood, the tiniest glance in the mirror, and wrapped her pink steaming self in the towel.

Neville Chamberlain.

Chamberlain wore studded, winged, collars. And Patrick had one. For Christmas midnight mass and 'family occasions'. He hated it, it pinched his throat and he wasn't about to spend precious brass on another – and – the wearing of it meant a scrubbing. Standing in the copper, Mabel bruising his miner's nakedness with a stiff-haired brush and carbolic. And the ritual ended with her towelling him dry. 'Cos you do it softer than a man.' And, Enid realised much later, his arousal and their love-making and through the walls her mother saying, 'It's only the sex as'll get you to a christening!' And they would laugh and I would listen and it was their laughter I cherished most then, and remember best now.

She dried herself.

And that laughter became rarer as Chamberlain appeased and father wrestled with the paradox that as regards Adolf, he agreed with Churchill.

'That strike-breaking Tory bastard, sorry Mabel, Enid.'

'Pains me to share the steam off – never you mind – but to share my opinion with a Tory ...' He would trail off, horrified.

War. That ever-growing elephant in our tiny living-room. I buried my worries in books, and prayed Adolf wouldn't close the Library. Worth my Dad fighting to keep that open.

Pull the plug. My bathrobe, Dad's armchair.

She would settle with her radio after deciding, yet again, there was nothing on the television. Think about the marking, but leave it for Saturday.

Creature of habit. Ritual.

Our Saturdays was always the rag and bone man on his cart, shouting something I never understood, and neither did mother. She called them 'gypsies' – in her lowered voice - and cried when they came to the door, babes-in-arms to trade a sprig of lavender for any coins she could spare. Mother would hang the lavender from the mantlepiece till it stopped smelling nice.

And now I recall Fridays was the 'pop' man. Horse, cart and crates of fizzy weekend delight. Dandelion and Burdock and throat assaulting ginger beer. Father forbad us to even try 'American Cream Soda'. He said it was the same as the horse's poo, left for the flies and the boys on the estate to giggle over.

One or two of these essays show promise. Promise in the sense of hope. Not a certainty. Not a vow.

Something troubles me here. She laid her red marking pencil aside, took off her spectacles, stood and headed for the kitchen to refill her coffee; I begin to question some of the shibboleths of Grammar. This coffee is stale. Make some fresh. Twenty more essays to mark. I teach, I have been teaching, the Absolutes of Grammar. The Rules. Carved in stones. For thirty years. But a couple of these essays, in wilfully (or perhaps instinctively) ignoring some of those rules; well, one or two of these students have found an originality. An individuality.A voice. Their voice. A truth.

On Sunday morning Enid nodded to her fellow parishioners of St. Augustine's. Still thinking. And the doubt still un-resolved.

As she took her prayer-book and hymnal and found her usual spot she found herself arguing all writing, her own included, needed, axiomatically, to be a personal voice. Not to conform to a rigidity of Grammar.

Is that true?

I fear it is. I fear enough of it is.

Not all writing, no. Letters, non-fiction. But expressive writing, yes.

But, Good God (Sorry, Lord), but here's the rub; this is heretical to my drilling - and I do drill – the recognition of assonance, alliteration, simile, metaphor, adverbial clauses, conjunctions etc etc ad infinitum (for each particle of Grammar has a title, a way of identifying it); and my drilling it into those malleable minds - the vicar was coming forward to begin the service – is only for them, my students ('suffer the little children') to come as close as I can guarantee to their passing examination at English Language 'O' level. To claim that monolith, that mainstay of employment hope. Wasn't that now, in far too large part, my job? My duty?

Yes, Lord. I am listening.

Paying attention.

Is it the elegance in this centuries-old language that so engulfs the faithful? For look. All our heads bow.

But the most interesting essays were the ones where the voice broke free. Disinterested in, unencumbered by process.

Yes, let us pray.

🐏

Once a decision is accepted, then a wall of detail - The Great Wall of Detail, is before you.

But it's detail and that's all it is.

Life only begins again when the decision becomes flesh.

I like that the church, the service, the ritual allows my mind to stroll. In an incensed space.

How often have I wondered why I don't have incense at home?

What is that? What is that in me? Separation? Home. Work. Church.

Across the nave a youngish woman with a perhaps five-year-old girl had taken Enid's attention.

Possibly, even probably, because the vicar had – again – chosen verses from Ezekiel as the text for his sermon. Enid had read Ezekiel and had appreciated it only a very little, on both occasions.

I assume these two are mother and daughter. They could be sisters, she could be an auntie, a baby-minder, neighbours even, but something in the familiarity between their bodies, the easy hand-holding and in the child's demonstration of her impatience with this place allows me to settle on mother/daughter. Hypothetical, but let me further imagine that the child has only this mother. Now.

Imagine then, five years previously, a young family, here for the christening of this daughter, this then cherished miracle. Who represents so precisely, so perfectly what their love-making looks like. Not hard to picture the shared doting, the shared wonder, the shared delight. And now he, the father, had left. Not died, left. A separation. Divorced. Enid swept those irrelevant details aside as she concentrated on how the child must have changed in the mother's eyes. She, the daughter, let's christen her Marla, could not be held in the same affection she had once been. Because she was no longer a shared wonder. She could not, had not bound the family together, so, yes, while she was ever a wonder, now, for the mother, she had to be a solo wonder. She could be shared with her grandparents, the mother's friends, this congregation even, but not with her maker.

Unless one counted God as her maker, which, in His house, in this instant, Enid didn't.

Enid did not doubt, watching them two pews ahead, the mother's love; tender and patient. She considered only an inherent anguish wedged now within that love.

As the vicar developed some theological point an Everest over the child's head Enid wondered why the mother, had come here. Enid had not seen her before and she settled into a trawl of possible options.

To be, to feel, blessed.

To show the child Something. New.

To sing. To share. Take Communion. Literally.

To bore the babe so thoroughly she would never dream of repeating the experience.

(Because perhaps the parents had once been married in this same spot, by the vicar, one glorious hope-drenched day? Was this the first time the mother had returned here? To lay some ghost?)

To kill a few lonely Sunday hours.

To win a bet?

To take the blood and the bread one last time before renouncing religion for ever?

She was an alcoholic and the wine was free?

Now her brain was fizzing nonsense Enid veered inwards to ask why she was thinking this. What was it?

Her own childless state. Envy? Pity?

No, no. My time has passed. Those vile flushes, o how I hated and resented them and their passage through me, their unpredictability, their will of their own, their mocking of this barren body. No, surely not that. I knew years ago I would not have children, have a family, a man, a partner, not since that night. I knew and I accepted it. Sadly, yes, but I did. I no longer asked. Looked. Was no longer prepared to be open. To all that.

So why am I asking now? Thinking this now?

Heavens but it is something in that young mother's haircut, something about her skin, her shoulders – what? There's something flamboyant in her hair. In the way it bounces when her head moves. And I am ever Vanya's Sonya – plain and what good that I know that? Accept it?

I know that my life is teaching. Has been teaching. Teaching and my own writing and o vicar, do stop droning on and let us sing that passage in the creed I so love – 'And on the third day he rose again, according to the scriptures,' – and go.

Out.

Into fresh distractions. I feel so weepy. Suddenly trapped. That daughter, that child, is free to be bored out of her mind and I am not. Because of years. My years. And the handcuffs of Form. Formality. Those years I have worn at standstill since becoming what I am. Myself. A teacher. O thank you God. Amen, vicar. Ten more minutes.

As Canon Kirkby descended his pulpit, slow as his years, so

the mother and child rose and left. The child skipping free. People tutted. Demonstrating and sharing disapproval. And perhaps now thinking things a good deal worse than I did – but, essentially, because those two have escaped.

It was rude, yes. And it was not form. But was it wrong?

No, I can't say that.

The early evening radio played Saint-Saens and Enid read the small print of the Observer travel section. With her red marking pencil. Just doodling. Evening-dreaming.

🐑

She dressed.

Clean ironed blouse. Fresh. Cameo brooch. Tweed suit two. Brogues. Glance at the weather forecast. Lightest jacket, then. Breakfast.

Thoughts of the bureaucratic forms that needed to be written (had to be written, nothing *need* be done) for the government ghouls. Oh! Turning Education into shopping. God! And using us, the darned teachers, to do their research for them. On our time!

You could say, if you were in that frame of mind, Enid, getting colleagues to condemn themselves out of their own mouths. Only one thing truly truly counted in Education. The number of students in a class. Teacher-pupil ratio. And they were rising. Wrong, frankly. Wrong.

Teaching itself, set aside the planning of each lesson, is difficult enough, time and energy consuming enough (come try it, Baker, do!), without any of this extra nonsense. Inset days! I do see why people swear. It's release.

Don't forget the handkerchief.

There had been a questionnaire in one of the glossy sections of the weekend papers asking what was one's most embarrassing moment. Enid had shaken cold, instant goose-pimples at the memory of her one handkerchief-less morning and a sudden abundance of what the Germans call nasalschleim. She flushed even now, alone in her home, fifteen years after the event and pocketed a tube of lavender mints. Five minutes to the bus. Brief case, marking, keys, money. Out.

And that had not been her most embarrassing moment, not by a sordid long chalk.

Close the gate.

The 21 bus was Monday morning Manchester suburbs quiet, busy but private.

I always sit downstairs, on the left-hand side if I can, by the window for choice, looking at the same things I've seen almost all my life. Why never upstairs?

Here is my mental list of things I've never done, I'll never do. Learn to lip-read. Go to Laos. Ski. Swim. Have sex or children. Speak Czech.

I have lived all my life in these streets, apart from University. That enchanted poisoned island. That o so very mixed bag.

I don't believe these thoughts are indicative of a crisis - but

I do believe

that

that woman

in front of me

is reading one of my books! 'Women Without Men.' My first!

The one about Mum. Mum, raising me as a single woman in the war. Fictionalised. Partly. Enough.

THE SOLDIER'S HOME

O My God.

I flush.

O the temptation to lean forward and ask, 'Are you enjoying that?'

I could. I could do that. Say I've read it, too (true enough). No photo of me on the cover, thank heavens. And it's not even in my name.

She flicked that page over quickly. She is enjoying it?

I remember Paul Theroux once, one of his travel books and he was depressed if I recall correctly to be back in drab cold London from South America I believe a train journey book and he saw a woman on a commuter train reading one of his books and he soared. I know that feeling! I soar. Well now, there's something off my list. Soaring. No. not true. When the publisher, Gerard, 'my publisher', wrote to say he would 'love to participate' in publishing that very book, I was airborne then, too. He wished to 'make me an offer.' What a joy-drenched phrase. I read it a thousand times.

The bus turned right, west, at Swinton Town Hall (where they wed) and only four stops now to school. I hope she gets off, I hope she closes the book happily, slips it into her bag. That would be just a lovely treat, so it would.

I had spent four pounds more on a bottle of Chablis that evening. Drowning my Pride. And a loneliness, too.

Because although Dad would have been thrilled for me, he would have been shocked, too. But he couldn't be, because I didn't tell him. Fool that I was. Am.

And the second book, a straight novel (that woman is not even looking out of the windows - she's nowhere near her stop) had spurted forward.

One more stop.

She is completely engaged...

The bus, my bus is slowing. Children rise all around me. Some look at me. Some choose to wait, politely for me to rise, thank them and go ahead of them. I don't. Puzzled, they move past.

The bus stops.

School.

Get up and off. Your body knows.

What are you *doing?*

The woman read on, oblivious of the earthquake around her. The bus emptied of its children.

The bus moved indifferently on. Taking its drama with it.

Enid Makin watched children on the pavement staring at her. In genuine amazement.

There's another then. Never inspired amazement before.

A smile began. A grin. They'll tell on me... 'Naughty' is not something I've ever indulged in, either. How I wish I'd poked a face at them. Stuck out my tongue.

Still the blessed woman read. And perhaps she too had missed her stop, so engrossed was she. In my prose, in my story-telling...

One side of her brain flashed she could catch a bus back, or a taxi and easily make her first lesson. A different side wondered where this bus went, beyond Worsley. I catch it every day of my working life, it says Leigh on the front.

One of Dad's favourite jokes – 'Says India on the tyres but it's not going there...'

What if this woman is going to Leigh?

The woman turned another page briskly. O. That flick of that page. I know that! She's 'in'. Where was she, page 200? Mum's first stroke?

Just one smile and I'll get off and taxi back.

No, I won't.

Should I lean over and tell her there's three more by that author?

God, this is so – heck! - exciting!

The woman looked up, checked where the bus was, Walkden village, and Enid heated inside at something in the settling of her shoulders as she plunged back in…

I am wilfully going to miss a class.

A day of firsts, then.

I do not quite believe this is me and yet I will honour it.

Her mind ran through a Kaleidoscope of excuses, and being a teaching 'lifer' she had heard so very many.

She resolved to tell her Head, Rob, nothing but the truth. He would believe her, and if she chose to ask it, she knew he would be discreet. He might even embroider. Enid did not know. Sitting on a bus going she knew not how far, she knew not for what precise reason.

Exciting. Have to pay the extra fare when I get off. Like a naughty school-child.

Little Hulton. Four Lane Ends. Where was this woman leading her? Another page flicked quickly. Where was she going at this hour?

Her reader seemed to be as engaged reading as she had been writing it.

She was watching a woman read.

What for, exactly? At any second this book will surely be closed, marked and closed, and the woman and Enid would get off, and she would be faced with a bizarre journey back, to a bizarre situation.

How quietly thrilling. To A Bizarre Situation. Completely new…

Sure enough, the woman tucked her ticket into their book, closed it, rose and Enid followed her. And, shot for a sheep as for a lamb, having alighted, and not offered to pay the extra fare, she now followed this magnetic woman. Round a couple of corners – God, I feel like a private detective. Hilarious, Enid. Miss Marple Lives – and she was going into a hospital.

A nurse? She was a nurse? Starting a shift at 9? A Doctor? Wouldn't a doctor have a car? Snob Enid. She's visiting a sick relative.

She let the woman go, and loved her.

And in this wonderous dancing swirl, thought, 'Well, I might never know sex, but right now, I don't mind.'

🐑

On the bus back there was a Scottish man. Or was he a Scotsman? An open question in English grammar. Except in this case he was a broadcast. In a Scots accent. Talking far too much. And too loud. Seeking and needing attention and as he performed, oblivious to the lack of interest he was garnering, Enid wanted to gently strangle him. Another first. This entire morning was full of them.

And Enid wanted peace to think her new thoughts. Examine them. And still he over-articulated on. She had no sympathy with his bad leg. He possibly got it, broke it, tripping down a manhole he hadn't seen - too occupied revelling in the endless din he made. Ostensibly he was talking to an acquaintance – a relative? – across the aisle, but as she noticeably avoided eye-contact – as did almost everyone else – so he rattled, endlessly self-assured, onwards. And then, the person sitting next to him engaged him with a question and he lowered his voice; and Enid almost laughed as suddenly she wanted to hear what he had to say!

Her stop. School, from the other direction. She alighted. An hour and more late.

THE SOLDIER'S HOME

As with the children at Friday's bus-stop, and the vicar, and even the bore on the bus, Enid listened not to what, but rather to how, Rob spoke. She absorbed his care, his assumption she was 'obviously not perhaps feeling herself' today. His eyes as always were kind though he looked a good deal more tired than – well - Enid could not remember when she and Rob last sat down and talked face-to-face, when she had last had a chance such as this to study his face. Truth was, as she surprised him by interrupting his flow to say, 'We don't really talk, do we, Head?' He blinked. 'I am your Head of English, and a metronomic successful dinosaur. No need to talk with me.' The Head sat back. 'I take nor intend insult. I am neither drunk, nor ill, sire,' she added, 'nor am I insane, but this is me resigning, Rob.' There was a tiny beat, before, 'I should say my resigning because resigning is a gerund; and a gerund is partly noun and therefore requires the possessive pronoun 'my' not the personal pronoun, 'me'. But, in this case, there is a comma after me in the phrase 'this is me, resigning."

two

06.37. FIRST LIGHT, ALMOST. I am here. I am on this first Thursday train leaving Manchester Piccadilly for London Euston. A tube across the capital to Victoria, then a Southern train down to the coast. Hovercraft. Train three, Calais to my beloved Paris – metro – blow Paris a fleeting kiss this time, and catch the last Thursday train from Gare d'Austerlitz to arrive near midnight in Figeac. To be met and driven to Somewhere Else. And at the end of this teeming hectic day, to be asleep and to dream in France. Breathe country air all day Friday. And Saturday – begin. New life. House-hunting. O Excitement. O foot-drumming, toe-curling excitement. Come on train, time to leave.

Don't let it stop, this will. This new will. Stay this 'me' since Monday and the bus. Going forward.

I am tired of being Miss Makin. I shall become Enid as I travel. Voyage. Enid of the South. Enid De La Sud. Buying one-way tickets! I have never done that before. And yes, of course I will return, but, o please God, it's then I shall buy return tickets!

In the luggage rack over my head the same square-cornered tan leather suitcase (Mum's) I took to University.

(God, Enid, the clothes aren't *that* different.)

The last time I took a serious train. That one had been a steam train. 1952. 'When we had railways.' Dad. This one seemed formed from moulded plastic. But still, the self-same serious excitement only Adventure generates. Thirty years of service after...

That was a whistle. Some shouting.

06.40.

O! I'm briefly a child again. Stay there, Enid. And, well done, you.

The train moved. No steam, just a considerable jolt, which struck Enid as exactly what had been required. O heck - but goody!

'Au revoir, Manchester?' I don't know.

Good. Good that you don't know, Enid.

She settled deeper into her seat, didn't care for the rigid arm-rest, laid her ticket ready on the table. Bottle of water. Sandwiches and fruit and no appetite of any kind! Time. Space. To myself. Good. Journeys are good for thought. Made for thought.

I was fourteen when my excellent report, (Lord, what a swot I was – and have stayed?) my regular-as-clockwork excellent report, invited my parents – a direct comment from The Head - to consider now the thought of my eventually going to University. And, much more important by far, the change that letter sparked in post-war Dad.

Round another dinner-table the report was passed, read. And he spoke. Father spoke. He wasn't a mute but this was him beginning something.

'Think high, Enid.'

We, his women, had blinked.

'You want Oxford?'

A silence he took for assent.

'Start there, then – and when they say 'yis' – then we'll fret about the how.'

She and her mother, Enid viscerally recalled, had held their breath. And as he settled to eat, so they ate too. Chewed.

Tasted.

Suburbs. Back-to-back Lowry terraces; or I should say Coronation Street? Longsight. How did that get named? Perhaps it had a marvellous view at one time. Hard to believe today. Literally wall-to-wall suburbanity. That's not a real word. And? Who's to care? Or mark it with a red pencil?

I took the Saturday job, on the markets and I contributed. And apart from the years at University, when I scrimped as they did, I always have. Contributed. Till I took over.

Why am I thinking of this? Oh yes! Dad's recovery. One week after they both went to the Legion for the first time without Ted, I came home from extra cramming for my Higher C's, and found a piano taking up one wall of the living room. And Mother, with a huge smile in her silent eyes mouthing, 'Don't ask.'

I said, 'He can't play.' And she whispered, 'He bloody will.'

And he did.

Taught himself to play that ever-so-slightly out-of-tune piano. Dad. It was painful in one sense and in a larger one, sweeter than everything Mozart ever managed.

Not a sheet of music ever appeared. 'Pit frigged me lungs, not me ears.'

Heaton Chapel station

And after a year and more of practice he fashioned the bottom of a shoe box to lay just above the keys so he couldn't see them, and he learned to play that way too. And, never ever never to forget, arriving home early that Friday winter evening from my first thrilling term at Uni, bursting to tell them anything and everything, and Mother, a light glittering from her soul saying, 'Leave your bag there and keep your coat on, clever-clogs.'

I sipped lemonade at The Legion – no wine there – with nobody telling me a thing until, after a second Guinness, Patrick, my dad, to applause and o so tangible warmth, sat at the piano and played and played until all the world's favourite songs had been sung to the rafters and my clinging to Mother's arm as we cried.

'Soppy dates,' Dad said, wiping his cheeks.

Stockport.

Stopping here. Don't want a companion, I don't want to have to talk. Happy to think, please.

Good. No-one's joined me.

Three years later, hurrying towards my Masters, Mabel had her second stroke and that one took her. Hanky, quickly please.

I came home. And I sat to write a eulogy for her. For her funeral service. All the time thinking I can't read this, I'll just blub – but who else could, who else should? And, I had written what became the first chapter of the book that woman on the bus was reading before father pointed out it was only supposed to last five minutes. I was bitten.

No, kissed. Kissed by the bug of expression. It gave me a release for the grief and the loss, yes, but also the place to spend private energies.

Poynton.

Lovely. That canal. Parts of Cheshire truly are lovely.

'Old money, Enid.'

Life with Dad with Mum cold in the ground.

'I miss being a miner, Enid.'

I don't believe I did more than physically turn my body toward him. Inviting him to elaborate.

'It's daily facing the possibility of death. With other men...'

'Like the War?'

'Nothing like the war. I'll never tell you about that, Enid.'

'I know, Dadda.'

A deep silence. Then I added, 'And that's fine...'

And he said, 'And I miss the doing something I could do.'

I started teaching and I took over the house, basically. He washed and cooked a little, less as time and events eroded him and I worked and paid the bills. He also swore more, without Mabel. Apologised less, certainly.

I had a birthday and I don't recall which one, but I must have glanced at the newspaper column telling you who shares that date, because this I do recall.

Lady Jane Grey, poor doomed soul.

Lillie Langtry.

Art Tatum. A pianist. I bought a long-player which Dad listened to a lot and finally pronounced, 'Too bloody brilliant by half.' After he'd nodded along a fair bit looking at the cover, at the grinning black face.

And, a happy birthday to the new member of parliament for Finchley. A woman. Margaret Thatcher. It didn't even say which party she represented. And, for reason as shallow as a shared moment in calendar time, I became 'fond' of her, or more correctly, if this isn't a linguistic contradiction – and I don't care any longer if it is – vaguely interested in her. I never held any truck with astrology, so no fleeting wonder about shared characteristics; no interest in horoscopes, that thin end of some supposedly mighty cosmic wedge. Was I seriously to consider of a humanity divided into a dozen archetypes? I sound like Edmund in 'Lear'. What did he say? 'Fut, I should have been as I am had the something something star twinkled on my nativity...' Quite.

And I was always fond of that passage in Conan Doyle where Watson lists all the things Holmes has no interest in at all.

'You tell me, Watson, the earth orbits the sun and the moon orbits us (a sad paraphrase but it is forty years since I read it...) but it's of neither use nor interest to me. How many steps are there on the staircase up to this room?' And Watson, of course, hadn't noticed.

Nothing proves anything, except – some say – mathematics. Which I imagine is what explains the bizarre (to me) passion it can engender. It offers an absolute. I'm with Sherlock Holmes, then. So what? Pass me my violin.

I like this mood.

Prestbury.

Slowing down now for Macclesfield.

'High Tory Territory.'

After Mabel passed, it, Dadda's language did change. Sharply. On certain subjects. Made me wonder if, at times, and in some ways, Mabel had constricted him. What was certain was he made no concession to any sensibilities I might or might not have. Or be supposed to have. And in the privacy of his home I pretended no sensibilities. Offered him no sense of being offended, I hope.

It was language after all, Anglo-Saxon and undeniably rich and rhythmic. How he referred to the good burghers of Macclesfield for instance, 'A Festering Bunch of High Tory Twats,' had an iambic lilt. The language of the pits?

I would never have allowed a dot of it in any student's work, of course. Disaster guaranteed in an examination paper.

Macclesfield station coming into slowing focus.

I feel sad *and* released at the same time!

Because look at what had become my raison d'etre.

Results. Quantifiable success. No longer, as I once so fervently hoped (and believed my duty to be), to fill the hearts and heads of the young with the sublime purity of the possibility of the written word. And to engender a passion for that and to encourage them to revel in it and express themselves. No. I became what I am – I was – a hugely successful exam-passer. There's a truly vile phrase. Enough. I resigned. I have resigned. I heard myself say it, heard myself mean it. And now, right now, I am training towards something I don't know. Scared but proud. Like the last time I did this. When I went up to University.

'bye Macclesfield.

Next stop London, and no-one to disturb me. Good.

Good. Where was I?

I didn't read the content of Mrs. Thatcher's maiden speech, but I noted the event of it, and, how odd some humours are, I hoped it had gone well for her. My fellow Libran. My fellow 13th Octoberian. There can't be such a word. There is now. I just this second assembled it.

Shakespeare added six hundred words and more to the language.

Where was I?

I wasn't anywhere. I was doodling with memory.

And suddenly racing, hurrying south of Macclesfield.

Hurrah.

Dreaming of Oxford.

Where her heart was set. Ever since her father had said 'think high' - oh but she had.

The spires, cloisters, chapels, the squares, the gardens, light falling through plane trees, willows draped in the Isis river – the average length of a punt; Enid lived off finite information.

Before she sat her 'A' levels, she had read the prospectuses from St. Hugh's, Somerville college and her favourite, her choice, St. Hilda's. Where she would devour written culture, bloom herself in the sumptuous gardens, and leave book-bloated and with the world at her literary feet. She would lodge in the room once the accommodation of Edith Russell and breathe the same air as Cecil Woodham-Smith. 'The Great Hunger', her book, had been left by Enid's bedside when she was 13. Enid, used only to fictional narrative was, as her father intended, appalled. 'The English won't ever be teaching you that tale, girl...'

Oxford loomed. Its bells boomed in her heart.

She would make friends there. Boom. Love even. Boom! Argue about books! O boom on you big bells.

Enid knew what a fairy-story was and indulged in hers for its most potent currency – hope. What ending is better than a fairy-tale ending? Er - plenty, she thought. The Brothers Grimm were aptly named...

Dreams of Oxford.

The Headmaster wrote a letter to Patrick, suggesting a meeting, at his and Mabel's earliest convenience. Perhaps an evening after school?

The following Friday the family were sipping tea from china cups before a plate of Garibaldi biscuits and listening to The Head singing their daughter's academic and behavioural praises. And explaining options and possibilities for Enid, as he was in no doubt whatsoever she was University material. Both parents blushed and so did their daughter when Mabel said, 'Well, we're sure we don't know where she got it from...' The Head responded with, 'Mrs Makin, ours not to reason why. The issue here is the sky is the limit for Enid, academically. And how can we help her reach it?'

Patrick, over-proud and for want of any available words, took two Garibaldi biscuits. He heard Mabel's breath screech 'Tch', and put one back. As he sensed some vast new shame he toyed with picking it up again. 'What?' he wanted to say. But didn't. Instead he said magic words.

'Oxford, like?'

'Or Cambridge,' said Gerald Smith M.A. Cantab.

'Each college,' he said, 'has its own entrance examinations...' and no doubt Enid would pass them. Gain her right to entrance. 'This, I will opine, is a given. But,' he said, 'the question we must address is – how much might this cost and how is it to be afforded?'

Bringing both parents forward from 'in' their armchairs to 'on' them.

And Enid, nearing sixteen, felt Doubt. Iron-cold and horrid.

Her shining knight, Mr Smith, now produced a hand-written list of all the possible public sources of financial help. 'These we must write to.' A second list with two columns of figures. Of university fees, books, accommodation and living expenses. 'Or food, Enid, as students call it...' The first column was marked 'Ox

THE SOLDIER'S HOME

& Cam', the second, 'Redbrick'. Patrick looked at figures larger than any amount of money he had ever seen, and certainly held in his hands. Both columns with totals in three figures.

'And is this what you went through yourself, Head-Master?'

'Ah, no. My parents could afford to support me...'

'We can't.'

Enid was impressed by how simply he responded. 'I understand. Now.' A third list. 'We apply to the colleges of Enid's choice – for scholarships. I am happy to write any number of references, but the fact is scholarships are rare, means-tested, and, much more likely to be awarded to boys than girls.' He shrugged, sadly.

'And, you must write to your Board of Education.' He indicated the address and, opening his fountain pen, underlined it for them. 'They do have grants available. But,' he sat back in his winged leather chair, 'but... they may very well buck at the fees for Oxford and Cambridge. And so, Enid, you must prepare yourself for that possible disappointment. And finally, to give ourselves the best chance of no disappointment, we must write to charitable organizations...' a fourth list, 'to any individuals who can, do, and have endowed either educational establishments and/or individual students like Enid. This list I suggest we both cover.'

He spread his manicured hands, shared a warm smile and all things felt possible. Doubt to be combatted by Effort.

Enid attained the exam results required for university entrance. She passed the entrance examinations for all three of her favoured Oxford colleges.

The sun shone on Pendlebury.

Mabel, baking bread, asked, 'What is it you want to actually do, love?'

'Read. They say you read for a subject, read for a degree – I want to read English. Drown in it!'

'And then?' Dad. From the front room.

'Well, I'm only 16, dad. So. I don't know.'

'Needs considering.'

'I know I don't want to be a nurse.'

Three letters in embossed envelopes, typed on vellum paper and personally signed by The Vice-President of each one of the three Oxford colleges, arrived with elegantly expressed regrets on their sadly being no scholarships available. And so, regrettably… Heartfelt best wishes for Enid's future naturally and, in two cases, lists of possible benefactors who might be approached. And, should she find the necessary fiscal success, be assured a place would be found for her etc etc…

Enid heard the flightless bird falling.

'Costing us is this – stamps and ink and this posh paper… This begging.'

'One pint a week, less, Pat.'

'And the rest.'

The annexe of Manchester town hall was high-ceilinged, tiled and echoing. Mabel's first thought, 'I wouldn't like to heat this.' After waiting on an upright green leather bench, they were ushered into a wood-panelled, seriously polished, office whose walls were covered in huge portrait photographs of men, each wearing a Neville Chamberlain collar and a serious regard. The family met the present incumbent, a man with a damp handshake. 'Representing the Grants sub-committee of The Manchester and District Board of Education.' He had an ordinary collar and a three-piece pin-stripe suit, with a gold watch and fob Patrick didn't doubt cost more than anything he, Pat, had ever owned.

THE SOLDIER'S HOME

The man sat, opened a box-file and took out some papers. Everyone else sat when he looked up at them.

'The situation,' he said, 'is threefold. Has three inter-linking strands.'

That desk's worth more than our house.

'We have no policy, nor precedent, nor will we make an exception in your case, um - Miss Makin...' a quick look to check her name. '...to fund further education at either Oxford or Cambridge. No matter your Head Master's florid recommendation.'

'Secondly', - Patrick thought, he thinks we're thick. Well, we are, but Enid isn't – 'secondly we always bear in mind when allocating precious public funds to any and all of our female applicants, the very distinct possibility of wedlock and mother-hood.' He spread his hands in a strangled what-can-one-say gesture. 'And consequently, the probable waste of the time, money and the education.' Enid blushed. Guilty for her gender.

'However, and thirdly,' he leaned back a little, and there was something oddly distasteful in his smile as he said, 'in recognition of her obvious talent, this Board is willing to award Enid a grant for a Redbrick University entrance, to fund three years of study.'

O, such smiles from her parents as the man took a breath.

Before.

'Provided – as is normal in these circumstances - Enid 'pledges' to teach, once qualified. For a minimum period of five years. Preferably within this education authority. And, further, without this promise she will agree to pay back this grant, which would then have to be seen as a loan, only.'

He sat back to wait.

Enid, for the first time she or her parents would recall, expressed anger.

'That's blackmail.'

All eyes turned to her.

Also for the first time, she felt an instant sweat freezing on her skin.

'What this is – is public money, young lady. Tax payers' money. And – you could learn some manners.'

A full seconds' silence of shock. Echoing.

'Aye, tax payers' money,' Daddy cut through the quiet. 'Not yours.'

The new silence was icy.

And the man in the far better suit broke the eye-contact, fearing he might be about to be struck, and, voice wavering, said the meeting was probably at an end and would they all please consider the detail in the sealed envelope he now offered to Patrick and which Mabel intercepted, and let him know their decision as soon as possible as other tax-payer's children would most certainly be affected.

Patrick stood, his chair scraping hard on the parquet, the other man flinched as Patrick stormed from his office, then returned instantly to stand glowering by the door and usher his women out. His finger gesturing speed. Now.

It rained all the way home.

Enid and Mabel looked at numbers. Figures. Sums.

'We can, we can make these ends meet, love. Take in a lodger. There's washing. Sewing. Always a way. We're not the first, won't be the last.'

Patrick received a letter from the Miners Union promising his daughter £10 p.a. for three years.

The Army regretted, but…

He talked with a pal about doing a football pools collection round. Never mind he'd always said the pools were a tax on the poor, never mind the damp winter evenings of the football season, it would be cash in hand. Mabel would take the dinner-lady job.

Another quiet meal, after the meeting with the man in that office and Enid said, 'It would be best all round, if I went to – applied to - Manchester. No halls, no accommodation, no spending money. Just a 57 bus-ride?'

There was quiet.

Two meals later Patrick said, 'I've not talked about the war - and I'm not starting now, but. When I went to the Army. That shock of not being at home, not being safe, having to do for yourself – that's a part of this. This next bit of your life, love.'

Quiet at the table. Enid could sense Mabel was proud of Pat and what he'd said, and why.

And beyond their net curtains a cloud lifted. Two more days and Patrick added, 'Breaks our hearts so it does – as we can't send you to Oxford. Sorry, Enid.'

The sun glinted off the plastic tablecloth.

'And,' Mabel leaned forward, 'what have you thought about this teaching pledge thing, lovey?'

'I've thought do I have a choice…'

'Aye… Bastards. Sorry Mabel, Enid.'

Quiet.

Nottingham was September sun-filled, youth filled, noisy, excited, energetic.

A different Land of Hope…

The Florence Boot halls and Enid's room, her cell, were plain.

And no-one of great pith and moment had slept or studied there.

Enid unpacked, rebuked her snobbery and determined to read

this local author, this D.H. Lawrence. Who was trumpeted a little by the college. And Byron.

Her first night away from home, and she did think of the cliché 'hearth and home' as she ate her mother's sandwiches, drank water and read all her introductory literature. There was a giggly racket coming from downstairs. There was a determination never to let her parents down coming from her room.

Her first lecture, tomorrow at ten, her first morning proper, was on Mediaeval English.

And she would have a seminar, later in the week. A seminar.

No matter how enthusiastically she reasoned the experience later the lecture was dull. The tutor, a Mr Bateman M.A., had delivered it before; and Enid, watching his method as much as absorbing the content of his hour upon the stage, bore in mind three years from now she too was going to have to be a teacher, and resolved to do better than this. Yes, of course one might have to teach the same thing as each new academic year came around. But not like this. Like a soulless metronome. Enid quietly dreaded her seminar and got a first University surprise when Mr. Bateman not only mocked himself and his 'dreary dearie' content, but steered the conversation sharply away from Medievalism and towards what, if anything, 'My dear young Miss Makin might have written?' Because, each year, he published a modest volume of the best of his student's verse… She left his room flustered, engaged, and not a little shocked. Flustered because at one moment he had rested a hand on the back of her chair and she had felt his man's heat; engaged because he had talked passionately about writing, and shocked because here she was wondering if she might attempt something. A first week passed and Enid had survived, had asked a question or two, and was both thrilled and very grateful to be here. She wrote home to say just that.

THE SOLDIER'S HOME

In the canteen, counting her coins carefully, she slowly found - let me not be too forward, she thought – companions.

Janice and Judi from the North-East and Lyndy, her father a pig-farmer, from Stirling. And, to their collective delight, from an entirely different world, Belinda. Her father was 'in television' and over that tumbling first-term she it was who weaned the others off their stout or port-and-lemons and onto wine. Enid, who had no need of the weaning, enjoyed that learning curve. Some giggly evening with wine of two colours and gas-fire toasted muffins Enid unofficially promoted her companions to 'friends' and marvelled at how they were so fiery, so lustful, so sparkling. And at how they liked her.

And, within that first term, Judi took a lover. And described him, and their behaviour, in some detail. Jaw-dropping. Then – My God - lovers. And Belinda too. An older, married man. Heavens. Education indeed. Janice lifted her nose a little at this 'looseness', whilst Lyndy sat on the fireside rug hugging her knees, eyes 'on stalks' said Judi, laughing; and Enid decided best not to mention she went to church every Sunday. Nor would she mention any of this in correspondence home. They would come straight down and take her back.

They talked late, giggled long, shared and compared notes on The Venerable Bede, Chaucer and other men. On essays or their individual and collective assignments they argued long and louder as the wine ran and Enid considered herself within a realm of Delight. And to be growing. And learning. And at least as much from her contemporaries as from her tutors.

One night a week they would go to a bar.

Enid watched rituals being practiced she did not yet understand, nor could confidently interpret. A way of lounging with a drink, of looking over a glass, a way of knowing who was where in the bar without ever seeming to look around it. If she had had to name it she would have settled on 'sophistication'.

Alone in her room, reading D.H. Lawrence in linear sequence (the College Library Her Biggest Ever Sweet Shop) she wondered what she might do if a man found a taste for her. She rolled over, stared hard at the ceiling and knew she would most certainly squeal. In shock.

Turning over onto her side, she could imagine someone completing a literary version of a her. A dormant rose springing to life... And yes, another fairy story, beneath not shimmering Oxfordian willow, but by the grey-brown Trent and in the chillier winds and fresher air of The East Midlands.

Enid was not yet besieged by suitors.

The student bus discount was a precious asset and the journey to Dovedale, the prettiest place Enid have ever smelt, passed through Lawrence's village. Eastwood. No accident, surely. She deliberately finished 'The White Peacock' in Dovedale itself one cold Saturday and the College Library, that teeming waterfall of dreams, was certain to have 'The Trespasser.' She wasn't entirely sure what she felt about David Herbert yet but decided there was no need to mention him till she was. If indeed she was to be. Who knew? But he was different. And, she had walked where he had walked. That was new. Each day seemed to contain an adventure. A voyage forward. One evening of pink wine and cigarette smoke, Lyndy played a record of Mahalia Jackson and Enid wished she had been born negro, poor, religious and with lungs like that. Her friends laughed at her excitement. She laughed at their laughter. Well, I am poor and religious. No wonder it rings.

O youth.

Meetings discussing politics, even Communism, smoky jazz clubs – all places where one could meet men and/or have fun. Enid had no aversion to fun but as regards men - her nerves seemed to communicate so quickly, so completely. How to break that?

'Those that go searching for love only make manifest their lovelessness,

and the loveless never find love.

Only the loving find love

and they never have to seek for it.'

Lawrence, she had discovered, was a poet, too.

And that verse begged questions unpleasant and difficult to face and harder yet to answer. It made Enid more self-conscious, a little more concerned than she wished to be; and it made her question too whether her friends were finding Love, or simply exploring sensation. Which D.H.L. certainly seemed to encourage. As a path. As a first path.

She began to read, for the first time, newspapers. Periodicals.

To be aware of, and to cautiously explore, a wider world. Aware too of sharply different uses and styles of language. Her truth was that stylistically, journalism didn't engage her, not compared to non-fiction such as, 'Five Guineas' or 'A Room of One's Own'. A biscuit to a meal. But, sometimes, with the right cup of tea at the right moment a biscuit could be perfect, yes. One biscuit a day, then. Since they, containing sugar, were still rationed. So yes, some news. Her father wrote to tell her to register to vote. Churchill won the election, so she knew when she got home he, Father, would be pained, and livid.

The term hurtled by, the prescribed melange of Chaucer, Caxton and Gawain and the Green Knight study set against her private reading of Byron and Lawrence; and her decision not to attempt verse for Mr Bateman, who loomed physically nearer each tutorial. Fulfilling Janice's instant assessment, 'He's a grubbing old letch, him'. 'Sons and Lovers' contained passages of writing that left her breathless. Eager for lessons to finish so she could run back to her cell and continue to be shocked and thrilled enough to begin exploring masturbation. Their First winter break came and she trained home to tell. To Share. To celebrate.

And shared and celebrated that evening at The Legion, where the symphony of the piano and voices raised in raucous song and her father's rehabilitation became Everything she'd ever wanted.

Father wore 'the collar' to midnight mass, and Enid, Lawrence-fuelled, hoped it produced some glorious sex for them.

At a January Students Union meeting, called to discuss a motion condemning a continuing war in Korea and the U.S. explosion in the Marshall Islands of a hydrogen bomb, she saw him.

Her hydrogen bomb.

Bertrand.

The meeting was dreary and Enid felt only guilt she was so ignorant of the issues, which the meeting did not help her grasp, concerning Korea. The bomb was simpler. Statistics about survivors in Japan suffering new horrors made it so. The motion would be passed, this righteous rubber-stamping was a waste of good 'The Rainbow' time.

Then he stood.

He urged them all to consider a bigger picture. Alongside soldiers from sixteen member-states there were United Nations troops, fighting in Korea. Fighting which had begun by being titled The United Nations Joint Command. As he spoke now that title had been changed to Unified Command. Led now, from front and rear by the US. General Macarthur commanded all the UN forces, President Truman his empoweree. So, this war between

THE SOLDIER'S HOME

Capital and Communism was being waged. He set aside any opinion or preference, 'That, mere politics, is not the point here', he said, passion entering his voice as mutterings of disagreement rose in the room. 'My point is the role of the United Nations.' He paused for one second and did their eyes meet as he scanned his audience? 'Until we dare, we the citizens of this tiny spinning rock, until we dare empower our idea, the United Nations...' his voice rose and his French accent became more marked, '...to have control of all the world's weaponry, to be the World's policeman, we are doomed to have endless debates condemning endless wars and endless slaughter. The question here, mes amies, is - do we have that courage? The courage to deserve and empower a real United Nations? Humanity grew from necessary tribalism into what we now call Nationalism. I dare us to become truly United Nations.' When he sat Enid's applause was the clearest noise.

Enid shocked herself that she even approached him, delighted herself she managed to make conversation, and some entirely new emotion entered her when he stuttered in making his responses. Nerves, he said, apologising. He felt confident discussing politics, much less so about himself. He was from Dijon. Older than her. Ten years older. Here studying architecture, prematurely bald, seemingly possessed of next to no personal vanity and this first conversation only became stilted when Enid realised she was thinking about her mother dancing that first dance. Smitten. On air.

She thought she should not tell him what was beating in her. So she asked wider questions and bathed in his principles and passions. And when he asked, and she had to make blatant some of her feelings she said, truthfully, she liked his brain. He thanked her warmly and then added quietly that his heart had no faith in the rest of him.

He had hers, on a string. For his honesty. Skipping home on the gossamer wings some song she'd only recently heard described, she couldn't remember who had asked who if they might meet again – only that they would. The weekend.

Time gaped empty till then.

Classes, education, food. All passing detail.

Lawrence? Fiction… And fiction, she had read Byron saying, 'Was the talent of a liar.' Quite right My Lord.

This, Bertrand, this and only this was True. She could feel it. In bed Enid vaulted over all the gushing precious narrative details, whatever they were bound to be, so she might only enfold him in This Love and heal all of him and have him like her in return.

Her friends could tell Something. They asked, she told them and an avalanche of advice followed.

'Rush, girl.'

'DON'T rush.'

Lawrence said, 'Do it. Let yourself fall in love, if you haven't done so already. You are wasting your life.'

The weekend.

They walked the most beautifully drizzle-filled Saturday from Dovedale to Milldale and back.

Stepping stones across the river Dove, Reynard's giant cave. Tissington Spires. And Lover's Leap, where a sign read –

'There are many mysteries and stories surrounding the history of Lovers Leap, most of which are based around the heart broken lady who is said to have taken her life here and others of how a young disgraced but in love couple took their lives to be with each other.'

They held hands leaving there.

O such a baptism of the flesh. How could a hand hold all that heat? And hope. It did. For now. For starters.

Enid wondered would they kiss, and wondered if he too was hoping they would. And she hoped she wouldn't have to lead that first step across their own Lovers Leap. And if she did, what happened if she didn't like it? She didn't dare risk. Not today. And Glory be, there was no need. Too glad to concentrate on her hand in his, and when they had to part, his hand searching for hers. She longed for a kiss-gate to invade their path. And for him to not know its ritual. None did.

Wet and yet almost too warm on the bus back, they parted French style with his three soft kisses very near her cheeks, and a look in each other's eyes that was the essence of poetry she thought – the Uncatchable. She couldn't capture it when she sat to try. But she loved the trying. No, she Loved the trying. The thinking on him.

And their next time they would, could, be together.

All of her friends came to a meeting concerned with some 'fascist' taking over Cuba. Enid wished for her Father to materialise and not only explain Latin American political history to her, but to see and hear her Bertrand and approve. 'Good lad, Enid, there's a fine lad.' Just as vast and as simple as that. Approval.

Which is why she had invited her friends.

Oh no.

Enid's very virgin heart was suddenly seized. In a giant icy glove. Called Panic.

Why had she asked them to come?

Why? To boast, Enid. You bloody bloody fool. To have them be envious. Yes, only so they would like him and she could bathe in that glow. Traitor Enid. Traitor to him.

Next instant. A fresh terror.

One of them would be as dazzled as she had been and dazzle him and take him. And think nothing of it. 'All's fair in love and war.'

Or, O God, the opposite. A fantastic hot contradictory idea. How might it feel if one of them did 'fancy' him and still he chose her, dumpy virgin Enid?

Or - O No! – Worse. Much worse, the pits, my pits – they would all be bored by him. She would be utterly belittled by indifference. The whole 'us' of him.

So. Is this what my affection, my attraction, actually is? A search for Status? O God I Hate growing up.

As he stood to speak her heart beat ice. Fire. Ice.

As he began, and as his voice didn't waver, only grew in the strength of his convictions, an entirely new wonder flooded Enid.

She didn't care a fourpenny fig for what anyone else thought.

Or did. Or tried to do. She liked him and she trusted herself. And – him.

She stood, just watching him and not truly listening, on this highest peak of her life, on this glittering summit.

She introduced him to her friends and none made any connection 'of that kind', nor he with them. His hand reached for hers to calm his stuttering. It did.

So far D.H. Lawrence hadn't described quite this particular rapture…

Now.

How to leapfrog everything else? How was that done?

Bertrand gave off no confidence he knew. Enid knew she didn't. Driven hard by their o so eager delight and desire and ignorance, they dared plan a must-be-silent night in her room.

And I do lift my aching arms to you,
And I do lift my anguished, avid breast,
And I do weep for very pain of you,
And fling myself at the doors of sleep, for rest.

Shocking and exciting each other first with kissing, with the cold wetness of their tongues, the fumbling with buttons, and it all

THE SOLDIER'S HOME

happening without music and even for her, the ignorant, surely too too quickly. Enid had assumed he knew. Something. Had some experience. Suddenly some dimly court-yard-lamp-lit nudity, but better that than bald naked beneath her central un-shaded light-bulb – and finally swept up, rushing helpless and heedless from on to in her narrow single bed, their bodies wrapping, folding into huge impulse and his, yes, it was his, his acceleration and something private to him happened, something instantly wrong, unplanned, unwanted, chaotic. Sticky. Colding. And silent.

*

And the worst, and most crucial, a total failure of words.

Of the words, any words, to be bravely honest with the other. It was bad. Instant and solid bad.

By the end of that night Enid had signed the Pledge in her head.

She lay awake, pleading with the sun to rise and take him, release both of them. She knew he wasn't sleeping. It was not good.

The dew of the morning
Sunk chill on my brow –
It felt like the warning
Of what I feel now.
Thy vows are all broken
And light is thy fame;
I hear thy name spoken
And share in its shame.

He left her suddenly, long before dawn, without a drink or a word or another kiss and she washed and dressed and buttoned herself higher and put her head firmly down for the next two years, to be rewarded with the highest honour the University could bestow and, O what a Blazing Day for her, an offer of a research scholarship. One more year to study to be a Master of English. Mabel had her second stroke and it took her and all was over and done with. She hurried back, phoned her old Headmaster and Mr Smith was 'absolutely delighted' to welcome her home. As a teacher.

I wrote Mabel's eulogy and began my life with Patrick.

Another single, one-way ticket. Hurrah, again.

For the Underground scrum to Victoria.

No wonder they all dive for the seats she thought, holding to her strap with one hand, suitcase in the other; and new people kicking by her, so blatantly irritated by it and her, this out-of-town frump; but all seemingly too de-humanised to make any actual eye-contact; not even so much as a baleful complaining eye.

And weren't we told, and believed, and cherished it, that these tube tunnels contained the very soul of the British spirit of the War? Community in a Blitz? All I can feel is Thank the Good Lord I never lived in this.

The train down to the coast was magnificently rank. The ninth year of Mrs. Thatcher's government and it was impossible to see through the never-cleaned windows; dead beer-cans rolled amongst the ancient hamburger packets colonising the floor, and only the terminally desperate would risk the lavatory. Enid listened, fascinated, as an articulate American woman queried the guard as to whether first-class was, by some British Quirk, a whole lot better.

'Not really, dahlin' - 's all filfy.'

'That was said almost proudly, sir.'

THE SOLDIER'S HOME

'All Millwall fans now, luv. We're crap and we know it. Tickets, please.'

A seat on the ferry, an hour and a half and this adventure could truly begin.

No-one could have noticed her toes squeaking pleasure inside her sensible brogues, or the way her knees rubbed together, but some might have wondered at the smile that kept creasing her face. This, she realised, is my fiftieth birthday present to myself. Only five years late.

three

A TEENAGED HEART-BROKEN First-Love gone bad Zoe re-opened the house and spent sweet sad hours repairing in its solitude. Heat and dust rose around her, sitting on the doorstep, soaking in the view and the solace.

She returned again, in happier times, summer holidays from University; walking there three times in one week to sun-bathe naked. She did her rather fine line drawings of the house and that autumn framed them and her photographs which now occasionally still caught her eye as she bustled through the salon to the kitchen. She recalled 'the secret place' but it no longer frightened her, since she now considered Janatou to be her secret place.

Her English degree secured, Zoe returned from three years' work experience, teaching in Portsmouth, and (Sara considered for want of anything better to do) fell in love with Gilbert. Sara had to own that he was a charmer - but she'd known a charmer herself and nothing could induce her to fully trust the man. Still, it wasn't her life and her daughter was old enough and daft enough to make her own mistakes...

They set up house together and slowly Gilbert's parochialism began to be at first less than charmed by her travelled erudition, then embarrassed by it (since it had the self-regarding scent of boasting in it), then embarrassed by her and her refusal to conform to his notion of a role she was utterly unsuited to, and it was not long before he began to turn it into a mental stick to beat her with; and as verbal abuse threatened to include the physical, so Zoe rose to every bait. She became the victim of a headstrong determination not to be defeated by her own mistake. It became their shared obsession.

She became addicted to their spiralling arguments, to the way her superior logic would lead inevitably to his heavier hand; and she was ghoulishly fascinated by the minute gradations of restraint he had to show in the actual striking of her, a restraint she shared, always stalling at scratching his face; of making their violence public. And, it was true, both craved the brutal orgasms that climaxed the confrontations. She became tunnel-visioned - determined to win. He would accept her. Without qualification. She would conquer his moods. She could vanquish and extinguish his rages. He would become cultured in some way.

They were two years down this track when one July afternoon Sara called to see her daughter and heard, 'I'm in the bath, won't be a second.'

Bustling in Sara called, 'Nothing I haven't seen before, Mademoiselle.'

It was, though.

Zoe's ribs and upper arms wore livid bruises and ignoring her daughter's shrill and demented denials, Sara demanded a neighbour give her a lift down to Maurs, where she marched into Gilbert's bicycle repair shop and announced not only her daughter's immediate departure from his life, but his imminent and certain denunciation to The Mairie, The Gendarmerie, the local papers and 'from the bloody pulpit if needs be', should he ever appear in her or Zoe's eye-line again.

Zoe was beyond fury with her mother's 'high-handed interfering' - but there was a quiet in Sara's, 'That is never acceptable,' that sobered her, and out of outrage grew a grudging gratefulness, and in time, an accompanying respect.

Her considerable energies she channelled into money and pleasure. Skiing became an obsession and to fund it Zoe managed a series of shops, a make-up salon and ran a neighbouring village café for three years before the owner, a sour postman called Serge, refused to let her 'modernise' it - install hot-food facilities and perhaps even a television for the big sports occasions - and in a spectacular and still talked about fit of pique, she slammed out. Also still talked about was Serge's instant installation of all her ideas.

Her cousin, Marie-Jo was down from Paris. She worked for the Departement Nationale de Tourisme and had been charged with compiling a demographic report as to why quite so many English were crossing La Manche to set up home, or buy a second home, in France.

'That's not rocket-science!' Zoe laughed.

'Cheaper property, better food, better climate.' Marie Jo chorused her top-of-the-head thoughts. 'And actual culture.'

'And they hate that Thatcher woman.' Zoe assured her. 'Oh yes. The ones who come here.'

'So, we're getting their champagne socialists?' Marie-Jo made a mental note to write that up as 'A Failure of Socialism.'

'And what are you going to do now? Next.'

'You've just given me the idea,' said Zoë.

She set up her Immobilier business and tirelessly scoured the surrounding countryside for properties for sale, offering the

THE SOLDIER'S HOME

sellers 'more competitive' rates, building up her lists, and carefully targeting the English through ads in their quality newspapers, magazines and periodicals offering French Country Cuisine in her Chambre d'hôte - whilst house-hunting in paradise. Five years ago. And now, her first American had called. Mentioning the word chateau. Oh yes, please!

Over the three and a half decades since Jacques' barely attended funeral, the different Mayors of Lauresse and their committees sometimes mentioned they could claim unpaid taxe d'habitation and taxe foncieres on Janatou. But this always foundered on the question of from whom? With the result - no effort was ever made to find the owner.

'It'll fall down of its own accord one day,' some wiseacre would say and someone who'd been there would mutter, 'Not in your grandchildren's lifetime it won't...'

Being so remote it represented neither health hazard nor danger. Forget it. More paper...

When Janatou crossed her busy mind, Zoe considered it to be, in a way, hers.

When Sara infrequently thought of it, she felt older yet.

🐑

A foot passenger in Europe.

Oiling my rusty French back to its uncomplicated efficiency will be a pleasure.

And a further place to hide.

O. From whom?

No-one. No-one knows I am here.

Then, hide what?

Tout droit Enid, to the station.

The vasty fields of France. I can see them through the train window. Do I assume that's because we're in a Republic?

Having to live with Dad after Mum went. 'Having', Enid? Choosing, surely.

Didn't exactly feel like choice.

The watching over his getting older.

Finally, just me and the house. Claiming it's sudden silence and solitude for mine.

And Ownership.

Leave that. That's past now.

Elvis Presley.

He swept through the school so completely even I knew him by his Christian name alone.

My second year of full-time teaching. And yes, he alarmed me. He became a competing obsession to my own; that these children develop a passion for the language they would use for ever. He seemed to not only be re-writing it, but debasing it. 'You ain't nothin' but a hound dog, c-crying all the time...' It was wanton. He sounded gleefully wanton.

And by the time one had learned to quell him, to achieve and maintain an acceptable level of concentration in one's class-room/ work-place, the young ladies' skirts were rising, the boy's hair descending and there was talk of a generation gap. It was surely a different youth from the one I had grown with. And so soon. I was hardly 25!

A year or so later and Margaret Thatcher, now Mrs Thatcher, won her Finchley seat. I was idiotically disappointed to learn

THE SOLDIER'S HOME

she was a Tory but she did beg the question, 'Well, what was I?' After Bertrand I lost any interest I may have feigned in politics and lazily I re-cycled, scatter-gun style, my Father's belief in the Sanctity of working-class solidarity in an ageless struggle against 'them'. So, I voted Labour yes, but thinking back, it was a shameful act. Containing no genuine thread of either interest or knowledge, nor even, more honestly, an opinion of my own. I had no great opinion on Elvis either for that matter, beyond a conviction he was of no practical use to a teacher of English Lit and Language.

O no.

O no.

Thirty years too late – I should have *made* them write about him. Invited them to channel their passion. Express it.

O blessed retrospection.

Elvis. His blatant peddling of sex disturbed me too, yes, and I chose to ignore him because of it. It took me far too long to realise the man could certainly sing and by then he, like Mother, was gone.

A person needs must forgive themselves for who they were.

This person must. Will.

Starting here, just leaving Amiens.

I bored myself, bored myself and others with my holiness of purpose.

I encastled myself in my certainty. Was I rigid? I fear I might have been.

See, I have no friends, not really.

Val, yes I was close to Val for a time.

Our first two years of teaching together, sharing our conviction. This is sudden sad – she was the last person I giggled with. Her marriage to John burst on the banks of his insatiable infidelities and she emigrated to Australia. I was shocked, my God I was, by her first letter detailing the characteristics of her new love, Eve, and their intimacy. Sex. When Val next confessed I was the only person, previous to Eve, she had ever considered 'in this way', I believe I came to some sad rigid lonely conclusion (frightened Enid - tell the truth rolling south! – you were frightened) and mea culpa, our correspondence dwindled to birthdays and Christmas and now, last year only Christmas and – I never even sent her either of my last two books!

I will write to Val, from Paris. I will. She'll be pleased for me. She'll be proud of me.

Maybe I will be, too.

Rain, now.

I am confused by the word 'soul'.

I know – it is my profession – language evolves. It must. Or we'd all end up speaking and thinking like the book of common prayer. Or worse.

But.

Where is this train now?

My head is a jumble. A jangle.

Yes, it is. You threw the rule-book away. Called it handcuffs.

I want to linearise the past. Is there such a word? Yes, now there is.

Because if I can put the past in order, and behind me – then won't I be able to see clearly, a path forward?

Well, Enid Makin, you don't know and you must try.

How fearful Daddy and I were to be left alone.

The poor dear man completed one recovery – only to lose

THE SOLDIER'S HOME

his partner and guide. And be left with me, unfit, unlearned, for emotional tasks.

The title of my book in his memory, 'Cruel, Cruel Life.'

And in losing Mabel he completely lost God and consequently he and I lost one whole ritual – Sunday.

I never asked him what he did while only I took communion and prayed for the strength and the right to forgive the Almighty for His vile robbery of both my parents. And he never asked me. A thing. We would not speak till we were around the Sunday tea-table. That's a sizeable silence in a school-teacher's weekend.

When it changed, it was The Miners' Strike. And because he needed to. Talk. Couldn't stop himself. And, I now believe, he heard the clock ticking towards 'finite' and needed us to make up lost time. Which we couldn't. No-one can but I don't want to be sad, again.

Then leave this. For now. Linearise tomorrow.

What does the word 'soul' mean? In 1988.

I think of Mabel's soul gleaming when Daddy bought the piano. I saw it shining with delight for him. That *was* her soul. If it wasn't we're missing a whole new word. And it used to mean immortal. The everlasting part of a being. Didn't the judge say, 'And may God have mercy on your immortal soul?' And the Sacrament was the 'body and soul of Christ'. And it was born somewhere deeper than rational. 'In your soul' was a sacred inviolate place. Morality clung there. 'He's a bad soul' – how utterly damning that was. I read once that no flowers grew on Billy the Kid's Grave. Bad soul?

And Daddy's soul? Where was that by the time Burma was survived? It felt lost. Left scattered there, with the horrors that silenced him.

And, why didn't I ever ask him? Sad.

Did England have a 'soul'? Some would say it had surely been Churchill, and his inspirational command of language. Some might say now it was The Royals, but not I. Is it then a changing thing, evolving like everything now – in a rush. A race. The human race? The soul dragging behind somewhat, left. Stalled in Religion? Has my country of birth lost its soul? Was the soul obsolete in a world of house-brick sized walking telephones? Was Mrs Thatcher a version of the soul of Britain? And if yes – and she herself certainly gave off an impression of believing that – then am I on this train to escape that?

Yes. In part. In some part.

I am on this train, in part too, because of the all too audible sound of my father's heart breaking.

Or was that not, indeed, his soul?

I will – and did - defend Mrs Thatcher this far. She approved the creation of more comprehensive schools (which, though I taught at a grammar school, I came to believe in as A Future) than any other Education secretary, before or since. And yes, she became the Milk-Snatcher, but being honest - my memory of crated school milk? It was horrid. Yes, calcium, yes teeth; but from this teacher's point of view, that soubriquet, 'Thatcher Milk Snatcher', was a glib and convenient way of pigeon-holing her, pillorying her, and her (then) liberal attitude to education was conveniently obscured.

Daddy hated her just for her politics, for her party, certainly at first. Later it became personal. And that is something else about Mrs T; she demands a personal response (Like being on this train, racing away?). Few are genuinely indifferent to her. I respected that quality, stemming from that energy, for as long as I could. Because I felt she was also hated because of gender, and some

THE SOLDIER'S HOME

collective perception of her being unfeminine. Unattractive. I related to that, so I did. And what a nest of worms that is. And how deeply unqualified I feel to hold an opinion on any aspect of it. Even, seemingly, in my soul.

Does your soul need experience? A participation?

If yes, then in giving up teaching, have I lost mine?

Paris. Soon. Metro to Austerlitz and last train into the evening and be there, Figeac, for a late late supper. Marvellous. All this change in one beaming day.

It's Dad.

In the end, and I loved and adored and I respected my mother, my head and heart are still wrestling with the only man in my life; and the life I lived with him, after Mabel had gone.

The train is slowing. Suburbs, les banlieues, are sprouting.

I never told Daddy about the first book. The one about his wife.

I never told him about any of them.

Was I ashamed of him, or them? Or me? I never told hardly a soul about my books. Val. Lyndy. I preferred it that way. I still do.

🐏

Bustle. Enid had heard people say, 'I can't take Paris. Too noisy, dirty, too snobby.'

As she stepped from the train at Gare du Nord - they were the snobs! How could you not love this city? Shame to have no more time than to cross it, this evening, but, it would always be here. And God willing, soon only one train away.

I'm a Francophile snob, she thought.

Well then, I'm in the right place. Aren't I?

And my snobbery extends to pretending not to notice the travellers on the metro are as indifferent as those on the Victoria line. Big city life.

Austerlitz. Last lap. The station seemed quiet, so a last seat to herself, then?

'Un aller-simple pour Figeac. I believe there is a train in twenty minutes, arriving near midnight.'

Enid had her money ready from the separate section of her purse.

'Non, madame, there are no trains south this evening.'

Paris gaped.

'What? No. You are – have I misunderstood you?' Nooo.

'Your French is excellent madame, so I imagine you know the word 'greve'?

Oh Paris, how could you?

'A strike?'

'Voila. Je regrette, madame but the next train to Figeac is eleven o'clock tomorrow morning.'

He was talking in slow motion. What would it take for him to say, 'April Fool!' or, 'Just an SNCF blague madame…'?

He was now looking at the queue behind her. Helpless her.

'Madame?'

Enid moved away, everything in slow-motion. Forgot her suitcase. The next person in the queue handed it back to her. She took it. Held it. Turned. Which way.

THE SOLDIER'S HOME

She was alone in the city with nowhere to sleep. All momentum stalled. The journey, the adventure, the escape squashed. For a second she was even scared. And that cooling thought prompted a welcome surge of practicality. You have money, this city is awash with hotels. The nearest decent one to this station, please Ms Sensible.

The station hotel was too ludicrously expensive to consider and the concierge, tacitly agreeing with her, offered options of *pensions* close by and a map which he marked with an arrowed path for her to follow.

Rue Poliveau.

Passing a phone-box she found change and the number, dialled Zoe and explained. Zoe was full of commiserations and would be there, never fear, to meet her tomorrow. 'Best laid plans, eh?' she said, surprising Enid with the quote. She gathered her suitcase, the map and following her arrows, arrived at an uninspiring building.

🐎

'Poor thing. But, still six this weekend, Mother.' Zoe didn't disguise her pride.

'And all wanting those dangerous breakfasts?'

'Not all of them are from the North of England, no.' Zoe slid into patient-with-your-parent mode.

'Those beans...'

'Yes, mother - and the bread fried as I showed you.'

'And that spicy mud?' Sara didn't disguise her disgust.

'Ours not to reason why mother dear.'

'That's as well, then...'

'Come down with me to shop? Figeac. To the Supermarket?'

'You go,' Sara shuffled away. 'I hate those places - no-one talks to you. I'll do the rooms.'

'Just two singles - for the English woman and the American. Give him the south-facing one.'

Zoe knew that as a rule, Northern English people considered a croissant and a coffee to be a long way from an acceptable first meal of the day. She had worked hard to convince an under-manager at Leclerc's in Figeac. The man had weakened to her lipstick and eye-lash batting, but was convinced only when she brought in statistics Marie-Jo faxed at her request. There they were, in Governmental triplicate. Influx of the English...

Bien.

Baked beans, back bacon and HP sauce there would be.

🐑

Enid accepted a single room with a single bed, left her bag there and crossed the boulevard to the Café Nuage for a light evening meal.

It was functional and her appetite was thin. The wine was poor, really quite poor. She felt marooned in her favourite city. Awful feeling. And at the moment she told herself to stroll, take an evening stroll, the drizzle, la blasted bruine, began.

The room, if it had an atmosphere, was at warmest, unwelcoming. Almost damp. The kind of room one didn't want to undress in.

A greve. A strike. Damn.

Damn their blooming strike.

Enid's blood ran cold.

What did you say? What did you just this second think? What was that thought?

That thought was damn their strike.

Good heavens.

That is some betrayal.

Outside the Parisian traffic roared. Damn that, too.

'I fear, Ratcliffe, I fear.'

He was 21, Shakespeare, when he wrote that. Scholars say. How do they know? How did he know?

I fear too, Ratcliffe.

I am afraid of my shallow breathing.

Aware and afraid of a temper. Rising in me.

And what is the fear? What is the temper, Enid? Miss Makin?

It's dad. It's always Dad. I want the toilet.

That was cold and damp too and she hurried back and lay on the bed. Pulled the cover over herself. Stared at the dreary ceiling.

I'm in fear of events – strikes - overwhelming me. Sending me back. Tail between my legs.

I'm afraid of events I can't control, or predict. What was exciting – and distracting – when the trains rolled is now black ice and I slide and fear to fall.

Like me and Dad after Mabel went.

Everything starts with Dad. The only man in my life.

We buried Mabel and we clung together there at her graveside. Babes in the wood. Canon Kirkby droning platitudes and generalisations about her – I do understand why Father broke with both the Church and it's earthly representative in Pendlebury – and we clung together through the sandwiches and cakes, the stories and remembrances of her friends and neighbours and we clung together by the door, seeing them off and we cried when there was just us, tidying up, and tidying up to how she would have wanted it left and then we went to our rooms and we could never ever be, were never, that close again.

We got on. Didn't we?

Did we?

We got on with our lives.

Mine fuller and more occupied than his, left alone to ruminate – telling me how he missed the companionship of the pits.

At first, each weekend I would suggest an outing. Go for a drink even, or a walk and just the once he came.

We took the Sheffield train to Edale, and we gently climbed gentle Mam Tor and him at the summit, weeping, weeping into the wind. Perhaps it was the sight of the open cast mine and it's belching huge chimney but as we turned for home he squeezed my hand and said, 'Good, love. Thanks.' And I don't remember us going out together again.

Stray thoughts.

Turn them off, with the light.

She did. It didn't work. The curtains too thin. The thoughts too fat.

The traffic was passing from continuous to sporadic. There would be no silence. Not in a twenty-four-hour city.

Enid had removed nothing more than her shoes.

Dad and me and the Other Woman. That would be the title for this book, this chapter, this long pain.

He'd hate me.

He's hating me now in heaven for saying 'their damned strike'.

I can hear you.

Disappointed. Not for the first time. That was D.H. Lawrence.

Remember Enid. Recall. Be clear now. Be brave.

Penguin books were prosecuted – at the Old Bailey no less - for publishing, finally, the unexpurgated Lady Chatterley's Lover.

Father sat in his chair, read the newspapers, listened to the news and re-cycled their opinions as an opening for a conversation. I didn't welcome it, as I feared I would disagree and, typically I tried to say nothing. Father, I believe the phrase is – I don't know its provenance – yes, I do, it's betting at poker – Damon Runyan - upped the ante.

'Disgusting.'

I said, 'What is?'

'Trying to publish filth.'

'How do we know it's filth?'

'It's an obscenity trial. And I can read.'

'And have you read the book?'

'No, and I wouldn't want to.' Then. 'Have you?'

'Yes.'

His eyes widened. He turned to look at me. I remember screwing my courage to the sticking place. 'Yes father, I have.'

'You have read those words, Enid?'

'All those words. In their context, yes.'

'How? How have you read them if it's not published?'

'I read it at University.'

O Jesus Mary and Joseph but that cold beat of silence. That precursor to worse. He almost snarled at me, at that word. 'O...'

I said, 'He's a local writer. They're proud of him.'

'He's a disgrace.'

'He's a miner's son, father.' And as he didn't speak, I dared add, 'And you heard those words down the pit.'

'Aye, I did. Where they belong.'

'Oh, Dad.' Now I made my mistake, if mistake it was. 'Trust me, I know. I've read almost everything he's written. The man is a beauty. You're wrong.'

Nothing more he could say, now I had exposed his literal ignorance. And perhaps he tasted condescension in my voice. A teacher's voice at his table.

Six days later I was 'proved' right. By law. And I had proved to both of us he was capable of being both puritan and reactionary.

Did he forget? And forgive? There is a delicate moment in the parent-child and now adults-both axis and he made me feel I had forced something.

He sulked and rumbled and picked petty squabbles he could win and I wished I had more life outside the house.

Did my breadwinning take what little was left of his masculinity? That, his masculinity, and what he felt he ought to be able to do with it – Everything – become a lead dead weight. He became a knot, my father. And the Guinness loosened it, yes. But it was Mabel who took him to drink and without her the drink came to him, alone. Not the same thing. And, worst, no piano playing. He buried that with his wife.

She took the tunes with her.

My head hurts. Why this dank room, why this night, why now?

Why can't I be where I want to be?

Why am I being held here?

I don't want these thoughts. This room, this cell.

Because of a strike.

'Yes, daughter, like The Miner's Strike. That I gave the last gasps of my physical energy for. My being.'

'Whose Side Are You On?' became England; and my Father in his seventy-fourth year got dressed, made a lunch, brewed a flask, said, 'Duty calls,' and caught a train to join a picket line across the county border in Yorkshire. He came back as I had never seen him - frightened. He only said, 'Coppers with no numbers on their shoulders? She's pitched her army agin us.' Thinking now, being frightened must have reminded him of the war. And, to be reminded of that, on England's green and pleasant land.

By Her.

The Other Woman. In our ménage a trois.

Margaret Thatcher. Replacing Mabel.

Right from her winning the leadership of the Conservative party.

And, because she brought him back to the table, I almost liked her.

He'd been in his armchair, sunk in depression. He even said it, 'I'm depressed, Enid.'

When I asked why, thinking it must be memories of Mum and that it might be good for us both to talk about her, he rose from his chair, lifted the cushion and showed me the newspaper, and the photo of the smiling, dead, bearded Che, surrounded by soldiers. He sat back down, and I don't remember his next – what – seven years until she got elected Tory leader. Until she galvanised him.

As a middle-aged woman some part of me was touched by her ascendancy.

I kept that quiet. In his house.

'Just wait while that cow gets her hands on real power. And she will. Like dawn comes, she will.'

And I, O irony, I defended her. Which drove us apart and was exactly what he needed.

I was the rock-face, he the pick.

I asked him once exactly how had he formed such a poor opinion of her, and so very quickly. His slow look told me he knew when he was being patronised. 'There's no art to find the mind's construction in the face,' he said. There was me put in my place.

In my defence of her I said I was pleased a woman had achieved so highly. My father said, unpleasantly, 'I married a woman. That's not female.'

Do I ever remember thinking I should leave him? No, I don't believe I did.

More likely I might have thought I couldn't. And resented that. And buried it?

And here I am tonight, mining myself...

That folded paper with the news of Che is still there, under his cushion.

And yes, I do remember what filled those years till Maggie. Vietnam. That must have triggered memories of far-eastern horrors and now, nightly, television war indeed. It felt like permanent rain on the roof.

And I did not deal well with him.

He swore more, talked less and in what was - must have been - a retreat from him and a search for the route back to him, I began my book about a man who went off to war and came back someone else and the music that saved his ravaged soul, and all too aware of the irony I might never finish it until he did. And, like my other books, my secret me, I never told him. He didn't share, why should I?

That is truly pathetic.

I was. I am. I can be.

So could he. Mabel's birthday or their anniversaries he would cut me out completely. Wanted all that sadness for himself. Mean. Understandable when I feel charitable. Tonight, in drizzly endless Paris, plain mean. Bad parenting.

He is angry with me, ashamed of me, I can hear him through the night.

Running away. 'You put your shoulder to the wheel…'

And I'm running from that Other Woman, from her destruction of my profession, for her ideology. That Dad saw years before I did, was repellent. Like Napoleon she believes we are a nation of shopkeepers and everything can be sold. And Education, too.

Oh God, but this is all self self self.

When he gave gave gave.

I'm betraying all the thought and all he taught or tried to teach this teacher.

Yes, and lying here making a martyr of him is a waste of life, too.

Honour thy father and mother – and I do – but they can't live your life, Enid.

I resent the hold you have on my soul Dadda.

Let me be. Open your claw.

Some clock church tolled enough numbers to be close to midnight.

Orange neon and passing car headlights. If only they would stop…

What will I find in this room? In this night? What might kill me? Nothing.

What am I doing?

Where am I going?

To never-never land you sad foolish creature. Over the French rainbow.

Face this.

Face it.

Listen –

Nothing in your life has worked.

No love.

No children.

I never even left home.

Why should it change now?

Billy Liar's mother said, 'You put your troubles in your suitcase with you…'

She's right. All here in this cell.

Enid rolled off the bed, opened her suitcase and took out every single item. Laid them out on the carpet and laid herself back on the bed.

Go back? Fight the good fight that killed him? Honour him?

Why?

I have had my life with him. And the silences. The secrets. The shames.

'She can't see the consequences of her thinking. Makes her inhuman.'

There was a sense of some incoherent rage transferred from somewhere – Mother's passing? - into an implacable cold hatred of this successful Tory woman. I'd see it in my face one day.

A Sun journalist, if that isn't an oxymoron, coined Prime Minister Callaghan saying, 'Crisis, what crisis?' as rubbish bags and Shakespeare's phrase, 'The Winter of Discontent' dominated the news and he, Father, saw the future clear as could be. 'She's in. She's coming. Need only play a straight bat. And she fucking will.'

She did.

She stood on the steps of Downing Street quoting scripture and all he said was, 'We're fucked now.'

I loved him. I loved you.

When Michael Foot became leader of the Labour party how he hummed with admiration and respect for the man.

And. And he dressed and went out of a Sunday morning.

For me, that was so thrilling.

To see him polish his shoes again was thrilling.

He went not to Church but to buy 'a proper Sunday paper.' He would return and read Everything.

'Telly news - Tory propaganda, Enid.'

I chose not to point out almost daily government rhetoric about a 'left-wing bias' at the BBC. Because I was happier that he was energised. That he was my dad. Not a shell in a chair.

She, 'The Bitch', appointed Mark Carlisle as her education secretary. Who said he had 'No experience of the state system, either as student or parent.'

Giving him my Christian benefit of the doubt, I thought, well, you're in the right place to learn, then. Or at least ask. If you've the mind to.

Mark Carlisle. The cause of the worst of us.

Ever.

Face this then too, my lady.

For want of conversation I mentioned his, Mark Carlisle's, creation of an Assisted Places scheme which allowed bright working-class children to gain a free place at a top public school. The silence that followed should have warned me, but ought I to have known what else would rise?

'Good idea to let clever proles mix with the upper-classes, is it?'

'What could be wrong with that?'

'The evil bloody notion of a better education for Money!'

Like I was an idiot.

'But then, you would defend it – you had that privilege. Of a kind.'

I said nothing only watched his eye-balls darkening to bullets.

'Didn't you?'

'You mean Nottingham University?' And he pounced, it all erupting from him.

'You're a fucking snob Enid, and you always were. If we'd had to scrimp for your precious fucking Oxford you'd have killed your mother a fucking sight sooner.'

I didn't fight back. I never fought back. I wish I had. O but I do.

I could only hear the both of us breathing and nothing else.

For ages.

Years it felt.

It was at least a week in a silent house before he offered, 'You weren't to know. As she was weak.'

THE SOLDIER'S HOME

Two more days and, 'And I didn't know how weak. Physically.'

I read some American philosophy of how one must scream 'I hate my mother' to 'move forward'.

Are they all insane? No, because sometimes I did hate my father. I did. But I don't want to remember that. Why should I? To what end?

Another toll of a church bell. Shorter, by far. Come quick Dawn, and release me.

O God. Selling off council houses, creating a 'property owning democracy.' Thatcher.

'The whore.'

'I'm trying to eat my tea, Daddy...'

'She's bribing the working-class.' He threw the paper across the table at me, folded at a photo of her smiling, handing over the deeds of a house in Essex to a grateful nuclear family.

'That's bribery, Enid.'

I put my cutlery down.

'Isn't it an old Labour Party policy?'

'Course it bloody is, and quite right, too – but do you not have the eyes to see what she's doing with it?'

Another mistake, I said, 'She might be rewarding those who voted for her. In big numbers.'

He gave me a bad look, pushed his food away and said, 'I am ashamed of the working-classes.' And as he fell back into his chair, added, 'And whose fucking side are you on?'

A question to which there was no healthy answer.

He said, again as to a child, 'She's invoking Envy. That's a deadly sin, Enid.'

And there was, must have been a realisation for him I was never going to produce an heir; and his piteous attempts to discuss it as he tried to be both mother and father and bless both their hearts he couldn't ever be. And how angry the expending of that effort made him. Angry because he failed. He and I, we didn't have a language to discuss 'things like that.' Shame on us and shame for us.

He threw satsumas at the television. At a Labour politician criticising Michael Foot for wearing a donkey jacket – 'it's a fucking working man's coat you shite-hawk…' at the commemoration 'of the working-class dead you execrable man,' at The Cenotaph. Almost the very last burst of anger he physicalised and me thinking, 'I didn't know you knew the word 'execrable' – and I would have thought – bet, even – that you didn't.'

What a cow.

I hugged him and he had no idea why and he shrugged me off and I hated him in that moment, too. For my own failure to speak.

A cold tear welled and waited.

More bells. Less cars. Be no sleep now.

Galtieri invading the Malvinas.

'O fuck me, here's her fucken rabbit. Get her out of her three million unemployed hat. And he, he is MAD. Mad to pick a fight with the English', he said. 'The English love fighting, we're good at it.' This from a man raped by the steadfastness of his combative courage. 'And scoundrel's last refuge here we come. In red, white and blue spades.'

A woman on a televised phone-in pinned Mrs. Thatcher on the direction the Belgrano was sailing when she was sunk.

'She is a fucking lying cunt, Enid.'

I wanted to say he had finally bought Lawrence's language into the house. I didn't. Just sat there as he, shocked and sad, said, 'She just bare-faced lied in our front room.' I heard his sorrow that a leader should. They did, all the time and he knew that, and she was a sworn enemy, yet somehow, somewhere she wounded my father deep. His concept of public morality shattered. He sat in his armchair like a sculpture. Grey Rubble of a Decent Life.

It took years off him, that tiny incident.

When she began re-structuring my wages and my profession and my profession took strike action my father and I, we began to tread a path back towards one another.

He went out campaigning for Foot. He shouldn't have. I shouldn't have let him. I wouldn't have dared try stopping him. Daily, knocking doors, leafletting. It weakened him further and her vast triumph was a nightmare, and he lost Politics. And without that... what was he? He used to joke, 'It's only class hatred as gets me out of bed in the morning...' Longer and longer he sat in his saddening chair.

Until The Miner's strike.

'Damn their strike...'

He supported Arthur. As a coalminers daughter, so did I. Less emotionally, less informed and with less of a sense of the Apocalypse he, father, promised. Hoped for. His whole life, his being, his beliefs, his soul, 'on the line'. 'Where they should be.' An enemy as worthy of conquering as Hitler. His regret at his age and his history preventing his being active tangible.

News film of Orgreave. We watched a brick open the head of a policeman. Miners beaten by club-wielding horse-riding police. He said, 'Orwell were right.'

And, all the time, daily, horrible, their voices. Hers heartless ice, his that of an hysteric. I was sick of both of them. They deserved each other and there we were all paying the price. My dad more than most.

When she survived the IRA bombing of her Brighton hotel he only said, 'She's killed Christ in me, Enid. I wanted her dead.'

His eyes sank into hollows of despair, and what dug deepest was the Miners' defeat. He had struggled for a belief in something all his life, his concept of 'socialist principles' and now here he was, his time and energy reduced to a journey between his bed and his leather arm-chair and a looking at a waste of his life's efforts. My heart went out to him and stayed there, with him, helpless as he faded.

One day near the end he handed me one end of an envelope, holding the other in his veined claw.

'I know we've had secrets. And. I don't want to know yours now. Too late for me. But this one's mine, so I'll share it.'

And he talked about the War. He told me how five years after he got home there had been a campaign to get men like him compensated by the Japanese and they had been and he had put it all in an account and it had grown enough. Then he let the envelope go. I thought it must be a cheque as it clearly wasn't cash.

It wasn't either.

It was the deeds of our council house, which he had bought.

It was an earth-quake.

'You sold your soul Daddy? You took her bribe?'

'I did my duty, Enid. To you. You can sell this now and you could get a place in Oxford, I'd like to send you there.'

Less than a week later and I was alone.

But I am not.

THE SOLDIER'S HOME

Duty.

What is *my* duty now?

To who? Whom? Now I've reneged on the children?

To write your romances from a glade, bee-loud, in France? That's a duty? What did he die for, then?

He died for his. His sense of duty. And I am not him, nor no longer his. He is no longer my responsibility, dead these three long years, at peace with Mabel; being eaten the pair of them by indifferent time and worms. The cycle. Complete. My duty is – please – if I may - to complete mine. And in the most banal of all thoughts, to try to be happy. Finally. Before it runs away. The time.

Bloody hell. 'To be or not to be' – that *is* the question.

'We put our shoulders to the wheel...'

O but the comfort of quotations.

'Rest rest perturbed sprit...'

And still her breath came in gasps – her chest rising and falling too quickly. Something final to resolve?

In the morning over the coffee and croissant and the concierge's sympathy, 'Strikes, eh? I wish we had your Mrs Thatcher...'

And Enid said, 'Yes, I do, too.'

When what she thought was, 'You're fucking welcome to her.'

And left her father's spirit there to argue with this man.

four

O GOD - that book. It's, it's mine. That's mine. The book. The book on the metal spinning thing - it must have a name – metal-book-holder-spinning-thing – it's mine.

Of course, it had been translated. She had a copy, but there it was, on sale, in the Gare d'Austerlitz.

Which meant someone had ordered it, and ordered more than a single copy, in expectation of sales.

How thrilling.

How heart-lifting. Like that beautiful woman on the 21 bus.

Her smile almost hurt.

She looked round and no-one at all in the whole teeming station seemed to be aware of the beam-of-light connection between the metal spinning book holder thing and the middle-aged grinning English woman. Self-conscious, she turned the grin off and it sprang back into place. Her brogued feet wanted to dance.

Enid didn't believe in omens, but she did believe in books. There was hers. There might be more – there *must* be – at other stations, at the end of her journey. In her future.

She composted her ticket, picked up her bag and felt like Marie Von Trapp singing, 'I have confidence...' in that treacly film.

She had watched only the three times in one week.

She went back to the metal spinning thing, bought a copy, had the young lady wrap it as a gift and posted it, with her fondest love, to Val.

In the note she wrote, 'The next one of these will be authored by your proud, dear and hopeless friend, Enid Makin.'

Then she got on the train.

Pulling out of the Gare d'Austerlitz, the concrete grey suburbs of South Paris slid by and you would have to be a maniacal romantic to find that inspiring, she owned. And she also owned - I feel a little free. Free-er.

I don't think that would be allowable at Scrabble.

I don't think that matters, my dear.

A new start deserves a clear-out. Needs it.

Bon courage.

'Voulez-vous quelque chose du chariot?'

'Non, merci.'

Look at France, dad.

Leave dad in peace, at peace.

God, but these suburbs go on. Couldn't live here. Concrete.

I believe I have had my fill of concrete.

I'm looking for stone, not brick.

Another brick in the wall.

O.

O I hated that song. 'Blame the teachers.'

O, thank you *so* much, Pink – I nearly used that worst *gros mot* - Floyd. Making their glib millions.

I was angry, properly angry but once in my whole thirty years of teaching. 'Lost it', as the idiom has it, perfectly accurately.

Somebody hummed that tune in my class.

In *my* class!

If it had been Hamblin, the ex-army Biology teacher who had taken two 'bad' boys – Foster and Bevan – to the gym after school, laid out some mats, had them tie one of his hands behind his back and invited them on and beat them up easily and painfully – if it had been him I could understand it – but I!

I kept calm enough as I asked for the person to identify themselves. When they wouldn't, didn't, I did use the word 'coward'.

That got a layered response.

Miss Makin distracted – unheard of. Miss Makin personal – never. Miss Makin angry…

I sat them all in utter silence. After twenty minutes and some coughing and fiddling beginning someone said, 'It was Hughes, miss.'

I said, 'I am no longer interested in who and I have never held any place for ratters or ratting.'

The silence sealed for the remaining twenty minutes, one whole carefully planned lesson, till the bell rang. And even then I made them wait, silent.

O I was cross.

Well, that was a warming memory.

Father and I watched the World Cup Final together and I wondered (but again, did not ask) if the Irishman secretly hoped they would lose. When they won, he offered, 'O dear God, knighthoods for football now.'

The sixties.

No-one offered me mind-expanding drugs. If I was invited to a party I believe I talked too little to hold anyone's attention or interest; I didn't smoke, never got hilariously or wildly drunk and when some poor soul was murdered at a Rolling Stones concert in a place called Altamont the newspapers, far too eagerly I felt, announced an end to all the Openness. There was something in their tone that induced a bizarre nostalgia in me for a thing I had not ever participated in. The incoming decade felt cold and vengeful, somehow. A sense of 'You've had your fun.'

I hadn't.

Would I, will I, ever?

Vierzon. The flat-lands. Couldn't live here.

Just under half-way there.

Lovely day so far.

Enid even dozed.

When Thatcher shuffled her cards and appointed Keith Joseph to Education Father simply said, 'Well?'

'What?' I who knew nothing.

'That – thing...' I could see the effort not to swear as badly as he longed to, 'That - Joseph - has a theory the poor shouldn't have children. State-supplied condoms. That's your boss now, Enid.'

I was reduced to, 'What do you want me to do about it?'

'Educate yourself. For fuck's sake, woman.'

I did my best, father.

Brive la Gaillarde, and hills.

The roof-tiles turning from slate-grey to terra-cotta. Rurality; more animals than houses, more trees than people or cars. Bridges over sharply glistening rivers crossed and re-crossed and with each one England slid into a past as the train charged her into a future. A sudden tunnel.

Why do tunnels always make me feel like a child again? Excited and scared.

The train poured out into the widening valley of The Lot river.

A sign. Department du Lot.

Thirty-forty minutes more.

At some point in our lives together the money I earned from book sales surpassed my Head of English salary.

So, if I had told him, if I had shared, had he known, he would have had no need to even consider that gesture. Of buying the house.

So, I need to learn to lose my secrets, because that one grieves me.

Still. Feels I made him betray himself.

And me?

Enid, three years alone? Mrs Thatcher's aim, she says repeatedly, is to take The State out of people's lives. But she has tighter control over schools, colleges and universities than ever before. I feel a nasty – such a silly, lazy word, but accurate here to catch my feelings – a nasty change in education in progress. Once upon a time – and yes, now it feels like a fairy story – we believed schoolteachers, university lecturers, teacher trainers, local education authority officers knew best and could be trusted to act, not only in children's and parents' interests, but for the wider good. The government's role was to provide sufficient resources. From the 'victory' over the Miners she and her ghastly Baker behave as though education is an Industry. And an ailing, near-bankrupt one. They denigrate our views, demand Value for Money; and impose 'performance management', all vile hokum - *and* to insist on 'customer satisfaction'.

Disgusting. My blood boils and I honour my father's struggle, but.

I will stop, I will cease my struggle with her force. This is why I am on this train, slowing into this pretty little town.

She may have England and I will hope to share something better in Figeac.

'Figeac. Monsieur Mesdames - la prochaine arrêt est Figeac.'

Enid reached down her suitcase. The train's brakes were applied.

As the platform cleared of train and passengers an elegant black-haired woman strode towards Enid, hand outstretched, smile beaming.

'Ms Makin?' she said with no trace of a French accent.

'It is. Enid. Zoe?'

'Voilà. Bienvenue.'

'Merci.'

Before Enid noticed the handshake had melted into three tiny cheek-kisses and her suitcase was in Zoe's hand.

'Good journey?'

'Very. Thank you.'

'My car's just outside.'

The drive took them up through heavily wooded hills. Pine, chestnut, oak, plane trees, silver birch - till the road flattened into an upland plateau of tiny hamlets and scattered farms with curious locals stopping their late Friday afternoon work to see if they knew the car. Some of them did; to some of them Zoe raised a finger and to some a smile, too.

'So,' she said, 'If I might - what are you looking for?'

'A place. Just a simple place.'

Zoe turned to show Enid her smile. 'Good. We don't do a lot of Grand up here. Simple - we have plenty...'

'Your English is terribly good.'

'Thank you. It ought to be - I taught there for three years.'

'Not English, surely?'

'No! French.'

'And your accent is flawless, too. Where, may I ask?'

'Portsmouth.' Zoe answered.

There was a pause.

'What?' Zoe smiled, inviting Enid's response.

'No, nothing. Just wondered if you didn't find it a touch - primal?'

Zoe barked a laugh. 'The tattooed hordes? And the men just as bad!'

Enid said, 'I only went there once – but – yes.' Both women laughed.

They drove on in pleasant silence and Enid sat back, taking in the view, until Zoe quietly asked, 'And this 'simple place', is it for a permanent move?'

'If I find it. Yes.'

'Let's both hope then.'

Zoe thought, is this the spinster I might become?

The bedroom was simplicity itself, the carefully spread English magazines on the bedside table notwithstanding. The window

THE SOLDIER'S HOME

offered a dull view over the backs of neighbouring properties. Enid hung her clothes, arranged her few toiletries, pushed her case beneath the bed and heard new arrivals.

On shelves all down the wide staircase were books and Enid was able to browse the titles, delay having to be social - and eavesdrop on the conversation below.

'Like we said,' Jim over-enunciated for this attractive hostess, nonetheless a foreigner, 'we'll sleep in our camper-van but take the meals if we may.'

'Not a problem.' Zoe beamed her best smile. 'And no trouble finding the village?'

'None at all. Lovely quiet spot.'

'Well, certainly if it's tranquillity you're looking for - you'll find it in abundance here.'

Janet, relaxing with every long word this woman used, chimed in, 'We're just looking.'

'Well, you're very welcome,' Zoe beamed, indicating armchairs. 'Take the weight – is it 'off your pins'?'

Enid heard that Zoe knew perfectly well it was, and she then followed it with her piece de resistance, 'And can I offer you a pot of tea?'

'Oo, now.' Janet purred.

'That'd be champion, aye.'

Everything the husband said came as a pronouncement. No need for the conversation to progress unless he had more to add.

Zoe said, disingenuously. "Champion'? Then, tea for two.'

And she was gone.

'Crikey Riley Jim - you're not going to expect me to speak frog as good as that, are yer?'

'I don't expect you to speak English as good as that, love.'

'Charming.'

'Wasn't she?'

Enid slipped back up to her room, found her notepad and a pen and scribbled.

There were more voices as she made it all the way downstairs. A younger couple were making the acquaintance of the older pair over tea and what looked like Bourbon biscuits. Enid nodded to them all, and sensing the outskirts of a linguistic panic arriving with her, said, rather loudly, 'Lovely afternoon, isn't it?'

An almost audible sigh of relief.

In the pause the younger man rose to cross the room and offer her his hand and his name, 'Roy.'

'Enid.' The hand was warm, hard, almost calloused. A builder?

'Sue.' He displayed her warm smile proudly. The formality clearly impelled the other man to rise from his chair and offer, without the handshaking, 'Jim and Janet - from God's own country...'

Enid smiled. 'Yorkshire?'

'Like I said,' he affirmed.

Enid wondered why, at fifty-five she now wished a social trapdoor could open before her, into which she might slowly and ever so charmingly descend, leaving only the fragrant odour of discretion.

Instead, she smiled, nodded, and was relieved when the Jim-man returned to his chair and she could veer away towards the big dining-room and the sanctuary of some more book-shelves. I have never understood how it is that I can be so very confident in front of thirty-odd schoolchildren and so very ill at ease with a tiny handful of adults. N'importe, she told herself. And, as you've come here looking for solitude - that's correct.

THE SOLDIER'S HOME

The room was dominated by a huge table, neatly laid for six she noted - so one more to arrive. Deal with. A glassed stable front door at the far end opened out into the village square and she could see a couple of old men sipping what perhaps was pastis, outside the café in the early evening light.

A huge stone fireplace, topped by an oak mantelpiece had an ancient sword hanging above it. Enid felt it to be the only masculine thing she'd seen so far. Finding it difficult to imagine the kitchen would reek of men she concluded this bright woman and the mother she'd mentioned did not share this space with a man. Now. Perhaps the war had taken him; but to Enid's entirely unpractised eye she found it hard to believe that weapon had featured in WW II. A grand-parental relic?

Behind her the Englishmen were chatting routes and roads and the women were smiling and bored. There were a few paintings, none of which looked either original nor particularly interesting; until she came on a delicate line-drawing of a house. It could not have been simpler yet something in it - either the building or the sentiment moving the hand of the artist - arrested her. Accompanying it were two framed black-and-white photographs. The first, head on, showed the same house, classic box-simple farm-house; steps up to a front door, two windows on each of its three floors. Caves, ground and grenier. And looking isolated. The second had been taken with the edge of the house in foreground and focused on a stunning view, soaring to mountains in the distance.

The flowers on the table and by the telephone were charming and, sniffing the air from the kitchen, Enid realised with some gusto that she was hungry.

The last of their party came in from outdoors. He was holding a mobile phone, which looked oddly out of place here and from the expression on his face, was precisely that. His suit, though clearly of light-weight material looked formal. Zoe arrived from the kitchen to make these introductions. He greeted her with, 'One hundred per cent correct, Zoe. No sign of a signal.'

'It'll come, but not this weekend.'

He was American. Trim, middle-aged. Monied?

He punched a button on his apparatus and it made a quiet version of the noise from the door of ye Olde Offey. Satisfied it was now inert, he laid it down.

'Happily marooned,' he faked and turned to shake hands. Zoe started with Jim and Janet and Enid felt a trace of embarrassment as Jim enjoyed displaying his determinedly cloth-capped approach to the foreign. Even as a foreigner himself.

'Come to buy a chateau or two, then?'

'I have as it happens, yeah.' The man smiled easily enough. And, intriguingly, Enid didn't believe him. She noticed Zoe's eyes gleam, though. Natural enough.

The American turned from Jim to include Janet in asking, 'And yourselves?'

'Oo,' she smiled, also a little disingenuously, 'we're just dipping us toes in the water.'

'O.K.'

He said it slowly, as though translating her dialect into his, before adding, 'Well, here's good luck to us all.'

Zoe introduced Roy and his wife and those pleasantries were exchanged. And led him towards Enid.

'Jack Bentley,' he said, extending a hand as warm as his smile.

'Enid Makin.'

As their hands parted Enid asked, 'Where are you from?'

'Ah,' he laughed slightly, disconcerting her, 'I came from and I live in Louisiana.'

There was a beat.

Enid said, 'You say that as though it isn't entirely true.'

He tilted his head, nodded and added a smile. 'Quite so, yet it is perfectly true.'

Enid accepted the conundrum and asked, 'New Orleans?'

'Yes! You been there?'

'No, not at all,' her deprecating tone meaning to indicate how very little travelling she'd done. 'No, but it has always appealed to me. I couldn't say why.'

'The music?'

'Possibly.' A tiny look between them. Enid said, 'Hard to comprehend isn't it – an ignorant fondness?'

'Need for Romance, isn't it? Like Manchester. I've never been there, never seen it.'

Enid raised an eyebrow, she hadn't followed his thinking. 'And you're fond of it?'

'Manchester England, England,' he seemed to be singing, 'Across the Atlantic Sea...'

Enid had a sense of imminent embarrassment rising.

'Hair.' He said by means of an explanation, 'Hair?'

'I'm afraid I'm no wiser.'

'Musical,' offered Roy. 'Great album. That's a song from it int it?'

'Yeah.'

'Oh.' Enid said, 'Well, as a Mancunian, I should have known that. Passed me by.'

The American nodded, then guessed, 'Mancunian being – meaning - from Manchester?'

Roy said, 'It's posh for Mank.'

Enid offered him a soft smile and said, 'Pendlebury is not posh.'

'And let me guess, Mank is not posh for Mancunian?'

'Correct,' said Roy.

'O.K. One last question then. What's 'posh'?'

'Brass,' said Jim, a smirk starting.

'Ah,' The American was again graceful in saying, 'This is the two countries divided by a common language schtick, correct?'

He turned to Roy and Sue, 'And so where are you-all from?'

Sue said 'Leicester.'

'And that's one of those places only English people could pronounce from its spelling, right? Like - '

'Arkansas?' said Enid, almost blushing.

He grinned. 'Touché...'

Enid smiled back.

Now, that was enough. She had been quick-witted, which she most assuredly did not believe she was, and she had survived so could this interview please stop right now, please. Before more were expected. Please?

The man seemed to catch something off this brief quiet, and her rising blush, said, 'Lovely old house,' and picking up his phone he moved away enough to fake beginning a look-around. Enid, nodding in the direction of the sword, added, 'Mm, it is,' and, seemingly mutually relieved, they separated. She watched him for a second, sensing a privacy re-gathering. Yes, and perhaps that's transference, my dear.

Had she watched him longer she would have seen that after a cursory glance at the books he had stood, somewhat transfixed, by the framed line-drawing and even more so by the two photographs. He had no notion of how long he had been standing there when he heard Zoe's call to the table. He willed himself into his sociable mood, pulled out a chair for Janet as she arrived beside him, and prepared himself for this longest weekend.

THE SOLDIER'S HOME

Sara bustled around the table as best her ancient legs and, it felt to her, even older slippers, would allow. She received a medley of compliments for her soup, in French, English and atrocious Franglais, at all of which she smiled, muttered 'merci' and bustled out even a little quicker.

She and Zoe served platters of chicken and lamb, put the best serving spoons in the vegetable tureens, chorused, 'Bonne Appetite' and retired to the kitchen; Sara to deal with the obscene addition to her mille-feuille pastry tart, and Zoe, her back against the cuisiniere, to chatter.

'The American is rich, Mamman. And the younger couple are serious too.'

Sara looked unhappily from the carton of crème anglais to her daughter. 'What do you want me to do with this muck?'

'Thicken it Mother. With this.'

She pushed the tub of crème vert along the work surface. 'This could be a good weekend; can't you feel it?'

'And how much more sugar in it?' Sara was not to be distracted.

'Too much - they're all English. Except him. Mind you, he's American. And they're vast. But he's slim. He won't take custard.'

'Good for him. I could make better. Eggs, milk, cornflour...'

'I know! Tonight we comfort them, yes?'

'And start tomorrow with the disgusting breakfasts?'

Zoe replied by simply staring at Sara, with what she hoped was a fond but baleful air.

'And did you get those tea-bag things?'

'I did. And I think the single woman could be a buyer, too. Get their plates in ten minutes. Time for a quick fag.'

Zoe went out the back door to smoke.

Sara stirred the custard. And poured it into a jug. Waited.

Thinking. Thinking what? she thought. Nothing too much. Zoe came back in.

'The devil makes work for idle hands,' she said. Her mother looked offended. 'It's an English expression.'

'Oh. Meaning what?'

'Let's get their plates.'

Sara almost fell back into her chair by the stove. Breathless.

'Mamman? You alright?'

'No.'

'They'll need the cheese.'

'You take it.'

'You're not alright?'

'No.'

'What is it?'

'I need a moment.'

'What? What is it?'

'A moment to myself. They'll need the cheese, daughter.'

Zoe took the cheeseboard through to the table and her guests. Her mother had been fine. Grouchy but fine. She'd served all the dinners, gathered the plates and now she was in her armchair, white.

A ghost.

Sara, gripping hard into the oak of her chair. Her knuckles white as Jacques' shroud. Thirty-four years since.

You who hoped your heart would persist long enough to see a grandchild. Never mind Zoe was everything but maternal. You, whose heart is thrashing with some of that thought now.

And of an unending, unrequited love. For the father of the man now eating at my table, down that corridor.

THE SOLDIER'S HOME

That ghost. Who had walked back through the years and through the door and she'd served him soup and meat and only as she took his dinner plate and he turned to compliment her, in easy almost local French, had she properly seen his face and now here she was – an ashen teenager in an ancient body, gasping.

Why?

Why was Jacques' son-ghost here?
No idea. But no accident.

Zoe reappeared, carrying the pudding plates and leading with concern. Questions lanced at her. I don't need nosey now. Sara raised her eyes, found her daughters' and said, 'Leave me until I choose to speak. Please'.

And glory-be-to-blood Zoe moved to make the pot of English tea.

No accident. Hold that thought while you wait for the silence.

Sara heard the kettle, listened to the tea being made, the pot being warmed, the tea being brewed, the trolley being laid just so.

She felt a last glance from her child and the kitchen was hers again.

No accident, impossible. For him to be here. Impossible.

Simone is dead. He's come to find something?

Simone is dying? He's been sent to find – his father? Sara snorted. Sad, but possible. Simone doesn't know. She never knew.

I have to ask him.

Or he will ask me.

I won't ask him.

I might.

Slow down heart. I need to see all this through.

Someone, probably someone dead, needs me to see this through. So slow. Down. Heart.

This heart that last pounded like this when I hoped and I did pray, yes I did, I stopped and I knelt in the lane and I prayed I had a half-brother to that man alive inside me. Seeding inside me as I walked back from Janatou, walked back from that - our one bed time.

And the memory of that one intimacy is why this heart races. Races beyond this corpse's years.

That damned deaf God who didn't hear my prayers. Or ignored them.

O but Jerome would laugh so loud.

And now, this copy of the father is eating my food.

As he would have done had I grown him.

Were he mine.

I have sixty-eight years and I shake. I can shake. Still.

Should I be grateful? Scared. Pleased? To be chaotic, like this?

Why should I be anything other than what I am – shaken? Hard.

The past walks over me. Why?

I don't know.

Round the room the business of scrutinising Zoe's property lists began. Sue sorted a manageable pile of what-they-could-afford as Roy rolled an impeccably neat ciggie and settled with the others to read.

Zoe, serving digestifs, had difficulty keeping an entirely steady hand as Jack placed by the side of his chair her descriptions of two chateaux; Bessonie - which needed Work - and La Putine, which didn't; but either sale would give Zoe change from a new car..! The noisy man and his wife were looking at family sized places and Enid, good as her word, was sifting out the smaller, more isolated

THE SOLDIER'S HOME

places. Her choices would need builders and work. Or, Zoe had learned not to pre-judge, she might even do it herself. And if not, well, both the Commune and the Departement were sprinkled with English artisans.

She re-filled glasses, answered questions, made polite suggestions and mentally began to plan a route to please everyone at least once.

'Three in the morning, nice lunch, three in the afternoon, is best. Tomorrow and Sunday...'

A room full of nodding agreement.

When Enid joined Roy and Sue in wanting to view Le Sireyol Zoe jiggled her itinerary to include it in the afternoon and asked her, 'And is it only that one?'

'Well, no...'

Jack Bentley caught something in the tone of those two tiny words.

Enid lowered her voice, 'What I'm really looking for is something like that.' She nodded at the two photos and the line drawing.

'Ah.' Zoe's business face slipped to reveal someone younger.

Enid took a reasonable risk. 'You took them? You did the drawing?'

'Yes, both. I did.'

Unlike me, Enid saw, this woman makes no secret of her pride. 'They're lovely.'

'Thank you.'

Nor of enjoying being flattered.

'It's a lovely place,' Zoe said.

'Is it...?'

Enid let the question hang, obvious.

To her surprise, and Jack's, this bright woman didn't pick it up. Enid, curious now, had to add, 'Is it - occupied?'

'No. Not for years and years.'

'Ah. Then…' Enid turned to directly face Zoe, 'Would it be possible to see it?'

Neither of them noticed Jack place his papers on the floor, openly listening now.

'Well, yes, that is possible, yes - but…' Enid watched the younger woman choose her words, before settling on, 'It's not a property I can sell.'

'Oh?'

'It's a long story.'

'I like stories.' Enid said.

Zoe looked at Enid as if for the very first time - seeing the individual and not just a potential customer. She drew an upright chair alongside Enid and sat down, drawing the room's full attention. Especially as she too now lowered her voice.

'I could take you to see it…'

Enid sensed unexplained caution.

'Would you mind?'

'No. Frankly I'd love to see it again. I've no idea what state it might be in, mind you.'

Enid waited. And watched Zoe come to some decision in her head before she said, 'We could put it at the end of the day tomorrow…'

Enid smiled her appreciation, then said, 'I sensed a 'but' – earlier?'

'I will - make some calls to clarify the situation. There are complications. It may be possible it can be purchased. I'll find out.'

'Thank you.'

'My pleasure. My job.'

THE SOLDIER'S HOME

Both women smiled.

Zoe turned to Jack. 'And for Monsieur Bentley?'

He had indeed picked out both of her huge sprawling chateaux.

Zoe managed an only ever-so-slightly strangled, 'Uh-huh. We can see one first thing and the other in the afternoon.'

Draining his cognac Jack stood, 'If you'll all excuse me I believe I need some shut-eye.'

'Jet-lag, you'll have.' Jim nodded at his own statement.

'That and this very fresh air, for sure, yeah. See you all for breakfast. What time, Zoe?'

'Eight-thirty all right for everyone?'

General agreement.

'Recommend me a book, please. Not au fait with my European authors.'

Enid watched Zoe give the man a 'let-me-think-what-would-suit-you' look, and watched him share a warm relaxed 'how-do-you-see-me?' grin with her.

'In French or English?' she asked and he said, 'Either.'

She moved to a shelf and handed him one.

'Colette? O.K... I sure don't know her.'

'I liked it.'

'Women's stuff? Put you to sleep good style will that!' Jim said.

Janet said, fondly, 'Don't mind Jim, brandy always makes him jovial.'

Enid dressed for bed and thought about that house, the 'long story' and the 'complications'. 'Un-occupied for years and years' she'd said.

She told herself how ridiculous it would be to put all her eggs in this first basket.

She turned over. 'I am excited,' she thought.

And turned over. 'I'm excited on this side, too.'

An owl hooted. She thought, 'I'd hoot too if I could.'

A dog barked.

'So, even if the house isn't available, there could be a story. To pinch.'

She giggled at the thought, and her use of that silly word and how young the giggle made her feel.

The church clock struck a half-hour.

'And live alone in the bee-loud glade...' she thought. 'The French bee-loud glade...'

Along the corridor the book lay untouched as Jack stared again at his mobile phone – 'No available service.'

He looked at the contents of his suitcase. Comprehensively unsuitable.

OK. I wasn't to know, he thought.

'Nearly home, Mamman,' he said, placing the tiny urn on the floor by his bedside table.

Finally in a bed in France, he turned his thoughts to Sara and the shock he had given her and what he ought to do about that.

And sleep.

five

SARA DECLINED to serve her breakfasts. Zoe had the good sense to respect whatever was troubling her mother. For now.

The food was enthusiastically demolished, swilled down with gallons of copiously sweetened tea, and topped off with endless toast and jam.

'Who had coffee and a croissant, then?' asked Sara.

'The American and the single woman. Why?'

'Wondered, that's all.' Sara grunted. The French speakers, she noted.

Zoe booked a table for seven for lunch and checked all the food preferences for their evening meal.

Jim and Janet would follow in their camper-van if Zoe would promise not to drive, 'Like a Frenchman.'

She replied she would drive like a French Woman and had her smile ready in place for his inevitable, 'Well, int that worse?'

The chill in the morning air would lift with the sun rising into the almost cloudless sky. En avant.

As Zoe swung the Espace down towards Bessonie, checking her mirrors for Jim and Janet, Enid reflected that no-one could not but be beguiled by this countryside. The sky was indeed clearing into an emotive cliché - that shade of blue you had to associate with The Impressionists. Puff-ball clouds grinned their assent at the idea of moving to and living within this landscape.

Zoe took the left-hand turn out of the woods near Le Fau, and the plain spread out suddenly, a green and brown squared quilt, all the way to Aurillac, and the Puy Marie soared five thousand metres, still clutching at its glittering white underskirt ski-slopes, even in May.

'Gorgeous,' she heard Sue say.

'What's the town, Zoe?' Roy asked.

'Aurillac. Good shopping. Very.'

They crossed a stream, through a hamlet too tiny to have a name and passing the incoming village sign, Zoe pulled up in front of the gate-posts guarding the fifteenth century Hugenot Chateau de Bessonie. The morning sun gleamed into its vast sandstone facing wall, and danced across the slate-grey tiles of the four huge corner turrets and with an almost insolent flick of the wrist Zoe cut the engine, turned to Jack and quietly said, 'Voilà.'

Only Janet heard Jim's, 'Bugger me sideways.'

Which, she reflected, was probably as well.

The double-iron gates were so heavy, took that certain amount of force to push them open, that an odd respect fell upon the group.

'Is that like a church?' Roy asked, of a white-stone chapel nestling in a frame of elder trees.

'The family chapel; added in the nineteenth century,' Zoe said. 'It's part of the property,' she added.

THE SOLDIER'S HOME

Unnecessarily, thought Enid, but perhaps she's nervous. God, if she sold this...

'How many rooms, Zoe?' Jack's voice was crisply business-like.

So was Zoe's. 'Seventeen. Shall we?'

She produced a suitably ancient iron key, fitted it into the lock and using both hands, turned it and the right-hand oak door, the wood grey now with five hundred years of weather in and on it, creaked open.

Zoe clicked a master-switch down and an ornate circular chandelier, framed from a wagon wheel and so a good three feet wide and at least ten feet above their heads illuminated the threadbare and fading tapestries that covered two of the walls.

Directly facing the front door, a huge window displayed the sprawling grounds and a family of ducks hesitating on the edge of a lake large enough to have a rowing-boat tied to a mooring.

'Well now...' Jim's tone of voice was reverent.

'When Napoleon was defeated at Waterloo,' and Zoe had all their attention immediately, 'his most favoured commander and friend, Marshall Ney, fled here to hide. He carried a jewel-encrusted sword which he supposedly gave to the Gendarmerie of Aurillac in return for their turning a blind eye. He lodged in what has since become a small library. If we go this way...'

'Is the sword in there?' Sue's eyes were – Enid's mind flashing back to a University room with Lyndy - out on stalks.

'I'm afraid not,' said Zoe. 'Only the history.'

Jack couldn't not enjoy the blatant mix of envy, shock and even some anger from people who couldn't credit they were in the company of someone they imagined capable of affording this fabulous monstrosity. Both Roy and Jim privately promised themselves they'd clock the asking price when they got back to Zoe's lists.

As Zoe killed the lights and locked up Jim blustered, 'Nice little bed-sit that. Now show us summat proper eh, Zoe?'

Savadat, Jim and Janet's first choice, was indeed a smaller beauty.

Zoe nodded to the land between the south-facing veranda and the glittering wee stream. 'Vegetable garden.'

It was, like all the land, beautifully laid out. Zoe dared a glance at Janet and was rewarded by her approving and enthusiastic face. Jim caught Zoe's eye and his mouth straightened and his jutting chin invited Mademoiselle Estate Agent to open t'house. She did.

What looked to Roy like a beautifully worked walnut staircase led upstairs, but Zoe began by throwing a door to their left open, revealing a huge and gloriously sun-lit kitchen dining room. The vast dominating table and its four benches, Roy was sure, were oak.

'If we come here,' he whispered to Sue, 'I'll be on me bloody mettle.'

'We can't afford this!'

'No, I mean - round here. That's craftmanship.'

Enid guessed now his trade was artisanal. Making sense of the feel of his handshake.

Roy and Sue and Enid had picked out Le Sireyol. One of only four properties in an isolated farming hamlet.

Simplicity, French rural style. House, barn, and a well.

In front of the barn and sloping down to the front of the house was what might, with work, become a lawn.

'That needs mowing badly,' announced Jim, and Enid snorted a brief but blatant giggle.

Everyone stopped and waited.

Hugely embarrassed she waved away their attention.

'No, it were summat I said, weren't it?'

Enid looked at Jim.

'Only a misplaced adverb. I do apologise.'

'Go on. Please, Miss. I've been guessing there's school ma'am in there somewhere…'

'Quite right. Thirty years. A reflex, Jim. I believe the sentence could have been constructed, 'This lawn badly needs mowing.''

'O right. No detention nor lines?'

Enid smiled. 'I apologise. Please accept it and let us look at this house.'

'Fair enough. Zoe?'

The house was a sturdy stone box. Both Jack and Enid thought - it's the same design as the one on Zoe's wall. A bog-standard turn of the century farmhouse. The headstone confirmed it; 1900. Roy pointed out the barn's headstone was 1876.

'Mm,' Zoe agreed, 'Either the farmer made his living space in the barn, with his herd, or, more likely, lived elsewhere for twenty years or so.'

Zoe opened the front door and flies rose, disturbed in their sunbathing.

Enid liked the place.

Long views, secluded, south facing. Quiet.

When Jim and Janet went upstairs to see the grenier Jack whispered, 'That was elegantly handled…'

Enid was startled but responded, 'Thank you.' And added, 'I surprised myself.'

'And isn't that always a pleasure?' he said.

Lunch at The Hotel du Tourisme in Latronquiere was pleasing enough.

Enid picked at her salad.

She was no DIY person but Roy and Sue, who she thought were, had been intrigued by Le Sireyol.

The fifteen-minute drive to La Putine had spectacular views down the valley ridge on one side and endless serene pastured peace on the other.

Set a hundred metres back off the road, and commanding the sharp cliff-edge, it was easy to see why the chateau had been built in that strategic position. Nothing could approach it without being seen.

'An important point for a supporter of the King in the seventeenth century, when it was built.'

Zoë pointed to the sloped roof of the tower. 'At one time there was a turret, similar to the ones at Bessonie, but after The Revolution the homes of the bourgeoisie had their turret-tops symbolically guillotined.' Six pairs of eyes stared. 'I'm also told that's a local myth and it's much more to do with paying less tax. In rural France, either or both or neither are possible.'

She was making what she hoped was a decent fist of not mainly addressing Jack.

'It is French law, however, that one day each year the public has free entry and access to a chateau such as this.'

'O no. Wouldn't do me at all, wouldn't that.' Janet received a supportive grunt from Jim.

The front door opened and an elegant man in expensive cords, a noticeably tidy hair-cut and a cravat at the throat of his perfectly pressed shirt, kissed Zoe three times and welcomed them all warmly.

'Bienvenue chez moi, tout le monde. Entrez, entrez.'

'Wouldn't want to heat that for a winter. Would you, Miss?'

Enid smiled at Jim and thought, only one more and then - that place.

I'm pleased to be excited, she told herself, climbing back into Zoe's Espace.

Zoe, driving to Laborie, wished she could mind-read. Had Jack bitten? She couldn't tell and daren't stare.

Jack's thoughts were now on the major event of his day. He watched the country's beauties sliding by and breathed ever deeper. And shallower.

As they walked through the pretty little copse that marked the boundary of Laborie, Roy accepted Jack's offer of a cigarette, rather than roll one.

'Now then...' Jim properly purred.

His eyes lit up at the solidity of the two-storey house. He and Janet moved forward together, taken seriously for the first time today.

'Pool up here on this lawn?' she wondered.

'Aye. Tennis court an' all.'

Roy quietly said to Jack, 'You seriously going to live in summat like that first place?'

Jack smiled, 'No. I was just curious to see it. And that last one. And - I enjoyed fulfilling everyone's idea of how an American in France should behave...'

Roy smiled, nodded. 'Sneaky. I like it.' Then he trod on the cigarette. 'And that were pitiful, mate. I'll do you a rollie after nose-bag.'

Jack attempted a translation and failing, asked, 'Do I say thanks?'

'You will.'

Everyone else, for their own reasons, had no interest in this place and were more than happy for Jim and Janet to get lost in their transparent enthusiasm. When Zoe opened the house only they went in and didn't seem to notice or care they'd not been followed.

The heat was leaving the day as Zoe parked and led them down the cart-track to Janatou.

Enid stopped to take in the haunting grandeur of a giant dead tree and for the first time that day wished she'd had a camera. The blackthorn and the more ambitious spiders had colonised the path. Almost obscured it with nature.

Jack and Zoe became detached at the head of the group. He listening to her part in the house's history; of the summer she'd taken the photographs and sat to draw, and that this was a place she loved. Jack nodded. His mouth was drying. She said she came here to sun-bathe naked once upon a time, and when he didn't respond she wished she'd never been so unsubtle.

Behind them it was hard to disagree with Jim's, 'How you sposed to get shopping down here?'

'In a tank,' Janet giggled.

To Enid Makin every ancient cart-wheeled rut convinced her somewhere this private could suit her. Very well.

As the path wound on towards the end of the woods Sue and Dave were sure that this, whatever it was, was not for them.

Waiting till all of them would see it at the same time, Zoe pushed the dripping branch aside and there, in low late afternoon light, lay Janatou.

'Zoe,' Roy said, 'We'll wait by the car if it's all the same to you...'

'Same for us, pet,' Janet added. 'We'll go and have a smoke, eh?'

Zoe passed Roy the keys and said, 'We shouldn't be long.'

Roy nodded to Jack. 'I'll do you that rollie now, if you like...'

There was a tiny pause.

'Ah. No, I'll – I'm happy to accompany the ladies, thanks. Later?'

'Whenever, mate.'

As they strolled back Roy said quietly to Sue, 'Rum. First time he's looked owt but cool.'

Around the three of them the kind of silence that includes birds and flies folded. Enfolded.

The house waited.

The view, as the sun lengthened the shadows, was breathtaking.

'We've spent a day,' managed Enid, 'looking at lovely places - and now this...'

'I know,' smiled Zoe.

The house has a silent magnetism for each of us, Enid noticed. And the deepest silence is in this American man.

'That is a view.' Enid caught the choking note in Zoe's voice.

'It's like a secret place,' Enid said and was rewarded with the warmest flash of a smile from Zoe.

'It was – and it is.'

Zoe led her and Jack up the stairs.

One volet hung loose.

There was no lock on the door.

Zoe jiggled the latch just so and the feeble warm breeze lifted a carpet of dust to greet them.

Jim said, 'We find the owner, offer him ten per cent less under table and we'd get it.'

'And you've got the frog for all that have you love?'

'Money's numbers, love. And, I'll bet you every lawyer round here can manage cut-glass English when they niff their cut. What do you think?'

'I think we look at some more tomorrow - say us goodbyes and thanks, park up for a week, sniff about - and then...'

There was a fond beat.

'You're brains in this show, aren't you?'

Sue said, 'We could fix up that Sireyol place, us.'

Roy nodded. They agreed. Excited.

All three of them silent.

He seemed reluctant to cross the threshold. Or perhaps he was content to, or needed to, simply stand there for that moment, look, and breathe. Enid gladly followed Zoe.

The big room was plain, its simple furniture stacked against an un-plastered wall.

A long dead fire.

A bucket in a kind of kitchen space beneath the single window.

But the atmosphere of the place dwarfed all and any detail, Enid felt. Undefinable yet palpable. Through the open front door stood Jack, staring at the land and that view...

Zoe opened one of two doors in a dividing wall. The simplest possible bedroom. Bed, chair, chest of drawers.

Jack came in. He stood and he looked and Enid couldn't make eye-contact with him now, so private was he. So far from speech.

Behind the other door was a room empty of everything but dead flies and dust.

With seemingly next to nothing at all to look at, Enid was fascinated by how quiet and silently respectful – and slow – all three of them were in their movements.

She followed Zoe up a flight of wooden stairs to see the grenier.

Dusty too, and empty apart from one largish box against a wall. Enid hesitated.

Zoe hesitated.

Enid said, 'May I?'

Zoe seemed to shrug.

Enid ducked under one of the A frames.

She stopped and asked, 'Is this the long story? Here.'

'Some of it. My mother knows more than I do.'

Again, Enid felt compelled to ask, 'Might I?'

Zoe's gesture didn't deny her.

Enid knelt to see some plates, two paintings and a large pile of letters. Oh, glory but I would love to read those.

Jack's head appeared.

Enid stood.

Bizarrely guilty, she felt.

Jack looked around, saw the box, nodded to them both and descended.

They found him sitting on the edge of the bed.

He rose and joined them as they stepped back into day-light.

Zoe said, 'There's a source here. For water. But otherwise it's - primitive.'

'Mm,' Enid allowed, watching the setting sun falling slow towards its sleep behind the Cantal Mountains.

'Thank you so very much, Zoe,' she managed and vowed not to speak again till her heart had stilled.

When Zoe asked Jack was he ready to leave, he gave her a small bow and walked down the stone stairs.

🐑

Sara's evening feast had her fending off more bi-lingual compliments; and Zoe's guests were free, if they so chose, to discuss the day - and tomorrow. Zoe offered digestifs and Jack took the opportunity to slip into the kitchen, kneel into Sara's lowered eye-line and ask, in French, 'Could we speak tomorrow?'

'Bien sur,' she managed and allowed him to squeeze her hand and leave her.

I am overwhelmed, she thought. Thinking dead thoughts come to this kind of life. I want to hug him for an hour.

Roy and Sue admitted they were 'well interested' in Le Sireyol, but wanted, like Jim and Janet, to see more tomorrow. Zoe happily produced her lists whilst Jack declared he'd seen enough, and with her permission, might sit tomorrow out.

Making a choice? Zoe could only hope. For an American he was contained, this man. I'd always had the impression they were brash. He's not.

She turned to talk to Enid who quietly said, 'Je crois que vous savez bien ce que je pense.'

There was a beat.

'Oo now,' Jim announced, 'That were bordering on rude, Miss.'

Enid stifled a mounting blush by saying, 'I agree. In English, then - this is none of your business.'

'Now that's better. That was proper rude.'

'Again, I agree.'

'Yer after Wreck of the Hesperus - we're not soft, love.'

Janet's smirk needed slapping off her silly face, Sue thought.

Zoe nodded a quiet 'plus tard' to Enid and spread a calming order for coffees or teas. Roy rolled a ciggie for himself and Sue and an especially neat one for Jack.

'Now then, my colonial pal – this is a fag. None of that roasted bollocks.'

Smoke rose and a quiet fell. Zoe bustled back in with a tray. Enid took her tea to a softer chair. Watched Jack nodding approval to Roy.

THE SOLDIER'S HOME

She sipped at her tea.

The room stilled.

Jack took a chair next to Enid's, leaned towards her and said, 'May I ask, please - why you were attracted to that place?'

Enid blushed. 'You may, yes. And I sensed you were affected by it, too...'

'You're right. I was.'

He raised an eyebrow inviting her to answer his original question.

'Am?' Enid needed to know.

'Am?' He hadn't followed.

'You *are* interested?'

'Yes. I am.'

'Oh.' There was a pause.

Enid told herself to look this man as directly in the eye as she dared.

And as her eyes flicked from his shirt collar to rest back on her cup she had to admit it wasn't a very bold effort.

He saw the tension and asked, 'Any of the others appeal?'

'For me? No. That one - um...'

'Hit your G-spot?' laughed Jack and immediately wished he hadn't.

Why is he blushing Enid wondered...?

'That's not a phrase I'm familiar with,' she said, 'but it sounds accurate for all that.'

He'd like to leave this subject around about right now.

'And did it 'hit your G-spot'?'

Again, curiously, this man blushed. Enid smiled. He didn't.

'Yes. Yes, it did, yes,' he almost stammered.

'Why?'

'But that's the question I asked you...'

Enid stalled.

Jack relaxed as the G-spot faded away.

'There is a - a tristesse - there.'

He nodded slowly. 'Yup, for sure. Yes ma'am.'

Now he lowered his voice further and respectfully wondered, 'And do you enjoy sadness?'

'Not in the least.'

'But you're attracted to it?'

'By it, perhaps.'

They both nodded a little. In a little silence. A pause.

'And you? What were you attracted to?'

Enid watched him go to answer her, then think again and finally settle on saying, 'I - I guess you're right... It is sad.'

That was him quite deliberately saying nothing. Which was his right, his privilege. Enid puzzled.

They sat, both thinking.

'But you would like it, too. That property?' Enid finally dared ask.

Now he responded without consideration, 'Yes. Yes, I would.'

'I feared so,' she said, her voice thin.

He used the tiny silence to reach for an ashtray and stub out his cigarette.

'Well,' Enid placed her nearly empty cup on a side-table, 'isn't it all academic? Since our hostess says there are complications and it may not even be for sale.'

The man laughed. 'Everything's for sale.'

Enid was startled.

'That's - very American of you...'

He raised an eyebrow. 'Is this a pejorative concept I see before me?'

'I hope not.'

THE SOLDIER'S HOME

'It's only true, I think.'

It was Enid's turn to be silent.

And in the newest quiet he heard they were being listened to.

And further, he saw she had realised it – and still further, it discomforted her.

He stood.

'Would you care to take a stroll?' He leaned into the inherent Englishness of the word 'stroll' and elicited a smile and her standing immediately.

'I should love to...'

St. Cirgues was easy on its sightseers. Next to nothing.

They turned at the end of the graveyard when some serious woods began and headed back up towards the church square.

'And so,' Enid believed, after quiet consideration, this to be the point, 'you'll buy it one way or another?'

He looked offended by an inference of brashness.

'I don't believe I said or even implied that. I simply said it can be bought. Whatever the 'complications'.'

'Because?'

He went to laugh and stifled it back into a grin. 'Because there's profit for someone! That usually lubricates the wheels.'

They walked into the church square. A crass single spot-light illuminated the completely unremarkable church tower and clock. She pulled her cardigan a little closer.

'Why do you want it, Enid?'

The warmth in the casual use of her name surprised her. And, surprising her further, opened something in her.

'I write. Not very well I don't honestly believe, but it gives me and a small public pleasure; and I feel sure I could write in that place. And I have retired from my profession, and wish to retire from my country, and to be as honest as the evening invites me to be, I find it hard to conceive of a place so ideally suited to me. And my desires.'

She took a breath.

It was the most personally she had expressed herself in what felt like half a lifetime and the mere use of the word 'desire' raised a colour to her cheeks; which Jack noticed, and nodding his respect, he allowed her the space to re-gather herself.

Grateful for his discretion, she asked, 'And why do you want it?'

'I was born there.'

Their feet seemed to continue walking but somehow she wasn't sure they were moving.

'Well, not in that location. But certainly in that bed. I have it on the highest authority.'

And the air had now surely stilled around them. Enid didn't even bother searching for words.

She would like, she thought, to sit down now. Her eyes found a bench and her feet headed towards it. He followed, his hands in his pockets now; a relaxation coming over him, she thought, now he's said this out loud. She sat and he came and sat beside her. It was late enough for a goose pimple to be visible at her wrist.

'Then...'

And she stalled.

'Yes?' he gently prompted.

'As little as I understand French property law - the house is yours by right.'

'I am 'the complications', yes.'

'And Zoe doesn't know?'

'No. Or rather, she may, it depends on what her mother has said to her.'

A gust stirred the leaves. And laid them down again.

THE SOLDIER'S HOME

'No wonder you were beyond speech this afternoon.'

'Mm. Zoe is right - it is a long story...'

She looked at him.

He looked younger and older at the same time.

'I like stories...' she offered.

'Another time. Please, Enid.'

'Of course. Of course.'

Some night began to fall on an English ex-teacher and an American publisher sitting on a bench in a tiny French village. They let it.

When eventually she stood she said, 'I'm happy for you, Jack.'

He heaved a breath and looked up at her. 'I don't know – yet – quite what I am. But. I came to see it, amongst other things. I was sent to see it, rather. So, it's good. That I have.'

She looked down at him. 'Are you surprised that you've seen it?'

'Not at all, but I am shaken by what it meant. To me.'

She nodded, understanding. Sympathetic. Waiting, hoping, for more.

He stood. 'But, I'll take a night's sleep now, I think.'

She smiled and they took a pace or two in the direction of Sara's house.

He stopped and waited for her to look him in the eye. When she did he said, 'I'm sorry, Enid.'

'Not at all!'

She walked another pace, shook her head. 'Not at all. Jack.'

In her bedroom she felt the lady had protested that tiny telling tad too much. She should have said, 'Not at all, Jack.'

But what was to be done?

Go with the others tomorrow - see some other places. She had time. And, there were other immobiliers, other chambres d'hôtes.

Do this for a week? A month? Till you find the rainbow. Or - go home?

Eggs and baskets, Enid.

Be glad for him and for that place. The right person has the healing of it in his hands.

And, I am taken with the area.

There must be more than one fish in the sea.

Pebbles in the ocean.

Tears in my heart.

At breakfast Zoe showed Enid what had been chosen to look at today and, yes why not, she would come with.

Jack begged a word away from the table.

'What was in that box? In the loft?'

Heavens, thought Enid; has he slept at all? His eyes were full of something.

'I didn't really look; it felt private.'

He nodded just too quickly.

'As if it was yours, in fact.'

'Would you -?'

Enid looked up as he broke the sentence.

'Would you care to come with me today. To see. It. Again?'

For the first time Enid looked directly into this attractive man. Asking her an oblique question. She lowered her voice.

'Do you mean - hold your hand?'

He smiled, delightedly embarrassed. 'I do. Yes - I bloody do!'

With his laughter and deliberate pronunciation of the English swear-word, heads turned and ears cocked.

'Then I'd be flattered. And will I hear the story?'

THE SOLDIER'S HOME

'What little I know, sure.'

She saw him harbour a minute doubt.

'You sure you wouldn't prefer...?' he nodded towards house-hunters gathering their things.

'I'm quite sure,' she said primly.

'Do you want me to explain to Zoe?'

Enid gave him an old-fashioned look, walked to the table to gently touch Zoe's arm and said, 'I won't come today if you don't mind, Zoe.'

Zoe looked from her to Jack.

'Bonne journée, tous les deux.'

Zoe went to her car wondering if such delicate discretion on her part didn't warrant some positive reward from dollar-land.

When the house was quiet Enid asked, 'Do you know the way?'

'No, I don't - but I believe I know someone who does. Excuse me.'

Sara, alone in a rocker close to the cuisiniere, looked up.

'Madame...'

'Monsieur...' They spoke in French.

'Can I ask you something, Madame, please ?'

Sara stopped her rocking, folded her arms and said, 'It's Sara. To you. How to get to Janatou?'

He smiled.

Sara said, 'I can see both your parents in that smile.'

He said, 'They both adored you.'

'Pff,' she snorted compliment and truth away.

'It's only true, Sara.' A thick hand brushed at a tear that hadn't yet formed. 'My mother spoke of you like no-one else. You'd blush. The word 'respect' was made for you, she said.'

Sara rocked. 'She's dead then?'

'A month ago, yes.'

Sara nodded, and crossed herself. 'Take the Maurs road, to the red house at the top of the hill, turn right, keep to the left till the three post-boxes. The path is there.'

'Merci.'

'Rien.'

There was a quiet.

An idea occurred to Jack.

'Would you care to come with us, Sara?'

'No. I've been there.'

'O.K.' He stood.

'Would you take me one day to where the house was? Please ?'

He watched the woman consider that notion. She looked up and nodded.

'If you wish. Maurs Road, right at the red house, keep left, the three boxes.'

'Thank you. And help me spread her ashes ?'

Sara had to gather herself to say, 'That's not my place. To do that.'

'I know. I'd agree, but...' He waited for her eyes to meet his and then said, '...but I believe she'd be flattered.'

Sara rocked, nodded and was left with his kiss and her gathering tears.

Their day at Janatou passed in almost complete silence.

Enid did not hold his hand; but instead took the two upright chairs out to the bottom of the steps and there they sat whilst he went through the contents of the box. Simone's collage was a ruin of Time, mice and dust. The paintings were salvageable, the plates a curiosity only; unless you considered your parents eating off them. And the sun walked east to west across the panorama as he read his mother's correspondence with his father.

THE SOLDIER'S HOME

When he passed the first one to Enid she said, 'Are you quite sure?'

He nodded.

Perhaps two hours passed before she heard him say, 'Oh, oui Mamman...'

At another point he rose and went to look at the chimney.

A strangled 'Oh, Pappa,' were his only other words.

And a first tear from the son fell on the stones of the father.

If she had returned an hour earlier that evening Zoe would have found the novelist spinster school-teacher preparing their evening meal, and the attractive American and her mother sitting side by side weeping. Happily.

When Zoe tapped on the bedroom door, Enid was finishing her packing.

'Oh. Pardon.'

'Not at all.'

'I...' Zoe stopped herself saying 'hoped you were staying' and substituted a not entirely truthful, '...made enquiries about Janatou.'

'And it's not possible.' Enid smiled, letting Zoe off the hook. 'I know.'

Zoe's mind raced over whether it would be rude to ask 'how'.

'How?'

Enid decided assuredly not to reveal Jack's business, and instead wondered how to extricate herself.

'I don't. Know. I'm being negative about your use of the word 'complications'. What have you found out?'

When Zoe offered at first a silence, two bright women standing in a room, were both now quite sure the other was lying.

'Well...' Zoe began and Enid thought, this will be flannel. '... only that, for the moment, they are insurmountable.'

Voila. Relieved to have no more of this wee French farce, Enid did her best to nod sadly.

'Tant pis pour moi.'

'And you are leaving us?'

'Sadly, yes.'

Jack and Enid sat inside the Café Tabac with two glasses of white wine.

As gracefully as she had declined Zoe's offer of a lift she had accepted his. Of the short drive to Latronquiere and the room she'd booked at the Hotel Du Tourisme.

Now, like the rest of their day, they were quiet.

She could see his head was full. Teeming.

There was a tap at the door and Zoe poured in and sat hard on her mother's bed.

'Mamman. Talk to me please.'

Sara said, 'Tell me about Jacques. Secret-place Jacques.'

There was a beat of quiet.

'Tell you what?'

'What you remember about him, physically.'

Sara waited.

'O My God. That's - is that...?'

'His son. Yes.'

'Simone's son?'

'Exactly.'

Another beat. Of two hearts.

'Why? Why is he here?'

'She's dead. She asked him to spread her ashes.'

'Oh.'

'And she told him to listen to me. Talk to me.'

'And you have?'

'Through the blubbing.'

A beat of one heart, 'So he's not going to buy a chateau?'

'Why would he? He owns Janatou.'

Jack looked up. She had been looking at him.

'What?' he asked.

'I was just thinking of *not* asking you that same question...'

'Ah.'

A sip at his wine.

An ancien, a toothless old man, was their only company. His was a bottle of red wine. Arbel had nodded when they came in.

'What do you do – in America?'

'I run a company doesn't need running.'

'Does that pay well?'

'Yes.'

'Is the expression, 'Nice work if you can get it...'?'

He smiled, surprising her by looking carefully and warmly into her eyes.

She surprised herself by holding his gaze, and then saying, 'Are you bored?'

His smile warmed. 'Enid, I live just off Frenchman Street. A soul bored with that would be a tragedy.'

She said, 'And yet you are?'

He said, slowly, and directly to her, 'There is something so clean in the air here. Cleaner than even Manchester..?'

She nodded. 'The history is in the earth, here. It's different, yes.'

She took a sip, he a drink.

'I could come house-hunting with you tomorrow,' he said. 'If you didn't mind.'

'I'd like that,' she said simply.

He nodded.

She swirled the liquid and took another sip.

I like these silences, she thought. Why?

His eyes focused somewhere so far away she was free to watch him, look at him, with neither nerves nor embarrassment.

Well, she accepted, I like this man. He pushed his unfinished glass aside. She watched, waited. What is he thinking?

'Enid, what do the words time-share mean to you?'

She blinked.

'Um - something to do with Spanish beach properties.'

'No.' His face was serious. 'It's an arrangement between parties to share a property. Share Time.'

'Oh. I see.' Her tone indicated continued puzzlement.

She felt his eyes fixed on hers.

She watched the size of the breath he inhaled and released.

Before.

'I will give you Janatou. If you will allow me to come and share Time there. With you.'

Something happened to the colours in the bar.

Something smoky.

Something ephemeral solidified. Or perhaps something solid melted. Or perhaps a soul was born.

He watched her shallow breathing.

Her mouth fallen open.

'I'm speechless,' he heard.

'O.K.' He stood. 'I'll cancel your hotel and re-book your room for tonight. Hopefully your voice will return by the time I do...'

THE SOLDIER'S HOME

He walked to the door, opened it, and nodding towards the bar said, 'You think he stocks champagne?'

Zoe was making arrangements for Roy and Sue to make an offer on Le Sireyol.

Enid had not moved one centimetre.

Jack sat back into her eyeline, into her panorama.

'I accept. I can't express my feelings. Now. Yet. But I believe you know.'

'Good. I'm very happy.'

'So am I.'

For the first time in years, it felt, his back rested, truly nestled, into a chair.

And immediately he leaned forward.

'What do you do when you're happy, Enid? I don't take you for a big drinker.'

'No. I'm not. I do take a glass...'

They were moving along the precipice of Mutual Delight.

It was mutually delightful.

'You don't smoke or do drugs?'

'Oh dear, no. Do you?'

'I did. I don't. Did you?'

'No. I'm rather strait-laced, you see.'

'That sounds too English. What's the point in it?'

'Self-protection. I imagine.'

'So how do you unwind? Let your hair down?'

Enid thought. 'I take a bath.'

'O.K.!'

He smiled deeper than she'd yet seen.

'So, will you put a bath in Janatou?'

Enid smiled. 'There is an empty room there.'

'Mm. And no electricity, no sink, no toilette. How will your strait-lacedness manage?'

'None of your business, sir.'

'Well - it could be; when I come to spend Time there.'

Enid blinked.

'I'll take my holidays then...'

There was a beat.

'Enid...'

As she hoped and dreaded he would, he locked their eyes together.

'My deal said - if you spend Time there with me.'

She didn't believe she was exactly panting...

'Why - would you want to spend time - with me?'

'I don't know yet. I've hardly known you forty-eight hours.'

Their eyes smiled.

'I'm trusting my instincts,' he said and she could feel how pleased he was to believe it.

She waited for her own instincts... Then she laughed and he said, 'What?'

'I was waiting for my instincts!'

She thought his grin the kindest thing she had ever seen.

'And?'

Finally, she said, 'I'm considerably older than you.' And then added, 'Sometimes I feel I'm older than everyone.'

'I'm pretty sure that's not relevant.'

Enid Makin and Jack Vermande/Bentley entered a passage of light that fell only on them.

THE SOLDIER'S HOME

seven

FIVE MONTHS LATER, with late late autumn rouging the trees and the low evening sun painting pastel harmonics everywhere, Jack parked the hire-car, hitched his bag over one shoulder and walked the cart-track, wolfing the late blackberries. He skirted the trees behind the house, to surprise her. He made it to the back of the house and feeling like a naughty child tiptoed up the stairs to the door.

The latch stuck - you had to jiggle it just so.

Enid looked up from her vegetable garden.

'Hello stranger,' she called, making him jump.

His grin cut all distance between them.

'Hi, Enid.'

'You've come.'

'I have.'

She straightened the wide straw hat and rolled her shirt-sleeves down. Stood the hoe beside the sprouts and wiping her hands on her skirt, came slowly up the stairs. Thinking, he has come back. To be my lover.

'How long for?'

'Don't know.'

They stood outside the front door. He was wearing fond old jeans, a tee-shirt and jacket.

'You get a bath fitted?'

'No.'

'Electricity?'

'No.'

'Gas?'

'No.'

He smiled.

'You happy?'

'Very.'

'You writing?'

'Yes.'

'Good.'

He leaned forward and placed a first kiss on her blooming cheek.

'Did you get another bed?'

Enid Makin looked at her first lover.

'I did not.'

He kissed the other cheek.

Their eyes locked again.

This, she thought, is the first time in my whole life I don't feel plain.

🐏

In the morning he said, 'I'm going to buy me a rocking chair.'

'O.K.'

'Two?'

'As you please. But I have imported a leather arm-chair.' Her fingers rolled in a thick strand of her grey fallen hair.

On the evening of their first full day together Jack sat and rocked, his feet up on the stone of the staircase wall his father had re-built.

'May I read something you wrote, please?'

'You may.' She smiled and went inside, and emerged with a sizeable pile of neatly stacked paper.

'This is new.'

He nodded. 'You've been busy.'

'I've been happy.'

'Great.'

He turned a first page.

'The cat scratched at the window. I must fix that volet...' he read.

THE SOLDIER'S HOME

THE SOLDIER'S HOME

George Costigan has been a motor-parts storeman, a trainee accountant, another trainee accountant (both failed) a steel-worker, an insurance clerk, a wood-cutter, a bookseller, a record salesman, a book-keeper for a wedding-dress business - and then someone asked him to be in a play.

College followed and a career that started in children's theatre, then took in Butlins Repetory Theatre in Filey and eventually landed him at the Liverpool Everyman theatre. It was here he met some hugely influential people - Chris Bond, Alan Bleasedale, Alan Dossor and above all, Julia North.

His acting career has included working with Sally Wainwright, Willy Russell, Alan Clarke and Clint Eastwood. He has directed Daniel Day-Lewis and Pete Postlethwaite, and his writing for the stage includes several Liverpool Everyman pub shows and 'Trust Byron', for which he was nominated for Best Actor at the 1990 Edinburgh Festival. He and Julia North have three sons and one grandson.

THE SOLDIER'S HOME

THE SOLDIER'S HOME

acknowledgements

Acknowledgements are most sincerely due to Carol Dyhouse and Janet Howarth for their fantastic serendipitous aid in researching University Entrance after WW2; to David Robinson and David Hartley for their memories of Head-mastering and of the 'real' Ms Makin; to Min Roosevelt for her forensic proof-reading and to Stephen Bill for all his structural and other suggestions, all of which I have shamelessly nimmed and only he and I know how serious they were. And how eagerly pounced upon.

And to Judy Holt, Helen Parry, Linda Sheridan, Anita Vitesse, Mark Charnock, Hugh Fraser, Michael Monaghan, Sally Bretton, Sofia Cann, Kenny Glenaan, Joanna Daniels, Yvette Huddlestone, Claire Parker,Helen Snook, Jenny Secombe, Kate Hardie, Robin and Nicky Benger, David Fielder, Roy Richards, John Abulafia, Susie Wooldridge, Rob Porter and Cal Macanninch, amongst others I've shamefully forgotten, who gave freely of that Most Precious of gifts - encouragement - my bottomless thanks.

THE SOLDIER'S HOME

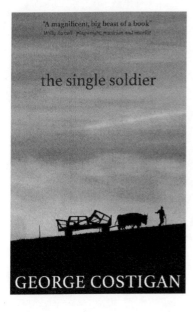

'A magnificent,
big beast of
a book.' -
*Willy Russell,
playwright and
novelist*

It is said that home is where the heart is, but when war rips a young man from everything he knows and loves, will he be able to find his way back to everything that matters?

In war torn rural France, amongst the devastation, physical and emotional, of German occupation, a man decides to move his house, using only a cow and a cart, six kilometres to the other side of his village. Where he painstakingly begins to re-build his home. By hand. Why would anyone do such a thing? The war was being won but would he ever find peace?

History, passion, love, secrets and painful truths collide in this astonishingly human, warm and emotive debut from writer and actor George Costigan.

The Single Soldier is available from Amazon and all good bookshops.

URBANE

Urbane Publications is dedicated to developing new author voices, and publishing fiction and non-fiction that challenges, thrills and fascinates.

From page-turning novels to innovative reference books, our goal is to publish what YOU want to read.

Find out more at
urbanepublications.com